D1824235

Down Trident

Chris Walsh

Chris Walsh joined the Royal Navy as an Engineering Artificer Apprentice in 1963 and served in a variety of ships and establishments until leaving the active service list in 1996 as a Lieutenant Commander. A very slight career change saw him begin a second career as a uniformed civil servant, retaining his rank, and employed at the home of the nation's Submarine based nuclear deterrent at Faslane in the West of Scotland. Chris completed sixteen years in this post which became the inspiration and catalyst for his first novel. Married to Marjory they have two children and four grandchildren. Chris and Marjory live happily in rural Kinross-shire in Scotland. Always a keen reader, Chris has been an avid short story writer for many years until the plot for a first novel evolved and caused a change in genre.

A Bardel Publication

Published by Bardel 2015
© **Chris Walsh 2015**

Second Edition
Down Trident

A small group of retired Royal Navy officers based at Her Majesty's Naval Base Clyde are charged with the everyday activities necessary to keep this nation's nuclear deterrent safe from outside attack.

They do not work alone but they are a very visible cog in a well oiled security machine. For this group a success rate of 99.9% is not good enough. For that period of time when their tasks are completed without mishap there is often little recognition and rarely praise.

However, if things did go wrong, or even not quite right, the fallout would be immediate and long lasting.

Their responsibilities are immense

So in part, this story is dedicated to these officers.

Acknowledgement

.

My thanks are extended to Bob Watson for the shove needed to get this manuscript back out of the cupboard and try to improve it.

The bombing of PAN AM Flight 103 over Lockerbie on Wednesday 21st December 1988 changed the world. The incidents of Tuesday 11th September 2001, known to us all as 9/11, changed the world for ever.

This story is set in the period between these two atrocities. It is a work of plausible fiction. For readers expert in the security of high strategic value military sites there may be a few actions or assumptions here that you will say are not possible.

Such doubts must be tempered by the suggestion that the human condition should never be underestimated

Chris Walsh June 2015

One

Daniel Coleman sat in front of his computer screen and felt the familiar buzz of excitement that came with the completion of another issue. Smiling to himself, he leaned back in his chair stretched his arms upwards and linked his hands together at the back of his head. Daniel drew in a deep breath, gave a big sigh and closed his eyes. To leave enough time for printing and distribution he needed to be finished with the editorial work before the third Thursday of each month. It was his only deadline.

He hit the keys to save his work, pushed the chair backwards and stood up. In what had now become a ritual Daniel crossed his living room cum office to the meagre drinks trolley and poured a small measure of Glenkinchie into a crystal glass. He raised his glass to nothing in particular and downed the contents in one swallow. This was the forty-seventh issue of 'Envirocare', and that meant his forty-seventh whisky. He had few luxuries and, in truth, had little need of them. At this same moment in every one of those forty-seven months he had almost persuaded himself that malt whisky was an indulgence he could not afford.

'Envirocare' was at best a periodical and at worst just a pamphlet. It was Daniel's brainchild and he was owner, writer, printer and distributor.

An English graduate from the summer of '93 young Coleman had set off in pursuit of a career in journalism full of ideals and expectations. None of the nationals would consider him. He once made it through the doors of the Evening Standard but was so nervous he performed badly at interview. For six months after graduating he wrote speculative letters to every registered newspaper and magazine south of

Birmingham, and a few of the more prestigious ones to the north. Nothing. Thoroughly demoralised he started, tentatively, to produce his own magazine and in the first months of 'Envirocare' showed a small but, to him, encouraging return. He decided to go it alone and leased a photocopier and a few office tools to supplement his computer.

Daniel William Coleman was a slim, bespectacled young man who sported a full head of ginger hair and a beard that could be generously considered sparse. From a typically middle class background, the young Coleman had wanted for little.

His father, a general practitioner in the Home Counties, had wanted his only son to follow him into medicine but was eventually grateful when Daniel gained a place to study English. Dr John and his wife, Barbara, decided to invest in a small basement flat in Fulham and Daniel moved in at the start of his first term. He was the only under-graduate in his year to have safe, rent-free accommodation all to himself. It should have been a ticket to popularity with the rest of his student year.

Coleman had somewhere safe and warm to party, even to share.

Perhaps if he had taken the lead and advertised that he had a spare bedroom available, things may have turned out differently. Perhaps the presence of another student, with friends of his own, would have widened his social horizons. He hadn't really considered it and it was too late now. Daniel was basically a shy person for whom relationships were never easy. His appearance didn't help; he looked studious, weedy almost, certainly not destined for the hard drinking, late night set. He set off each day on the bus, attended his lectures and went home to Fulham.

Now, four years on, he had lost contact with his entire University course. No re-unions, no phone calls enticing him out to the pub or even the theatre. Coleman had gradually and inexorably become a recluse. In the busiest city in the nation he was lonely. His life was work, supermarket, eat and sleep. Even the work he did at home. Human contact was restricted to those people he saw when delivering his monthly edition of

'Envirocare.'

At University Daniel discovered in himself a genuine love of language but was less interested in the academic aspects of his subject. For him, the simple juxtaposition of words was what seemed to matter. He knew instinctively that he wanted to write; trouble was he was none too keen on reading and didn't have the self-discipline needed to analyse and understand the work of others. Whilst his classmates were dissecting the great jewels of the English language Daniel wanted nothing more that to reshape them. He was short on original thought. He could work tirelessly attempting to improve a passage of writing but sadly for him there was no way he had the patience, skill or ingenuity to create his own plot.

All that left Daniel with nothing but 'Envirocare'.

At University he espoused just about every cause of his generation. He was anti war, anti nuclear power, anti pollution, anti profit, anti capitalism and opposed to the military. He was scared of acid rain and global warming. He marched to save the rain forests and the life style of Amazonian Indians. He was against fox hunting, all blood sports, testing cosmetics and drugs on animals, fur coats, and quarantine for dogs and sometimes found himself decidedly luke warm on the idea of coarse fishing.

'Envirocare' was essentially a 'green' issues paper and Daniel had a hard core of readers. If he sold every copy he just about covered his costs and fed himself. The little extras in life, the phone bill, and the gas bill, got paid when occasional sales were good or from his legacy. The good doctor and Mrs Coleman would, of course, have thoroughly disapproved of their son's life style and Daniel knew it. In his reflective moments he could picture his father, hands clasped behind his back, feet apart, swaying on his heels and advising a proper career.

To a large extent his parents were responsible for his lack of grit, their death, together, in a motoring accident at Christmas three years ago had effectively left their son independent financially. He could afford the indulgence of being a suburban revolutionary. The bills always got paid even if his savings were being gently whittled away. Daniel William Coleman was rudderless and knew it. That is what his father had called him the last time they had seen each other, before the accident; rudderless.

He plodded on day to day, month to month, year on year.

There was little spark and even less excitement. The trouble with being rudderless, thought Daniel when he remembered his father's words, was that you didn't really know what direction to travel in. You knew that things were going nowhere but had no idea how to break out of the cycle. Coleman continued to take the easy way out. He kept writing his monthly pamphlet. Secretly he hoped that some city editor would read a copy and track him down, offer him a job. It hadn't happened in four years so far.

This month's issue was much like the last. The articles and even the crossword recycled the same material every few months. Daniel had at least a dozen ways of extracting the word 'ozone' from his small but faithful readership. His one departure this time was the invitation for interested readers to come to his Fulham home later in the month to discuss issues raised. He had absolutely no idea whether anyone would take him up on the offer but felt strangely excited at the prospect.

Two

Compulsory redundancy hit Jim McCormack like a sledgehammer.

After sixteen years in the Royal Navy he thought he had a secure future until his fortieth birthday, maybe even beyond. It wasn't as if he was doing badly. In his last job at sea he had reached his goal and was the Marine Engineer Officer of HMS *Cromer*, a Sandown Class Minor War Vessel. He was head of the engineering department, the advisor to the captain of his ship. He was important; people listened.

If Chief Petty Officer James McCormack said the ship couldn't go to sea, then it didn't. Jim had considerable responsibility. It probably ran to millions of pounds when the value of a modern warship was considered. Now he had nothing.

Jim was bitter. As he finished his third pint of beer of the evening he slipped off his stool at the bar of the Kirklands Hotel and prepared to walk home. Lately his friends at the pub were beginning to find excuses for not joining him. He'd been drinking in the same pub for years, ever since he had moved to Kinross, one of the locals now; at least that was how he thought of himself.

Jim had little conversation except the endless anger and self-pity arising from losing his job. Trouble was he'd never considered a life outside the Navy and when the axe fell he still hadn't really accepted the news. He could hardly bear to talk about it to his wife, and until the fateful day when he walked out of the gates of HMS *Neptune* as a civilian he'd made no plans for the future.

Jim wasn't alone; there were ten other Chief Petty Officers of his specialisation made redundant in the same tranche. He was the last to leave. The others had completed the pre-release training that was on offer. They had attended various briefings on how to find new careers. All except Jim had succeeded in finding new jobs. For them, the future was a challenge. Jim hung on until the last minute. The problem would all go away or at least he thought it would. It was all a mistake, an administrative error.

It wasn't.

The first few months passed reasonably well. He scoured the papers for suitable work, visited the job centres in Cowdenbeath and Dunfermline and massaged his CV constantly. A few interviews were arranged. Nothing happened. He lowered his sights. He tried the dockyard at Rosyth.

A few years before he had been a respected member of a maintenance team working on warship repairs and directing the efforts of dockyard fitters; now he couldn't even become one. Jim moved away from engineering and was interviewed for a job as a van driver. At the first interview he found there were six other applicants,

He didn't make it to the second.

He had failed.

A bloody van driver; two interviews to be a bloody van driver, he couldn't bear to think about it. He'd been driving since his seventeenth birthday without a single bump, not even a parking ticket to his name. He had turned up in his suit, polished shoes, smart tie. He'd answered all the questions clearly and fully, and still he hadn't got the job. What did it take, that's what he wanted to know.

Luckily his redundancy payment still covered his mortgage. Liz was working full time, and Income Support helped. His mood worsened because he could see the end of state handouts looming large. Six months out of work and the rules would change. For a man who had joined up straight from school at seventeen and never drawn a penny from the state these months were the worst of his life.

Jim bade farewell to Bobby behind the bar and pushed his way through the door of the public bar, through the lounge and outside into the evening air. He walked out onto Kinross High

Street and started the short journey home. He loved it here. This was where he and Liz had bought their first house and he didn't want to leave it.

In the security of a job, Jim tended towards the 'get on your bike' philosophy famously offered by Norman Tebbitt some years earlier. In the rest room of the Naval Technical Department at Faslane he could be relied upon to offer an opinion about 'the lazy buggers who couldn't get off their asses and get a job'. Now he was beginning to understand the reality of unemployment.

At first he was a willing house-husband to Liz. He drew up schedules of when he would complete the household chores; shopping on Monday and Thursday, washing on Tuesdays, polishing and vacuuming mid week, all managed to a fine plan. He was going to have their little house cleaner than a new pin and better run than a destroyer.

Once the feeling of helplessness crept in, the schedule was abandoned. Liz went out of the door in the morning and the newspaper was open before she reached the end of the path. A pint at lunchtime if he was passing the door of the Kirklands gradually became a goal for the middle of the long day, something to get up for. Bobby even offered him a job behind the bar in the early months, but Jim laughed and turned him down. No way would Jim McCormack descend to bar work; he was much better than that. How could he hold his head high with his friends if he accepted Bobby's charity?

The subject hadn't been raised since.

Jim walked towards Sutherland Drive and the inevitable argument that awaited him. How much had he spent at the pub, how many pints had he drunk, had he found any jobs to apply for? The questions always raised more questions.

Liz understood the sense of failure Jim felt and was sympathetic. She knew marriage was a partnership, that for their ten years together he had been the provider, and a good one, she tried to show him hope and enthusiasm, to keep his spirits high. It was difficult. Liz was tired. The job at the bank was busy and her immediate boss, John Anderson, the Assistant Manager, didn't help. He was a *toucher;* Liz hated that. He didn't do anything outrageous but it wore her down. Like a dripping tap. If she were at her desk he would be close behind her with a hand on her shoulder.

If they were standing talking their conversation was punctuated by his touching her arm, even her cheek a couple of times. She loathed it. When the other women in the bank talked they all made the same comment, he was a slimy snake. But Liz didn't dare rock the boat, not now with Jim out of work. She longed for five o'clock each day and release from her torment.

The walk home usually eased her tension enough to face the increasing amount of housework and the prospect of cooking a meal. By the middle of the evening she would be ready for bed and then a new argument would begin. What had Jim done all day? No wonder he had energy for other things. All Liz wanted was sleep.

As the stress of a day in the bank subsided the thoughts of a different and altogether less manageable stress began: Jim.

Three

Annie looked into the large but ancient kitchen and surveyed the worktops covered in dirty plates and cutlery. *Not even a dishwasher* she thought. *At least I've got one at home.* She leaned on the wooden door frame and turned her head away from the kitchen and towards the open front door of the house.

"Darling, this kitchen looks like a war zone. Shall we leave the dishes until the morning?"

No reply came from her husband and she turned back to the kitchen and the mess.

"There isn't even a dishwasher. How can anyone be expected to entertain without a dishwasher these days?"

Annabel South had just endured her first dinner party as the wife of Flag Officer Scotland, Northern England and Northern Ireland. Her husband Alan, Rear Admiral Alan James South OBE to be more precise, had been in post less than a week, and had been a Rear Admiral the same length of time. Annie, as her friends knew her, had looked on her husband's new appointment with considerable trepidation but, ever the naval wife, she would make the best of it.

Greycourt, the Admiral's official residence in Helensburgh was all right, too big for the two of them with the children away during term time but she'd cope. After all was said and done her father had been an admiral so she knew the score.

Alan finished his farewells to their guests at the front door and walked through to join his wife.

"That's the last of them gone," he sighed, clearly happy to have brought that part of the evening to a close. "Did you say something, dear?"

"I said there isn't a dishwasher in this kitchen. Do you want to leave the clearing up until tomorrow, you don't have to go in to the office do you, it is Saturday?"

South considered his wife's question for a second before replying.

"I'd better go in for a couple of hours; there's an awful lot of reading to do before I'll be able to shake off the new boy in the area feeling. Weren't they a bunch of boring farts," he said, changing the subject and referring to their dinner guests. "If we hadn't invited the Commander it would have been hell."

"Yes, I liked her," replied Annie, "I'll bet she's a breath of fresh air about the place, Carolyn wasn't it?"

South nodded in silent confirmation and surveyed the devastation that represented the aftermath of dinner. He slipped his hand around Annie's.

"Don't tell me," South continued, "in your father's day he'd have had a full retinue of stewards to look after all this mess and we would be relaxing with a cognac before bed."

The defence cuts of recent years had bitten deeply into manpower levels; even admirals felt the pinch. For tonight's dinner, Alan had to go, almost cap in hand, to the wardroom at HMS *Neptune* to borrow a chef and a couple of stewards to assist Annie prepare, cook and serve the meal. The staff, in turn, was required to be up bright and early the following morning to provide breakfast for the live-in officers at the base and so he and Annie had let them go as soon as coffee was served. To be fair, the chef had cleared away all the pots and pans and that was an enormous help.

"It wouldn't be quite so bad if I'd enjoyed it," Annie offered, "but those two couples from the town hall were downright hostile."

She was right. The naval base at Faslane enjoyed a curious position in the community. It provided several thousand jobs, by far the largest employer in the area, but the local authorities were anti-nuclear, anti-armed forces and ardently socialist from a mould cast long before "New Labour" emerged. The peace camp outside the base had survived for years and years; even paid a peppercorn rent to the local council for their site in a lay-by. What an anachronism. The enemy camped on the doorstep and was supported by the people who drew their very livelihood from the presence of the Royal Navy. It made for a strained relationship.

"Do you know, I could see the Lord Provost, or whatever he is called, auditing the crockery and furniture whilst his wife was mentally costing out the meal. I'll bet they imagine that the government will pick up the bill. Perhaps you should have told them how much we paid to provide it."

"Yes, I know, darling," South replied, "but I do get some entertainment allowance towards this sort of thing and we must build bridges with the locals."

They decided to wade into the washing up so at just after midnight Alan and Annie South rolled up their sleeves and attacked the mess. As they worked together, a well-matched team, each withdrew into their own thoughts. Annie smiled and pictured their lovely home in Petersfield. The garden would be a mass of flowers by now and the lawns would need almost constant attention. It was a real struggle to leave her home to follow her husband for this appointment and she was already thinking about her return. Of course she was immensely proud that Alan had made it to Flag rank, younger than daddy did, but her pride was tinged with a little bitterness at what she was expected to give up to be the admiral's lady.

Her friends, her interests, all centred on their Hampshire home.

At least she didn't have a job any more. A year or two ago when she was working the move north would have been an even greater wrench for her. The Navy was still struggling with the concept that wives were people too; they had careers, expectation of their own. It was unfair to think of wives as baggage, appendages, to be shuffled around the country, even the world, just to support their men. What a dreadfully Victorian business it was to be a dutiful wife.

At first they discussed getting a tenant but Annie couldn't bear the thought of strangers sharing her home. They struck a deal; she would be a part-time admiral's lady, splitting her life equally between Greycourt and Petersfield. He would come south for leave and when his work demanded his presence in London or Portsmouth. Not ideal and an unwelcome drain on their savings trying to maintain two homes, but it was for the best. She had travelled up to Scotland earlier in the week to be here with Alan when he took up his post but even the week away from her home in Hampshire felt like a lifetime. Would the gardener turn up to keep the grounds tidy; he came highly recommended. Did they risk being burgled? What about frozen pipes. Surely that risk was well over by now but there were still so many worries.

Richard and Jane both had keys and had promised to look in on the house some weekends. Richard was the oldest, nearly twenty, and in his second year of geology at Southampton. He was also the closest to home. Annie didn't think he was the type to use the place for wild parties with his friends. No, Richard wasn't that type at all. Jane was in sixth year at Sherborne and hoping for Cambridge next year. Annie was proud of them both; good kids, she thought, and shuddered as she made mental images of the antics of some of their friends' children. They all seemed to want to drop out of university these days; hardly anyone finished the course they embarked upon. It was all about finding themselves, whatever that meant. Still, Annie was a '60s teenager and that seemed wild enough.

Alan's thoughts drifted to work and his new appointment. It was already clear that he would be under constant pressure to achieve cost savings. He knew he would have to be more a business manager than a NATO Sea Area Commander, and that his days would be full of budget plans and long-term costings. It was unlikely ever to be a question of what could he do to improve operational efficiency, always a matter of where could he save another half a million pounds.

The Strategic Defence Review had just been briefed to him before coming north to Scotland.

He recalled the pledge by the incoming government to review the armed forces role going into the next century and then match the resources to the need. *Some hope,* he thought, *here we go into another penny-pinching exercise, yet another bodge. More gapping of people.*

He found it most disturbing that in some areas he had twenty percent fewer people than were needed to do the job. *Hell*, he thought, *this is peacetime at the home of the nation's nuclear deterrent and I have to borrow a chef.* Of course he had to put a brave face on it. As far as Faslane was concerned, the buck would stop with him. What Alan found most difficult to come to terms with was the lack of morale in the Royal Navy. Young sailors were leaving in droves. It was a spiral, he understood that. If you have a shortage of people then you have to ask them to do more; if you make greater demands on their time people leave. For sailors and officers alike it was becoming a job. Even he, from his elevated position could see the cracks appearing.

Alan and Annie drifted off to bed, one locked into the problems ahead and the other taking comfort in what had gone before.

Four

The lift door opened and Laura Latimer breezed into the foyer of her South Kensington apartment building. John the doorman broke out in a beaming smile, ear to ear. He adored her, he fantasised about her, and he was almost puppy dog like in his admiration of the lovely Ms Latimer.

"Good morning Miss, lovely day," that was about all he ever managed before he started to get tongue-tied.

The object of his fantasy smiled back warmly, returned his greeting and continued out the door. Now left alone his thoughts and desires about her fell one into another and tumbled through his mind. As always she was dressed in a sharp, almost severe, business suit that accentuated every inch of her stunning figure.

She had a body to make even the super-models envious.

At close to six feet tall and with her raven black shoulder length hair and dark brown, almost black eyes, John thought she knocked spots off the beauties paraded in the fashion magazines. She had occupied the comfortable and exclusive second floor apartment for almost two years and John knew she worked somewhere in north London but wasn't sure where. He thought it may have been something to do with public relations but he had never had the courage to probe.

All he knew was that one sight of her and his day was made. Must be off overnight he decided, having remembered that she was carrying a small week-end bag as well as her brief case; he wondered who the lucky guy was and began to imagine her swinging her long shapely legs between soft silk sheets as she slipped into John's bed. John's thoughts were broken by the sound of the lift and completely destroyed by the appearance of the tenant from apartment number eight; you definitely had to watch your p's and q's with this one he thought as he followed the man's passage across the foyer and out of the front door.

Laura enjoyed a wry smile as she hailed a black cab outside the building. She was well aware of her looks and dressed to maximise the effect. She also knew the effect she had on the doorman and had long ago realised he would be totally unable to think rationally in her presence.

Laura Latimer had worked well for the young woman who boarded the cab and told the driver her destination. She had been Laura since coming to London from Damascus almost three years ago and her future looked good. Leila Latif, the real person inside the Austin Reed International suit, was very different from the woman John the doorman idolised. Her Palestinian father and Swiss mother had doted on their beautiful young daughter. But in war torn Beirut where Abdul Latif managed his business empire exporting jewellery life was never predictable.

Abdul and Karin Latif were gunned down in broad daylight the day before Leila's fifteenth birthday and she became an orphan. Remarkably, after the funeral, she continued much as before.

The family home was hers, there was ample, almost too much, money available and she would carry on with her schooling until she passed sixteen. She had no other family in the city and her father's friends worked honestly to close Abdul's business affairs leaving Leila a relatively rich young lady. Leila managed to juggle the disciplines of learning at school and running a home with ease. She could bargain for food in the markets as well as any of the more experienced Beirut women and her skills soon left her completely outside the concern of the thinly stretched authorities in the troubled city.

After a couple of months the young Leila, still less than sixteen years of age, started to explore her surroundings with a different set of standards. She needed human contact beyond the somewhat tentative and juvenile relationships she had developed at school and so she began to frequent the many street cafes in the early evening. Older in looks than her fifteen years she found acceptance in this adult world easy and began to make friends.

From the young men of Beirut she learned about politics, about political struggle, and about anger. She listened to tales of training camps in the hills, of successful missions against the oppressors of her land, and of the many causes espoused by Arab peoples. Leila was captivated. Her family had been honest and kindly people set only on a course to provide a stable home for her. They were motivated only by ambitions of wealth. Her new world became more alien with every passing day.

Inevitably Leila became noticed. Subtly, but surely she was introduced to the next order of man. She found her ideas and ideals being drawn gently by young men who spoke quietly and with more thought than the rather brash coffee shop youths she started out with. Largely un-noticed by Leila her background was investigated and her new acquaintances became aware of a wealthy young woman with no ties and a desire to share the romance and excitement of a world in the shadows.

At first her involvement was low key, testing. She delivered a few packages to the airport, passed on papers at an hotel, kept some ammunition safe within her house for a couple of weeks. She managed her tasks well. By her eighteenth birthday she was a regular courier within Lebanon and Syria and had a passport from both countries.

Her first trip to Europe marked a watershed in both her personal life and her involvement with the organisation. She was to accompany a man to Geneva. Leila didn't know what the man would do there but she knew they were to be a couple during the journey. Her contact in Beirut had played on the fact that she had the perfect background for the job. She had visited the country in her youth and could speak French and English fluently.

For all that she had learned in the last few years Leila was ill prepared for her meeting with Aziz. He was darker skinned that Leila and matched her in height. He was slim but clearly well toned and he had deep, penetrating eyes that were ever watchful. Leila judged him to be in his mid twenties and felt

24

almost a jolt of electricity when she shook his cool hand. During the flight from Beirut to Geneva Leila had to check herself, she knew she was talking too much but couldn't stop.

For his part, Aziz remained detached, giving little away of his personal life or mission. They arrived at their hotel without incident and were shown to a standard, if nondescript, room. Within minutes Aziz had left her alone in the room and returned some hours later without comment. They shared an evening meal, retired to the room and Aziz stripped for bed with an air of total unconcern.

Leila experienced a brief moment of uncertainty before following his lead.

Acutely aware of Aziz and the almost searing heat of his naked body beside her Leila once again felt doubts. In a silence that lasted for a few minutes but seemed like hours she laid perfectly still both frightened and at the same time excited by the situation she found herself in. Aziz turned to her, reached out to draw Leila into an embrace and she knew her life would never be the same again.

Their second day matched the routine of the first and Leila spent much of the time wandering around the hotel and waiting. When Aziz returned in the evening he declared that their work was done and they could leave in the morning for home. Leila was disappointed. She hated the feeling of not having control over what was being done but felt this uncertainty overtaken by the prospect of another night.

Over the next few months Aziz and Leila worked together several more times and although Leila wanted more from the relationship Aziz gave little. She was in love but could see that her lover took only the physical release of their union and wanted no commitment.

When a trip to London was discussed she assumed that she would accompany Aziz once more and was surprised when she was briefed that this time she would make contact with someone in London and that her companion would provide cover for her. Roles were reversed. Her partner proved to be a Syrian of about her age and Leila took a great pleasure in leaving him at their hotel whilst she trekked across London to perform her first task as the courier. That evening she took control of arrangements and finally in their shared room she used her young companion to satisfy her needs.

Leila set off the following morning with a smile of real satisfaction; as an Arab woman she was now the dominant member of the partnership. The man she had left behind at the hotel could kick his heels all day and she wouldn't care. As she travelled the tube to her second rendezvous she contemplated whether she would use him again that evening or just ignore him, a servant to be dropped at her whim.

Her task completed she returned to the hotel to find her partner in less than good humour. He was clearly bored from a second day of inactivity and decided that last night's intimacy allowed him to voice his opinions. Laura's mood changed in an instant and the cold glare she offered him failed to stem his complaints. Just as quickly she decided that this man was now a nuisance. He had served his purpose, her job was done and the prospect of sitting through a long flight back to Beirut with him did not appeal.

Leila raised a hand to stem the flow of words and suggested they take a walk to a nearby restaurant for an evening meal. Her smile worked its magic and within minutes they were on the pavement outside the hotel and heading for the lights of the West End. As she walked she played scenarios in her mind; what would her Control back in Lebanon say if she returned from an operation alone? Was this Syrian man expendable? Who was the more valuable asset?

Leila's decision made itself easy as she approached a darkened side street littered with commercial rubbish bins. In a single fluid movement she slipped a slender stiletto knife from her handbag, pressed the button to release the blade and thrust the needle sharp point into the man's neck. With hardly a murmur he dropped to the ground, raised a hand towards the blade and drew his final breath. Leila withdrew the blade, wiped the blood on his jacket and walked swiftly on.

In the deepening shadows of the evening she left the body of her accomplice slumped close to the rubbish containers, turned straight for the hotel and within minutes had disposed of his meagre luggage, checked out and was heading for

Heathrow Airport. An open return ticket would ensure she would be in the air before any fuss started and with the man's passport and travel documents securely inside her luggage she knew it would take days before identification could be made.

Leila Latif had become what her masters wanted. She was intelligent, beautiful and calculating, but much more she was capable of killing without a second thought. She would have a role to play in the world of intelligence gathering and international terrorism.

Laura, as she now thought of herself, stopped the taxi at the Edgware Road station and headed underground. The tube train was crowded as usual and she was forced to stand all the way to King's Cross. Emerging from the station she turned into Caledonian Road and walked the short distance to the office that acted as her London base.

She had learned the rudiments of the import/export business during her lengthy stay at a camp in the Beqa valley, sandwiched between training in weapons and explosives and unarmed combat techniques. She had been a good student and had learned well. The business was legitimate and she made an adequate living bringing goods in to England from the Middle East to supply the many dealers trading in rugs and Arab artefacts. Her private wealth, sensibly invested, allowed Laura the luxury of accommodation in Kensington and a life style which brought her into contact with the affluent of London's middle society. Her brief was simple; she was to merge in with her new country and report anything that offered a chance to cause embarrassment to the United States or Britain.

Latimer Imports occupied a single shop front in Collier Street and a glance through the window revealed little more than a small office equipped with a range of standard office equipment. Laura opened the door, picked up her mail from the floor, closed and locked the door behind her and moved into the office.

Leaving her briefcase and mail on the desk she moved swiftly through to a rear storeroom where she opened the weekend bag and took out a change of clothes. Wasting no time she stripped completely and redressed in Marks and Spencer's underwear, leaving the luxury of silk behind. She followed that with jeans and a sweater. Laura tied back her hair, moved to the wash hand basin and removed every scrap of make-up. Adding an anorak from a cupboard Laura left the office through the rear door looking a different person from when she had entered barely fifteen minutes earlier.

Five

The peace dividend in Northern Ireland created some unusual bedfellows and the sight of Padraig Flynn and Brendan O'Neill sitting together in the Drapers Arms in Wapping bore witness to that fact.

Flynn was an idealist.

He was, until last year, an active soldier of the Irish National Liberation Army, the INLA. Flynn alone had a kill record of six in an organisation generally regarded as one of the most extreme of the republican terrorist groups. Flynn had a reputation for never backing away from any action that would further the cause of a united Ireland. He would willingly bomb or kill or maim or intimidate and it mattered little to him whether the target was man or woman or even child.

For Flynn the cause was everything and the end could always justify the means.

Padraig Flynn had enjoyed dozens of different names in his ten years with INLA and had stayed one step ahead of the security forces throughout. He was talked about by the RUC and by Special Branch and in the corridors of MI5 and MI6 but only as an un-named, un-identified enigma who had successfully evaded arrest. He would not have been surprised to confirm that his name failed to feature in any security organisation file and that his various acts of terrorism were not even attributed to the same man. That INLA had managed to keep his identity and purpose a closely guarded secret in itself testified to his skill on the ground.

Brendan O'Neill had little in common with Flynn.

Where Flynn was cunning, resourceful, determined and careful, O'Neill was brash, short tempered and unreliable. O'Neill was a Belfast Protestant who had drifted towards the Loyalist Volunteer Force out of boredom and the wish to indulge in his passion for violence. O'Neill had flirted with hard drugs. Whilst Flynn kept himself to himself O'Neill was well known, he had a criminal record before he left school and by the age of twenty two had completed his first spell at Her Majesty's pleasure having beaten a young man nearly to death over an argument in a public house.

He was a bully at school preferring to use his fists before making reasoned argument and in a violent city had soon gravitated to stone and petrol bomb throwing. O'Neill was a soldier too but the comparison with Flynn ended at just the word. At the height of the troubles O'Neill was called upon often. He would turn out whenever a baseball bat was needed or whenever a knee-capping served the Unionist cause. His masters did his thinking for him and he was fed into situations where if things didn't go to plan he was expendable. Brendan O'Neill knew little of the history of the Province and cared less.

He didn't work and didn't really want to. He was ill equipped for a life beyond the violence of a divided Northern Ireland and failed to come to terms with the new future that Prime Minister Tony Blair had engineered with his referendum victory in the North and with the double referendum victory in the South.

The two Irishmen from different backgrounds found themselves without a positive direction. Flynn was putting out feelers on the International market to see if his skills could be used for a short period until the peace process started to creak under the strain. He was patient enough to wait for what he believed would be the eventual outcome; a return to the armed struggle. He kept O'Neill around him for much the same reasons as he had been tolerated by the LVF, he was useful for dirty work and was entirely expendable.

O'Neill drummed with both hands on the table. His mind told him that he was tapping out the tune to the latest offering from the Spice Girls but what Flynn heard was just an annoying distraction.

"Shut the fuck up Brendan," Flynn scowled directly at the man, "get up to the bar and get another pint."

"I've no fuckin' money," was the reply and a crumpled five

30

pound note transferred between the two of them.

Old habits died hard and Flynn looked carefully around the bar taking in the faces of the other early afternoon drinkers. Nothing suspicious. He could hardly remember a time when he was less threatened that he felt at the moment. Flynn had even found a job in London through some contacts from the old days and had a regular income working in what was referred to as the black economy. If his belief in an ultimate return to chaos in Ireland had been in the least bit shakeable he could almost have imagined himself on the path to respectability.

Latif and Flynn had met for the first time in Beqa when they had shared a training course in radio techniques. It was she who had tracked him down yesterday and suggested the meeting and it was she who had decided upon the place. Flynn had mentioned O'Neill to her and she seemed unconcerned about the other mans attendance. Flynn only knew the woman as Latif and so when he was informed that her name was now Laura he registered no surprise.

Brendan returned with the two pints of Beamish Black at the same time as Laura Latimer walked through the door.

Six

Laura entered the Drapers Arms and glanced around the bar noting everyone present. She saw Flynn and the man she assumed to be O'Neill and crossed the room.

"Hello Paddy, good to see you again."

Flynn nodded a greeting but didn't get up. He shuffled to one side along the wooden pub bench worn smooth and polished more by the action of countless customers than by regular cleaning. He made enough room for the woman to slide in beside him. Padraig Flynn introduced Laura to his companion and with the briefest of pleasantries completed O'Neill was despatched to the bar to get Laura a Perrier Water.

"O'Neill?" said Laura as soon as the man was out of hearing.

"Don't worry about him," replied Flynn, "he does what I tell him and isn't likely to think for himself."

"OK."

Brendan returned with the drink for the woman and noisily dragged his stool back to the table and sat down. He handed Flynn the change from the drinks order and was about to start up his drumming again when Flynn stopped him with a glare.

O'Neill lifted his full pint glass and took a long drink of the dark beer.

A moustache of frothy white decorated his top lip and he extended his tongue, almost crudely, to lick it away. Laura eyed him briefly and he grinned back in a way that made his thoughts obvious. 'One to watch,' she thought to herself, 'he may be just be muscle but around a woman he would always be unpredictable.'

"I'd like you boys to come with me to a place in Fulham

tomorrow," Laura announced, "I'll meet you at Fulham Broadway tube station at seven in the evening. It may be nothing but I want to check something out."

She briefly explained that she had read about a little meeting of environmentalists advertised in a pamphlet called "Envirocare" and she wanted to see what it was all about.

"There's twenty each for expenses," said Laura, and pushed a copy of the pamphlet across the table to Padraig. She lifted the corner of the page to show the man the four folded notes inside.

"If anything comes out of it maybe we'll do some work together"

Laura stood up and leaving the Perrier untouched she walked out of the bar without a backward glance. O'Neill followed her exit from the bar in complete silence, his eyes never rising above the waist level of her close fitting denim jeans.

"Quite a looker isn't she" said O'Neill, "I could handle some of that."

"If I were you Brendan I'd forget you even thought it, she's way out of your league. Just be grateful for the twenty quid and hope there's more to come."

"She's even left the water behind," said O'Neill, "if she'd had a pint I could have finished it but I'm not drinking this rubbish."

Flynn downed the remainder of his pint, folded the flimsy pamphlet in two and slid it into the pocket of his jacket. He indicated that O'Neill should finish his beer. The two men rose together and left.

***

Laura made her way to Collier Street by a different route and let herself into the office by the rear door. She changed back into her business clothes, applied some make up, and went through into the front room. For an hour she busied herself with the detail of running a business and at five o'clock she logged onto her Internet service and sent a brief e-mail to a CompuServe user number she knew to be in Damascus. Her controller would be pleased with the evidence that Leila Latif

33

was still active and thinking of her task.

When she reached her apartment building the doorman had finished his shift and the reception area was empty for the evening.

***

Back in his digs Padraig Flynn read through the copy of "Envirocare" and scoffed to himself.

"Bloody do-gooders, they wouldn't know a decent cause if it bit them on the ass."

Whatever his private thoughts, the prospect of doing something appealed to him and he began to look forward to the evening ahead.

Seven

Coleman was as prepared for the evening as he knew how. He had moved all his office equipment into the bedroom, bought a couple of wine boxes, some beer and soft drinks from the local supermarket, and had put two dozen vegetable "sausage" rolls in the oven. When the doorbell rang at exactly eight o'clock he imagined the evening would be a complete success. By half past eight there were ten people beside himself in his living room.

A couple of his guests he had met before and were regular subscribers to "Envirocare". They were tucking in to the red wine and talking excitedly about the seal cull due to start in Greenland this season. The two men were typically set in the Coleman mould, hair overlong for the latest fashion, bearded, jeans and sandals despite the fact that the weather hadn't really turned from spring to summer.

Their girlfriends made the perfect match, dressed identically to their men except for the addition of some coloured beads and brightly coloured knitted waistcoats. The four were a pastiche of '60's San Francisco. They seemed to think Coleman was doing a job of great value in producing his magazine and were bubbling over with ideas for inclusion in subsequent editions.

On the opposite side of the room and under a cloud of smoke stood three scruffy looking individuals, almost androgynous, who the host had concluded were two males and a female. They sported punk style haircuts, tattoos on their forearms and hands and from what conversation Daniel heard, as he attempted to circulate, they were pretty much monosyllabic.

Flynn had tried to engage this group in conversation but with little success. They were living in a squat nearby and had seen the invitation in "Envirocare" largely by accident but had come on the off chance that drugs may be freely available. Between the three of them they completely demolished Coleman's limited buffet and left at nine o'clock, each with a couple of cans of soft drink or beer in their pockets.

Once the punks had departed and Coleman felt more comfortable with his gathering he began to relax. Flynn and O'Neill added little to the substance of the discussion but aware that Laura saw some advantage in their attendance they did their best to appear interested. Laura made a fuss of Coleman from the beginning and it became obvious that she was a knowledgeable reader of his present and past efforts. She complimented him on topics he had written about and managed to draw the group together. For his part, Coleman was experiencing a feeling that was hitherto unknown to him. He was so clearly enjoying the attention of this attractive and intelligent woman that he talked more about himself and his work that he had done in years. Laura had found another acolyte.

Skilfully Laura probed Coleman about plans he held for the future. He had taken a document off the Internet from a group of activists called "Trident Ploughshares 2000" and he was unsure whether to give it any mention in his next edition.

Laura held only a vague recollection of this name and Daniel took centre stage as he explained to the gathering that the group had as their purpose the intention to damage one of the Royal Navy's four Trident missile carrying nuclear submarines. He mentioned that some time previously the group had caused damage estimated at some millions of pounds to an aircraft destined for sale to Indonesia in protest at the treatment of people in East Timor. Laura remembered it well.

"So how do this group intend to damage a submarine," Laura asked, "surely they must be the best protected weapons in the world."

"I know someone who used to visit the Peace Camp at Faslane," one of the flower people chipped in, "and from what he said the peace campers broke in to the base whenever they wanted to."

"They must have security, surely," she responded, "Soldiers or Defence police or something."

"Yeah, they do but the fence goes on for miles and the guards can't be everywhere at once. My friend says that the peace campers know all their radio frequencies and where the security cameras are fitted and everything. After all the peace camp has been there for years."

Daniel produced the paper he had talked about and Laura could see it was entitled the, "Tri-Denting It" handbook. The subject obviously held less interest for the flower people than for Laura and gradually they drifted off into their own corner of the room and eventually bade Daniel farewell and motioned to leave.

Daniel escorted the group of four to the door and Laura took the opportunity to whisper to Padraig that he should get rid of Brendan, stay another ten minutes or so and then leave himself. Padraig agreed and indicated to O'Neill that he should go. Left alone the three of them talked more about the Trident Ploughshares group and as arranged Padraig departed. As he turned back towards the living room he saw Laura silently signal to him that she would be in touch.

Feeling the comforting effect of several glasses of wine Daniel made no objection when his final guest offered to help clean up the mess and between the two of them they set to the task. Laura had long ago noticed the little glances coming her way from Coleman and she took every opportunity to rest her hand on his arm or accidentally brush against him. She was having the desired effect. Coleman blushed as he admitted that he wasn't in a relationship at the moment and was flattered beyond belief when Laura expressed surprise. The cleaning work done, Coleman was desperate to prolong the encounter for as long as he could and was delighted when the woman dropped leisurely into an armchair.

"Coffee?" inquired Coleman; "I have a little Whisky if you'd prefer?"

Laura settled on coffee and a delighted Coleman returned to the kitchen to make the preparations.

"Dan," she called into the kitchen, "is there a point when actions should speak louder than words?"

Coleman heard her but wasn't sure what to reply. He couldn't gauge the question well from a distance and so he returned to the living room and asked her to repeat herself.

"What I meant was," she replied, "is there a point when you feel so strongly about something that you want to take action stronger than just writing about it every month?"

"I suppose there is, I mean, well, first and foremost I'm a journalist, but I do believe in what I write so I must be willing to do more."

Laura slipped one foot out of its Timberland boat shoe and stretched herself in the chair.

"Dan, I've really enjoyed this evening with you, it's given me lots and lots to think about and I'd love the chance to talk to you again soon."

"Oh me too, Laura, I'm so pleased you were able to come."

"When do you plan to have the next of these little gatherings?" she asked.

"Well, I'm not sure, this was, sort of an experiment, I wasn't certain anyone would come at all so I hadn't thought about doing another one." Then, more as a question than anything, Daniel added, "Of course you would be welcome to come round at any time if you wanted to talk over anything, or even just for a visit."

Laura uncoiled herself from the chair, leaned over the seated Daniel and kissed him firmly on the mouth.

"I may just do that, thanks for the offer."

Coleman leapt to his feet as she walked towards the front door and managed to collide with her in the hallway. Laura kissed him again and this time he had gathered enough courage to return the gesture. She allowed the moment to linger rather longer and finally broke away seeming breathless and moved by the incident.

If Laura was moved by it then Daniel Coleman was shaking at the knees. As he closed the door behind his guest he found himself leaning on the door for fully half a minute whilst he recovered himself. If she had returned and asked him to jump out of the window he would not have hesitated.

Still sitting in an armchair an hour later Daniel's reverie was broken by the sound of his telephone.

"Hello, Daniel Coleman here."

"Hi, Dan, this is Laura. I took your number and just had to thank you again for this evening. I do hope we can get together soon."

Coleman retired happy, slept well, and woke in good humour.

Eight

For the next few days the office in Collier Street was a hive of activity as Laura carried out her enquiries. She had quickly tracked down the handbook seen at Coleman's gathering and was compiling a dossier on this group who called themselves Trident Ploughshares 2000. Information was easy enough to come by.

There was a promotional video expounding the group's views on why Trident breached International Law, there was the handbook itself, which spelled out the intention that the group be non-violent in their activities, and there was a host of detail gleaned from various Internet sites and web pages.

By the second day she understood the aim of the group and how they intended to function. She knew the hard-core founder group by name and knew they were trying to encourage the formation of small and medium sized affinity groups who could follow their own agenda under the umbrella of disarming Trident submarines.

Ploughshares had a diary of campaign activities spanning the summer months and were hoping that August would mark the coming together of all the groups at Faslane, in Scotland. There were sixty-two signatories to the Pledge of Commitment produced in the 'Tri-Denting It' handbook and that meant sixty-two people likely to turn up at the Royal Navy Base in August. In addition there were six, already established, affinity groups whose interests ranged widely from environmental issues to membership of the campaign to save endangered whales. These people embraced the philosophy of disarmament but not as their principal motivation. Laura judged that hundreds of such sympathisers could make the journey north in the summer and that suited her purposes well.

The potential for Leila Latif, alias Laura Latimer, was outstanding.

Once Laura was satisfied that she had the measure of the Ploughshares group she began to widen her area of interest to include the Faslane Peace Camp and its occupants. A rag, tag bunch, she discovered, who had occupied the makeshift site in a lay-by for sixteen years adjacent to the A814 road heading to the north from Helensburgh. In the early days the camp was a thriving community of a couple of dozen fanatics who were joined periodically by up to hundreds of others.

Half a dozen brightly painted caravans now marked what remained of the camp and numbers had dropped to about the same six. In recent months the new Argyle and Bute Council had attempted to gain an eviction order against the remaining group, which included a young mother and her child of about six years of age. The campers dug in. They dug some rudimentary tunnels intended as boltholes against the sheriff or the bailiff, and erected some tree houses. Some of the more notorious demonstrators from fashionable anti-road or airport groups lent solidarity, and presumably advice, to the beleaguered residents and finally the court bid floundered amidst a host of legal technicalities and the camp plodded on.

Laura worked steadily until six o'clock when she thought the time was right. Dialling the telephone number she had for Flynn a few thoughts were beginning to form in her mind.

"Yeah." was Flynn's response when he lifted the receiver at the third ring.

"Ever been to Scotland Paddy?" the woman asked, knowing that Flynn would recognise her voice and have the presence of mind to think before making comments likely to identify either himself or the caller.

Laura continued over the silence, "I've booked the three of us into a B and B for a couple of days, I'll see you at Glasgow Queen Street Station at five o'clock next Wednesday afternoon, travel light. There's ticket money in the post. OK?"

Flynn ended the conversation as he had begun it and hung up the phone.

Her next call was to a number in Fulham.

"Dan, it's me," she said clearly noting the lift in his voice as he realised who the caller was.

"Just wondered if you fancied getting together this evening for a drink and a chat?"

"That would be great," came the reply, "shall we meet here or, where are you now?"

They arranged to meet in the pub at the end of his street and Coleman headed for the shower, already planning what he would use from his meagre wardrobe.

For her part Laura went through the same routine as she had on first meeting Coleman, right down to the change in under clothes. She left Collier Street through the back door and headed for their meeting in Fulham.

"Yes mate?" the landlord of the Crown Inn on Lillie Road asked Daniel Coleman as he reached the bar. The landlord didn't need to have civility as his strong suit because he catered to the same customers each night. Like many London pubs off the main routes, his was a "local". It boasted a darts team and a dominoes team and enough regular drinkers to keep the business afloat. At least Coleman had been recognised by the landlord, if he hadn't, then the "mate" would have been left out of the address.

"A pint of Fuller's please," he asked for, and stood idly watching the barman as he pulled steadily on the beer pump handle. Two complete strokes and the glass was filled.

Coleman found a table and surveyed the bar; it was empty apart from himself and the owner. Looking at his watch he realised he was almost twenty minutes early. He rose and carried the glass back to the bar where he pulled out a bar stool and sat down.

"You're local aren't you?" from the landlord, "I've seen you about in the road but you ain't been in 'ere before." The implied question hung in the air and Coleman felt obliged to offer an explanation as to why he never frequented the public house.

"I'm meeting a friend," he muttered, "a girl friend," Coleman added, liking the sound of what he told the man and hoping to himself that it was actually true. A silence descended on the two of them and after a few seconds the landlord began to busy himself behind the counter and any opportunity for further conversation was lost.

The man behind the bar looked up briefly when Laura entered and noted the warmth of her greeting to the rather wimpish looking man he had just served. The pub didn't keep Perrier Water in stock so she settled for a half-pint glass of lager and the two of them moved towards the table furthest from the bar. As Laura turned away from the bar the landlord took a longer look. He noted instantly what her neatly fitted denim jeans did for her rear view and couldn't help but question what the woman saw in the man. By now the couple were seated at the table and just out of hearing range so the landlord satisfied himself with the thought that Coleman must be 'rigged like a donkey', and got about his business.

The couple spent half an hour in idle conversation, he sometimes haltering in his manner whilst she was confident and coaxing. Laura guided him gently and when the half-hour had passed felt him relaxed enough to probe further with her questions. Gradually she managed to point their discussion to the next issue of 'Envirocare.'

"So what are you going to put in your magazine this month Dan, I think it is so exciting to be doing something so worthwhile, I know I never could."

Coleman made the right noises in reply and Laura tried again.

"Do you have a main theme in each issue, or do you try to combine lots of topics?"

For Daniel this attention, centred on him, was like a powerful drug and just as she had loosened his tongue at their last meeting, so this time she gained the same result.

"Well, to be honest, I don't really have a proper plan. I just sort of add different articles when they interest me, and that way I manage to keep all my readers every month. I've got a big group of regulars you know, not just the few you saw at my discussion group."

Laura took a tentative sip from her glass of lager and wordlessly promised herself a glass of Champagne when she got back to South Ken'. Daniel remained silent for a moment and then turned full face to Laura.

"What do you think I should cover in the next issue?"

Laura felt a familiar surge of excitement as she realised that Coleman had quite unwittingly taken a step into the unknown. Now was the time for her to take care, now was the moment when she should mould this man to the shape she wanted. She felt a sense of victory.

"Is this your regular pub Dan," the woman asked. Coleman replied that it was his first visit.

"Have you still got any of that Whisky you mentioned last week?"

"My Glenkinchie, oh yes, I have a glass of that every month when I finish the magazine, it's a sort of tradition for me."

Laura looked disappointed,

"Does that mean I couldn't have a little taste now, instead of this lager?"

"Of course you can, shall I buy it here, or shall we go back to the house?"

"I think the house would be so much more cosy, don't you Dan?" was Laura's reply and they rose together and headed for the door.

"Bye," came the response from behind the bar but Coleman hardly heard the landlord's farewell as he held the door open for his girlfriend. Had he turned to engage the landlord he would have known instinctively that the man had directed his greeting to Laura and not him.

Nine

The evening sun sank slowly behind the hills overlooking the Royal Navy base at Faslane and bathed the Gareloch in an orange glow.

The wake of a slow moving launch caused strands of silver to flicker in the light and shade on the water. All was quiet. It was half past eight and Carolyn Smart was still in her office.

Another long day.

Carolyn was the Commander of HMS Neptune, the Naval establishment which provided the accommodation and hotel services to the Navy based in the west of Scotland and home to the First Submarine Squadron, the Third Mine Counter Measures Squadron and the Northern Ireland Squadron.

The former comprised the four submarines of the Vanguard Class capable of delivering their deadly nuclear warheads using the US Trident missile system, the recent replacement for the ageing Polaris of the seventies and eighties. SM1, as was the squadron's short title, also included the remaining submarines of the Swiftsure Class. The Third MCM Squadron was made up of eight Sandown Class, fibreglass hulled, Mine Hunters. Their advanced sonar system and Remote Control Mine Disposal System; mini, unmanned submarines, could be directed on to a mine, deliver an explosive charge, and withdraw to safe range whilst that mine was exploded from the mother ship.

The ships of MCM3 were a triumph of British technology and the envy of the world. Much simpler in their technology, the ships of the Northern Ireland Squadron carried out the "bread and butter" task of patrolling the waters of the troubled province in an attempt to prevent the import of weapons to the warring factions.

The apparent peace in Ireland did not halt the supply of

arms to either side, or to the many splinter groups of both the Republican and Loyalist causes. That process of re-arming and re-organising would continue unabated against the possibility that peace would once again prove beyond the grasp of the politicians and the gunmen.

She had almost finished another long day, in another long month, into her second year of her present appointment. Carolyn didn't think of herself as a rising star in the Royal Navy's firmament but others did. In what remained essentially a male dominated service she had made it to the rank of Commander at thirty-five and had done so, not as a token woman but on pretty well equal terms. Even her boss, the Captain, Tony Pounder, would grudgingly acknowledge that she was at least as good as many of the Commanders he had encountered in his long service.

She'd never be a submariner of course, and that made her a lesser being in Pounder's book, but then the Royal Navy had not yet signed up to the idea of women serving in the close confines of operational submarines. It was inevitable in the continual drive for change, but at the moment the submarine service was practically the last bastion of male dominance within the naval service. Next would come the Royal Marines. Tony Pounder genuinely believed that if she got through this job without a major cock-up, or worse still, without suffering some sort of breakdown, she would make it to Captain.

The Commander was totally absorbed with the subject of a group of activists who held the potential to spoil her entire summer. That afternoon she had chaired the third meeting of the Clyde Naval Base Trident Ploughshares 2000 Security Co-ordination Group. What occupied her attention this cool, but bright, evening were the minutes of the afternoon's meeting. Seated in front of her computer, as so many senior officers now found themselves, she typed away producing a digest of what had been said and laying out an action grid of who was to do what before the next get together in two weeks time.

Her post as Commander of the establishment carried with it a heavy, almost daunting, responsibility for security in what was most likely the most guarded military establishment in the country. She had already studied the reports of several boards of inquiry resulting from breaches of the base perimeter line. In one, during the previous year, a determined peace camper had managed to get on to the casing of a submarine berthed within the Base.

In a more recent incident an activist had stolen a Ministry of Defence Police inflatable boat from the nearby armament depot and tried to intrude into her parish. In her estimation security was a subject always likely to end in tears. As she shuffled her meeting notes into proper order it was not lost on Carolyn Smart that the person who had stolen the police boat was none other than Angela Young, and that she was the founding member of the Trident Ploughshares group.

Naturally enough, she had plenty of sound, even expert, advisors around her and the Ministry of Defence had an intelligence gathering organisation that drew upon all the well known groups like MI5 and Special Branch for their most up to date information. She had learned today that there were four "ploughshares" affinity groups already formed and active in Sweden and that they were all set to make the trip to Scotland in August. She knew too that the focus for the groups' activity was likely to be the nearby Armament depot at Coulport where the missiles and their warheads were stored, installed and removed from submarines. A piece of land adjacent to the armament depot had been sold off publicly during the last year and the purchaser had been a known anti-nuclear sympathiser. Since then there had been several gatherings on this land, mainly women's groups, but nevertheless a powerful force for disruption.

Carolyn decided that she had finished for the evening and began to look forward to a long soak in a hot bath back at her flat in the Officers' Married Quarters estate at nearby Rhu. She could almost taste the harshness of the whisky she would allow herself before turning in for the night. Trouble was, she knew, her Base had a perimeter fence, to the landward side, that was almost three miles in length and although it was bristling with security cameras and alarms it was still vulnerable.

The two major gates, at the northern and southern ends of the base were witness to the arrival and departure of over six thousand people each day. Some of them, maybe two thousand, were servicemen and women who had at least an instinct for security. Others made up the permanent workforce of engineers and accountants and cleaners and gardeners and cooks and the whole range of people who made the small town work. These groups were accustomed to the rigours of the security systems and by and large complied with the rules without a grumble. To them, at least, their jobs demanded this additional discipline and so it became a familiar nuisance. Still more of the numbers, often as many as one thousand people each day, were civilian contractors who came for a day or a week or maybe a month at a time to provide necessary expertise in a vast array of subjects. This group always had a sponsor within the established workforce and the status of their company governed whether they were permitted access to the base without an escort. In the course of a normal day there would be dozens of anomalies.

Access lists were incomplete or non-existent, sponsors would fail to meet their visitors, people would complain about delays, it went on and on. There were security passes of a dozen colours and types, each entitling the bearer to a differing level of access to different parts of the vast establishment. The task of issue and collection and policing of these passes required a complete sub population of security personnel employed round the clock stopping vehicles and drivers and pedestrians. The potential for chaos at the two gates was enormous. It took only one hold up during the busy periods, start and finish of the normal working day, and the traffic could be backed up for miles. Equally, it took just a small demonstration from the peace campers to effectively shut the place down for hours.

People were human and they suffered the frailty of imperfect beings. Security passes got lost in pubs, were still in cars when they were stolen, were not handed back at the gate on final exit. There were a million and one reasons why they went missing, and doubtless a new reason was just waiting to show itself soon.

The Gareloch was a public waterway open for use by small boats and yachts alike.

Only a small area of the loch was prohibited from public access and that area was patrolled by Ministry of Defence Police launches and small boats, and by Royal Marines of the resident Landing Craft detachment. Video cameras and Thermal Imaging cameras swept the water area continuously. Capable of registering a heat source the size of a seagull nothing should beat the surveillance system in place. But things did; even sophisticated systems had a human input, someone had to interpret what was being offered, someone had to ensure total reliability, if an alarm sounded every time a seagull moved its perch it didn't take too long for the alarm to be isolated. If a demonstrator rattled the perimeter fence and set off an alarm every five minutes for an hour would the response become jaded? Would the security forces at Carolyn's disposal make an error of judgement? Would they react slowly when they were under continuous harassment by hundreds of members of these affinity groups up and down the fence line and on the water in canoes, or as swimmers in wet suits and with blackened faces?

These were the thoughts that held the Commander's attention as she drove her green Audi through the South Gate of the base and off towards Rhu.

Ten

Laura settled into the most comfortable armchair at Coleman's flat and took a tentative sniff at the glass of whisky her host had provided. She had tried whisky before, of course, but couldn't claim any expertise in the puzzling world of the single malt. She studied the colour of her drink as she swirled it around in the glass, a delicate light colour like ripened corn or perhaps a pale gold. She sipped and swallowed. No sensation of burning in her throat, no heavy peaty or smoky flavour that she had experienced in the past, no, this was a brand she could enjoy.

Coleman poured himself a small measure of the Glenkinchie and surveyed the level in the bottle. He would have to buy another before the end of the month.

"Do you like it, Laura. Always been my favourite. I suppose I learned the habit from my father before he died."

"It's good," she replied, "I've always imagined whisky as being a bit like a hammer, but this has a subtlety that I haven't tasted before."

Daniel and Laura settled into a warm silence as both savoured their drinks. Laura looked around the room now restored to a working office again. Piles of back numbers of Coleman's magazine were stacked haphazardly on the floor. Books and magazines filled the remaining carpet space and were mixed up with packets of new paper, cartons of toner for the photocopier and boxes of floppy disks.

Laura was a tidy worker.

The need for security, secrecy, marked the way she ran her office in Collier Street and there was never a page of paper out of place. This was the opposite end of the spectrum, she thought, jumble and chaos, a disorganised mind and an undisciplined life. She idly leafed through old editions of

'Envirocare,' some of which she had seen before. Every month she read dozens of fringe magazines and publications, they were a useful source of information and intelligence. They offered a viewpoint at the edges of British life, always an opportunity for exploitation, for mischief, for opportunities to further her cause.

Laura broke the silence; "You asked me in the pub, what I thought should go in your magazine next month. Well, I think you should do a whole issue on Trident and that ploughmen group."

"Trident Ploughshares 2000, you mean," he asked.

"Yes that's it, the Trident Ploughshares. I'm sure your readers would like it and I know it would sell lots of copies. Besides, with all that activity the group has planned for August up in Scotland it makes sense to give it some more publicity. Perhaps some of your regular readers might want to go up there themselves and support the action."

Coleman looked up at Laura from his position seated on the carpet next to her chair.

"Yes," he said finally and with increasing enthusiasm, "maybe some of my readers could start a London based affinity group."

"Oh yes, Dan. That's a great idea, you could lead them, go up to Faslane yourself."

A slight frown showed on his face as he contemplated her suggestion.

"I don't normally travel away from London," he said

"But think of how good it would be to be able to see all the action first hand; to play a part in something so important to all of us, for the whole world."

"I could do a follow up edition of the magazine from the Peace Camp, action reports as things happen." Be a real reporter he thought to himself. Yes, maybe there was an opportunity here for him; maybe he could have a rudder to guide him at last.

Laura reached down and grasped Coleman's hand in her own. She squeezed his fingers firmly. "Dan, you could be the voice of the demonstrations." He was hooked.

The two of them passed ideas back and forth for an hour

with Coleman becoming more and more convinced that a departure from his normal mix of topics would make a welcome change for him and his readership. Laura started developing headlines and revealed a talent for producing attention-grabbing openings. Coleman started to scribble down notes enthusiastically.

She abandoned her seat and joined him on the carpet.

Very quickly they were in the midst of a sea of paper. They were drawing up short articles, some taken directly from the 'Tri-denting It' handbook that Coleman had produced at the discussion group days before, others developed between the two of them. Coleman could see that he would have more than enough material for the next edition of his magazine and he was keen to begin.

"Dan, I think you should contact the Ploughshares group and tell them all about what you are doing. Make sure that the organisers know that you are with them. Make sure they get the chance to make a contribution. All their contact numbers and addresses are here in this handbook."

Coleman required little persuasion and agreed to contact one of the principals the following day. Laura made a display of looking at her wristwatch and declared that it was time she left him for the night.

"This has been such great fun Dan," said Laura, "we make a good team."

Daniel Coleman expressed his disappointment that the evening should end so soon and with his courage bolstered by his beer and whisky reached out and took her hand. In their previous encounters Coleman had followed a lead, this time he felt himself a leader. Rising to his knees, he folded her into an embrace and a lasting kiss. Meeting no resistance, and sensing the woman's mounting compliance Coleman moved his hand gingerly until it made contact with her breast. With a light stroking movement he touched first one and then the other. Laura broke the kiss and shifted her position sliding gently to the floor, taking him with her. With an almost imperceptible movement she tugged loose her blouse from the waistband of her jeans and turned herself to make sure Daniel touched the bare flesh of her side.

As Daniel found the intended break in her defences and began his search of her smooth cool skin she reached out and started to unbutton his shirt.

Eleven

Laura expected Flynn and O'Neill to travel directly from London to Glasgow by train and that is exactly what they had done. For her, however, that would not do. She did not want to meet either of the men during the trip north and so she took a train to Edinburgh's Waverley station on the Tuesday and spent a night at one of the small hotels in the Morningside district of the city.

The Arran Hotel was totally forgettable.

It occupied a place in the market somewhere between the big hotel chain and the neighbourhood bed and breakfast. A dozen uniformly uninteresting bedrooms offering just above the minimum acceptable standard for hotel accommodation, it catered for a legion of commercial travellers and salesmen. Laura avoided the catering and the bar. She kept a low profile. The trouble with being tall and attractive, she had learned, was that people took notice. Men always turned their heads to look at a beautiful woman whatever they were doing and she had developed the ability to blend in with her surroundings. On the plus side, she knew, hotels like the Arran were populated by bored staff waiting impatiently for the end of their working shifts and they rarely summoned the energy for conversation, let alone inquiry. She would be safe here.

Having spent the previous two nights at Coleman's flat she was glad of the opportunity to collect her thoughts and review where events were taking her. She still lacked a positive plan. But, for all that, her instincts told her that the Trident Ploughshares 2000 group held the key, and Coleman would soon be identified in some way with the leaders of the group. Between the two of them they had all but completed a special edition of "Envirocare" directed solely at Trident and the group who intended to cause havoc at the base in Scotland.

The nights had proved interesting for Laura too. Coleman was a hesitant but very considerate lover. He was gentle and kind in his approach and Laura found herself moved by the sensitivity of his efforts. Their union lacked the intensity and raw passion of her previous encounters but as she reflected on their time together she realised that she had enjoyed herself. The next few days would hopefully present her with an opportunity to exploit what she had set in motion.

First thing Wednesday morning Laura hired a car, a three year old Vauxhall Cavalier. She scanned the Edinburgh Yellow Pages in search of a small hire company who covered the local market and found there were several. Laura settled on Leith Auto Rental and one look at their yard confirmed her suspicion, reasonably reliable cars but none of the frills offered by the big boys like Hertz and Avis. The deal was for unlimited mileage and Laura spent the rest of the morning driving around the city. She hadn't visited Edinburgh before, and with time to kill she took in some of the sights, including a trip as far as the Forth road and rail bridges, before checking out of her hotel and heading for Glasgow.

She parked the car in a nearby road and arrived at Queen Street Station at exactly a quarter past five. The two Irishmen were waiting. In the briefest of contacts she indicated that they should follow and in less than a minute she was out of the busy station concourse and back in the hustle and bustle of a busy Glasgow city centre. Padraig and Brendan had obeyed her instructions and each had a small travel bag that went quickly into the boot of the Vauxhall beside her own.

The drive from Glasgow City centre to Helensburgh was uneventful and took barely forty-five minutes. Laura quickly identified the Lomond Guest House. In the middle of the main street, it was a whitewashed Victorian house of two stories which boasted a sign at the front gate attesting to the fact that there were no longer vacancies to be found.

The front windows looked out across the road onto the river.

In the distance across the water Laura could see the waterside sheds of a small ship repair yard and in the foreground a few dinghies cutting backwards and forwards as they tacked their way towards the Royal Northern Yacht club and its moorings to the north. An elderly woman met them immediately inside the front door. She had a thinning scalp of grey hair and a pronounced stoop that caused her to bend her head backward at the neck to observe her guests. Laura took charge of the registration; a process that was no more than an acknowledgement that she had booked three rooms.

The landlady showed little interest in the group beyond showing them upstairs to their rooms and the two men and one woman made no attempt to engage her in small talk. The rooms were basic but clean and adequate and Laura selected the one that looked out towards the water.

"Get sorted out and meet me downstairs in ten minutes." she directed the two men and turned in to her room.

"Bossy bitch isn't she," said O'Neill, "I wouldn't mind shutting her up."

Flynn said nothing.

"I'll tell you how I'd like to keep her quiet if you want," O'Neill added needlessly as Flynn pushed open the door of his room and entered.

"Just be ready in ten, OK Brendan."

O'Neill continued to mutter for a second but soon realised that he stood alone on the landing with no one to listen to his complaints.

With the two men safely in their respective rooms Laura slipped back down the stairs and out to the car. From the car boot she removed her own travel bag and two old and battered leather briefcases that she slid under her bed and out of sight. She doubted the landlady would do more than offer the room a cursory search if she took time to visit it at all.

Laura was waiting at the front door of the guesthouse when the two men appeared and without a word the three headed towards the centre of town along the sea front. All three quickly took in the town pier to their right side and the parade of small shops facing the water of the river. A shiver made Laura realise that it was colder than when she had left London and she drew her anorak closed and engaged the zip. They were in sight of a range of eating places, a Fish and Chip shop, a Chinese take-away and a couple of typical sea front cafes.

O'Neill interrupted the silence first.

"I could murder a beer," he declared as they drew level with the front of the Imperial Hotel. The three exchanged a glance and Laura stepped towards the front door. Flynn and O'Neill followed.

O'Neill was despatched to the bar for drinks and the group selected meals from the bar menu. They took a table by the front window and sampled their drinks in silence whilst they awaited the arrival of the food. Laura and Padraig had completed their visual sweep of the bar and noted only one other group of drinkers, four men seated at the opposite end of the long bar.

"Not exactly good beer is it," complained O'Neill, who whenever silence fell felt the need to fill the gap with words.

Laura moved forward in her seat and rested both elbows on the table in front of her. With her open palms framing her mouth and her chin lightly resting on her thumbs she began to brief her team on what she had in mind for their few days in Scotland.

"Ok," she started, "tomorrow I want to drive along the perimeter of the naval base and have a look at their security arrangements. I want an idea of their strengths and weaknesses. I'd like you two to check out the peace camp; see if it is possible to talk to some of the residents, find out how well they are organised, see if they would be any help to us if we staged a break-in."

Flynn followed the woman's words silently and with his full attention. At the suggestion of a break-in O'Neill felt the short hair on the back of his neck begin to rise and suddenly his attention was focussed on the prospect of some real action.

"Most important," Laura continued, "I don't want you to draw any attention to yourselves. Can you manage that Brendan?"

"'Course I can," he responded with an expression of mock surprise, almost hurt, showing on his face, "I'm a fucking professional you know, I won't screw up."

As a waiter approached their table carrying a tray, silence fell. The food arrived and was distributed and the three began to eat.

***

"Creepy, see those three over there; the two blokes and the good looking dark haired bird. I reckon I know one of 'em," Corporal 'Sharky' Ward Royal Marines said quietly to his Sergeant and drinking companion of the evening. Sgt 'Creepy' Crawley looked up from his beer and took in the group at the opposite side of the bar. The three of them were directing their attention to the food in front of them. Two fish and chips and a quiche by the look of it, Crawley thought. The chips are always good here in the Imp'.

"Where do you know them from Sharky?" Crawley inquired.

"I'm pretty sure it was from the Int' briefs when I was over the water last year."

Crawley realised that one or all of the group must have some involvement with Northern Ireland. Ward had recently returned from a tour of duty with the patrol craft manned and operated by the Royal Marines Landing Craft Company and stationed on Lough Neagh, the large inland waterway that sat neatly in the middle of the six counties of Ulster.

"Which one is it" Crawley inquired.

"Check shirt, back to the bar," came the answer.

"Right boys," Crawley said to his group, "we've all been over the water, and we've all done this before. Sharky, see if you can come up with his name, outfit, and any other details. You just concentrate on check shirt."

Ward nodded agreement towards his troop commander and directed his attention back towards the man in the coloured check shirt.

"Jock," continued Crawley, "you take the other bloke. Start at the top of his head and work down making a mental note of everything you see. Don't make it too obvious."

"Right oh, Sarge," the Royal Marine replied. The atmosphere within the little group had changed instantly as the serious business of intelligence gathering began.

"Willy, you take the bird; same deal."

Sgt Creepy Crawley looked at his three friends and work

58

mates and recognised that they had understood his instructions completely. He had a sudden feeling of pride. The landing craft detachment were a small group of Royal Marines who worked and existed, at Faslane, pretty much in isolation from the almost overwhelming presence of their *navy blue* compatriots. It was satisfying that they should respond to his command without question, even when they were socialising together.

"I'm going up to get some more beer in two minutes so drink up but don't make it look like going home time," said Crawley. "Oh and Willy," he added to the youngest of the group, "I don't just want to know that she's got great tits OK."

Crawley rose and took the four empty pint glasses to the bar and asked for refills. The barman set about filling fresh pint glasses with the 'Eighty Shilling' ale that each of the Royal Marines was drinking. As he waited at the bar he looked casually at the group eating their meal and tried to remember as much detail about them as he could. He started to rehearse it in his mind.

He and his companions would need to churn it all out the next day for the Base Security Officer, himself a Royal Marines Major. Crawley cared about being professional. He was especially careful and conscientious where intelligence was concerned and even more particular when the problems of Northern Ireland were the subject. As a young Marine, years ago, Crawley had been shot at on the streets of Belfast. It was the only occasion in his eighteen years of service when he knew he could have been killed. The moment had stayed with him and even now he could hear the whine of the bullet that missed him.

The burly, six foot one Royal Marine Sergeant loaded the four glasses carefully on a tray and started back towards the table. The glasses off loaded; he returned the tray to the bar and took the opportunity to have one last closer look at his prey.

***

Laura finished her quiche Lorraine and salad and pushed her

59

plate away. The two men were also finished and with one swallow apiece had drained their glasses. Once again O'Neill was sent to the bar, this time to settle the bill as Laura and Flynn prepared to leave.

***

"Got him," said Ward quietly, "O'Neill; Brendan O'Neill, LVF; nasty bastard. He's an enforcer, you know, a knee-capper, a hard man. I'd love to get him on a dark night and give him some of his own medicine."

"Just sit quietly fellas," said Crawley, "they're leaving, so save it for the Base Security Officer in the morning."

The four marines continued their conversation as O'Neill and his two companions rose from their places and left the bar of the Imperial Hotel. Crawley crossed to the window and followed their progress along the road out of town. The manager was well used to servicemen and women frequenting his hotel and when Crawley asked him whether he had seen the group before he answered without reservation. that he hadn't. The Royal Marines returned their empty glasses, wished the barman goodnight and left to walk the short distance to the bus stop from where a routine bus service would return them the three miles to the naval base.

Twelve

The landlady was no more communicative in the morning and breakfast was served with the very minimum of conversation.

Laura had booked the Lomond Guest House for three nights but fully expected to leave before her booking was fulfilled. The meal was adequate, the two men tucked in to what was described as a "full Scottish breakfast" with relish, but what distinguished it from an English or Welsh or even Irish breakfast, for that matter, neither they nor Laura were sure. Laura decided that the offer of porridge probably marked the difference. The landlady produced a small bowl of the traditional oatmeal dish for Flynn when he agreed to sample some, but it looked grey and particularly uninviting so she settled for cereal and some rather crisp toast. At least the coffee was hot and served to wake her up fully for what the landlady obviously considered an early start to the day.

The three left the guesthouse and walked out into a drab morning and a drizzle of rain. Pulling their coats tightly shut against the morning chill and bending forward into the breeze they set off at a brisk walk and recovered the car at a few minutes past seven o'clock. They drove from Helensburgh north along the A814 and in the direction of Faslane. Too early for the bulk of the day's traffic the journey to the peace camp took less than ten minutes.

The occupants of the Vauxhall took in the yacht marina at Rhu and the point at where the Gareloch narrowed between Rhu point and Rosneath on the opposite side of the loch. Vast houses peeped through the trees and looked over the water to the peninsula. There was old money here at Rhu and along the coast; rich merchants leaving the industrial smoke and

61

noise of Glasgow and setting themselves up with a quiet haven.

The migration out of the city had begun in the last century and this area had been popular. Now the shipyards and shipbuilding was all gone and the noisy lower reaches of the Clyde were silent. Now the trend was reversed and luxury developments were reclaiming the industrial wastelands around the water in the city. Driving at a sensible speed the peace camp was quickly upon them and all three turned to observe the rather untidy site. There were six or maybe seven small caravans in various states of dilapidation and a central area where there was a campfire. An awning stretched between the branches of some trees provided protection from the weather.

As Laura slowed the car to a crawl they spotted some crude shelters erected in the stronger of the trees and a number of painted slogans on the road, on the fence at the side of the camp and on the caravans themselves. 'Trident is illegal' 'Ban the bomb,' pretty predictable stuff. One painted banner declared that it would cost £70,000 to evict the campers from their present site, a comment on their own vulnerability. There were no obvious signs of occupation although a brightly painted bus, an old van and one car were parked at the southern end of the site in the lay-by. Smoke rose lazily from the remnants of the previous evening's campfire and even with the car windows shut tightly against the chill the smell of burning wood was strong.

They continued along the road and immediately noted the security fencing running away into the distance, and, to their left, the Faslane base.

"Razor wire" said Flynn, "barbed tape coil. Notice there are more coils of it just inside the fence in a sort of no-man's land."

"See the cameras," Laura added, and both men noted the surveillance cameras spaced along the entire fence line as they drove.

As the road crested a slight hill their sight was drawn immediately to the massive structure at the northern end of the base protruding out into the loch.

"That," said Laura "is the ship lift where they can take one of the new Vanguard Class submarines out of the water for repairs. I've seen it in the Trident Ploughshares 2000 publicity video."

Laura had described one of the largest ship lifts to be found. A huge Trident missile carrying submarine could be manoeuvred into the shed, above a large cradle which would then be raised by a series of winches until both the cradle and submarine were out of the water. If it were needed the submarine could be moved along a network of railway lines and taken ashore onto a massive concrete holding area where the vessel could be worked on, leaving the ship lift once again ready for use. There were few signs to suggest that the ship lift was occupied and the large concrete area to the landward side of the shed appeared to be home to a small tug sitting tall on its docking blocks.

"Look left as we get to this round-about," directed the driver, "that is the northern gate of the base."

All three took in the sliding metal barrier at the entrance, and what appeared to be a further sliding gate some ten or fifteen metres inside the first. They saw too the armed Ministry of Defence policeman at the sentry position and the two security men of the Ministry of Defence Guard Service who were scrutinising the paperwork and passes of the driver of a lone car entering the gates.

"SA80's." noted O'Neill as he looked at the automatic weapon carried by the policeman.

"He's wearing kevlar body armour as well," confirmed Laura, although both men had already made a similar observation.

Laura followed the road around to the western side of the Gareloch, beyond the base, and drove along towards the village of Garelochhead.

"There's an Ordnance Survey map in the glove box Paddy, I want to go all the way down the west side of the loch to Rosneath and then stop for a look, okay."

Padraig Flynn retrieved the folded map from the glove compartment of the car and looked at the short route the woman had described. It would be a straight run down the water's edge on the opposite side to the Naval base.

Laura parked the car near the jetty at Rosneath for just long enough to retrieve a pair of binoculars from her travel bag. She set off north again, towards Garelochhead. After six or seven miles the group reached a point on the opposite side of the loch from Faslane and pulled off the road. From the car she could now see the ship and submarine jetties clearly and was able to recall the drawing in the Tri-denting It handbook that numbered the berths from south to north. She explained to her two companions that the 'finger' jetty formed berths numbers ten and eleven, and that the berth nearest to the huge shed was number twelve. These, she said, were the berths used by the Vanguard Class. Passing the binoculars to each of the men in turn she informed them that there was a submarine occupying berth number six and there were several smaller surface ships on the first few berths, numbers one and two.

Thinking back to the video she had obtained from the ploughshares group she remembered that the more important area to the north, where the Vanguards' would be berthed, had a floating barrier around the area as further protection and she took the binoculars back from Flynn to look at it.

"If you wanted to get inside the base the best chance is definitely from the water." Padraig Flynn offered and O'Neill nodded in agreement.

"Even better if we had a series of diversions around the fence." Laura thought aloud.

"I think I've seen enough, Paddy? Brendan?"

Both men nodded and Laura eased the car back onto the road and started back towards the village. Laura followed the same route back but stopped briefly just beyond the peace camp.

"I've got some thinking to do back at the digs," Laura declared, "you two go and chat up the great un-washed and see what they are up to, meet up again at midday at the pub we passed just before the marina."

Flynn and O'Neill left the vehicle and walked towards the camp. Smoke was beginning to rise above the lay-by from a freshly lit fire and as they arrived a couple of the residents were starting their day.

***

The peace camp always claimed to offer an open welcome to everyone and so it seemed as the two Irishmen walked though the tangle of caravans, fire wood, canoes and various odd pieces of furniture. A woman, in her early twenties, dressed in scruffy jeans and a sweater several sizes too big offered the men a tin mug each and pointed to a saucepan containing what they assumed to be tea. They both dipped into the pot and scooped out half a cup of the hot, brown liquid. Seated at the central table under the awning were two other adults and a child of about five years of age. The two men were invited to sit.

"I'm Jenny, and this is Petey, June and Rosey."

Flynn nodded in response and assumed Rosey to be the child.

"Pat and Bren', we'd like to do something to help."

The young child, looking decidedly grubby, ambled away from the table and entered a nearby caravan. Not the slightest interested in child welfare or even parenthood O'Neill was surprised when he found himself looking around to see where the child, or even her parent, could get a bath. Jenny, Petey and June were obviously accustomed to a life of little activity and of many hours spent around this same table in conversation.

Their normal routine seemed hardly disturbed as they accepted the two strangers into their midst and regaled them with tales of their successes against the enemy across the road. The two men remained in the peace camp, hardly leaving the table, until almost eleven thirty and promised to return that evening with some cans of beer. They had made it plain that they wanted to strike some blow, however small, against Trident, and that they knew something about the ploughshares group. Jenny, who seemed to be the leader of the small group suggested that 'Sheila' may be back later, and that she was definitely the person to talk to. Padraig Flynn and Brendan O'Neill bade farewell to their new acquaintances and headed south out of the peace camp and towards the town of

Helensburgh.

Thirteen

Time to stand and be counted.
  (Editorial comment by Dan Coleman)
  As a quite exceptional break from editorial policy this edition of Envirocare is devoted entirely to the subject of Nuclear disarmament, and specifically the work of the Trident Ploughshares 2000 Group. The United Kingdom continues to maintain a fleet of four Vanguard Class Trident missile-carrying submarines in direct contravention of agreed nuclear non-proliferation treaties signed by our government.

  These lethal messengers of death have got to be stopped and at last one group of dedicated workers for world peace are acting to make the voice of ordinary people heard. This group is known as Trident Ploughshares 2000. TP2000 form the core for activity against the nuclear weapons threat and as their name suggests they pledge to hammer weapons into ploughshares, symbolically making something safe and useful out of something harmful and useless.

  They are international in every sense, drawing membership and support from across the globe. Members are 'pledged' to the cause from America and Germany, from Sweden and Holland, from Denmark, Austria, Australia and Britain, from all countries where conscience is important and the continued existence of the human race is paramount.

  Their aim is simple, to rid the world of nuclear weapons by the turn of the century.

  How can you help?

  There are two easy ways.

  You can become a fully 'pledged' supporter of TP2000 by signing up as a core member. As a core member you will be expected to pursue the scrapping of Trident even at the risk of arrest and imprisonment.

The alternative to all out action is to form your own affinity group.

You may already be part of such a group, many Envirocare readers are. There are affinity groups from all over the world, each having their own identity, often their own individual causes to follow. What makes them special in the context of Trident Ploughshares 2000 is that these affinity groups also pledge their support to the banning of Trident and are willing to gather with others to further the aim. You can make your voice heard by lending support to this noble cause.

So what is the problem? Do you know what Trident is? What is its destructive power? The answers to these vital questions, and more, are in this months' edition of Envirocare.

The Vanguard Class submarine is a massive weapon of war.

Almost five hundred feet in length, four decks high and with a displacement of sixteen thousand tonnes this deadly war-machine circles the globe, un-heard and unseen, at over twenty-five knots, carrying within its belly an awesome arsenal of death. The submarine carries sixteen missiles, each of which has six 100-kiloton nuclear warheads. A total of ninety-six warheads and all of them can be targeted individually. Every single one of these warheads has a destructive capacity eight times more powerful that the bomb dropped on Hiroshima. The bomb on Hiroshima cost the lives of 130,000 innocent people. They were not soldiers or sailors or airmen, they were women and children and old people going about their daily lives longing for a peaceful settlement to another unjust war. Just imagine the killing power of one of these submarines, let me do the sums for you:

Ninety-six warheads at 8 times 130,000 lives: it works out to 99,840,000.

Yes, almost one hundred million people with only the weapon load of one submarine - we have four.

Our government policy requires at least one of these submarines to be at sea for 24 hours a day, 365 days a year, yes, every second of our lives.

Why should we take action when governments refuse to do so? Consider these points and you will see:

*   To use or threaten to use nuclear weapons of any kind is a crime against humanity and totally immoral.
*   Trident is criminal and illegal.
*   Trident is a clear breach of Articles 1 and V1 of the Nuclear non-proliferation Treaty.
*   Trident pollutes the environment with toxic and radioactive waste threatening the future of the planet.
*   Trident development does not respect international Nuclear Free Zone boundaries and exposes every person on the planet to the risk of nuclear accident.
*   Trident warheads are transported from one end of the UK to another exposing countless communities to the risk of nuclear accident.
*   Scare global resources and vast sums of British taxpayers' money spent on Trident (currently around £1.5 billion per year) are being diverted from urgent social necessities (eg. health and education) and from programmes that could tackle the underlying causes of international conflict.
*   A majority of world's nations feel threatened by nuclear weapons and want them disarmed. Many poor nations regard them as a terrible threat, which is used to protect the interests of rich nations.
*   Trident is anti-democratic. The decision to have nuclear weapons was made in secret without informed public debate. 70% of people in Scotland, polled in 1992, were opposed to Trident and a poll in 1997 of all British people found that 59%, as against 37%, now say it would be best for British security if we do not have nuclear weapons.
*   The British Government and NATO are not disarming Trident themselves.
*   Global citizens have a right and obligation to uphold international law, to behave ethically and in the interests of global community, and to disarm Trident themselves.

***

Daniel was pleased with his front pages and flipped through the remainder of his proof copy noting the other articles he had included. The magazine ran to twenty-four pages this month and that, in itself, was a record. He normally went for twenty. Much of what he had prepared had been taken directly from the Trident Ploughshares 2000 handbook but he had permission from Angela Young to reproduce it and he had given the group credit on several articles. At her request, and, he recalled at Laura's, he had printed the entire programme of events scheduled for August at Faslane and had encouraged people to form their own affinity groups and head for Scotland during that month.

He missed Laura badly.

She had called him that morning and she had insisted he had read his lead article over the phone. Daniel was delighted by her enthusiasm and was persuaded to add his name to the editorial piece, another departure from his normal practice. Laura talked about the two of them going up to Scotland during August to take part.

He would be a neutral reporter of course.

She suggested that he contact Angela Young again and tell her that he wanted to cover the entire ploughshares gathering as the official voice of the demonstration. Young had agreed readily enough but made him very well aware that publicity had to be meat and drink to the group's activity and that she expected the world's media to be there. They managed to agree that with his experience he would serve a very useful purpose as the group press officer. At Laura's second telephone call of the day she had dictated a final postscript article for the back page of the magazine and asked Daniel to include it in a prominent setting.

"No show without Punch"

An, as yet, unidentified Ploughshares affinity group thought to be based in England's capital has reported exclusively to an Envirocare staff reporter that the Summer festival of peace at Faslane will end, not with a whimper, but with a bang.

Details are still unclear about the intended showpiece action but the totally reliable source confirms that the eyes of the worlds will focus on Faslane during August.

Fourteen

She was waiting in the Ardencaple Hotel when Flynn and O'Neill arrived.

White painted and edged in black, the three-storey building boasted a curious balustrade at the roofline. Tables and umbrellas filled the small area between the front of the building and the road but despite the break in the weather and the afternoon warmth Laura elected to go inside. All the hotel's customers had made the same decision.

Two youths leaned on a pool table whilst their equally young companions played out their game. Pint glasses, half filled, rested precariously on the edge of the table and with each time they were lifted the seeds of another ring shaped stain in the wood were sewn. Colourful porcelain pool balls clinked together. Flynn and his companion moved away from the pool table to join Laura Latimer seated at the other end of the long dimly lighted bar. A middle-aged couple was engrossed in their bar meal, something unrecognisable with chips. The barman emerged from the shadows of a side alcove and prepared to serve his new guests. The men ordered beer and both waited as the hotel man poured the dark liquid into pint glasses. When the men were seated Laura spoke first.

"Did you notice that place over there?" she said tipping her head to one side and directing the two men's attention across the main road towards the water.

The hotel sat on the opposite side of the road from a Ministry of Defence site that described itself as the Clyde Off Site Centre. An ugly, prefabricated building sitting inside a high security fence, it was more an example of financial expediency that architectural elegance. The notice board at the gate indicated that, amongst its various functions, it served

71

as the press reception centre.

From her research she knew that this place would play a vital role in co-ordinating the actions of the many disaster control organisations in the event of a nuclear accident at Faslane or at the armament depot at Coulport further round the coast at Loch Long. She also knew that the Royal Navy had a one hundred percent record for nuclear safety, and had maintained that record since the introduction into the fleet of the very first nuclear powered submarine, HMS Dreadnought, more than three decades earlier. Laura imagined that this small fenced compound would play host to senior military, police, local and central government officials during the August demonstrations, and that this would be where the press and media would gather to receive whatever they were permitted to hear. She explained the purpose of the centre quietly and without emotion to her two colleagues. Brendan, as ever, was first to comment.

"You could certainly cause some damage to the big brass with a hit on that place, look at it, the fence wouldn't stop a couple of determined kids."

Flynn surveyed the compound through the hotel window.

"One unarmed guard by the look of it," he said, "Brendan's' right, that chain link fence is a waste of time, I can't even see a camera."

Laura watched and remained silent, deep in thought. After a few seconds she turned back to the two men.

"You're both right, it's a soft target. There's no doubt we could make a big splash there if it was manned up with all the top people but it wouldn't do much to publicise the ploughshares cause. I want them left holding a bigger baby than that one."

Laura took a sip at her glass of sparkling water and the men took long pulls at their beer.

"Well boys," Laura asked, "what did you find out at the peace camp?"

"For a start," chipped in O'Neill, "I could do with a bath, the inmates are hopping."

Over the next ten minutes or so the two men offered Laura an insight into the way the camp functioned and described the small group that they had encountered. There was no doubt that the peace camper's were a thorn in the side of authority. They kept the naval base security forces awake but in Padraig's opinion posed no serious threat to the base whatsoever. Both men agreed that whilst the peace campers were useful for nuisance value they were hardly cast in the mould of international terrorists.

"We've half arranged to go back later with a few cans," said O'Neill.

"There's someone called Sheila Boyd expected tonight and she is a player in this group you are interested in," explained Flynn, "do you want to come along?"

"No thanks Paddy," she replied, "I've got a few other bits of business to take care of this afternoon and I may need to talk to Dan Coleman again."

Laura went on to explain what had happened so far with the magazine and Coleman and Young. She told them that Coleman had dedicated the whole of his next issue to submarine disarmament and that she wanted to mount their operation during the demonstrations scheduled for August at Faslane. The two men listened attentively until she finished speaking and whilst Flynn sat in thought working out the significance of what he had heard, his partner could not wait.

"Christ, you've been shacked up with that ginger haired wimp, haven't you. I'll bet he hasn't got a clue what to do with his dick. He must have thought all his Christmases had come at once getting you in the sack."

Laura leaned across the table and stared deeply into his eyes.

"Don't press it, Brendan," was all she said her voice cold and tinged with a menace that even O'Neill recognised at once. She changed the subject.

"This Boyd is a big player in ploughshares," she confirmed, "I want to get her on our side. You two go down there again tonight and Paddy, see if you can fix up a meet for tomorrow sometime, away from the camp. I'll pick her up if she wants."

Laura reached into the back pocket of her jeans and pulled out a folded bundle of bank notes held firmly together by what looked like a small tortoiseshell money clip. She handed Flynn

73

a twenty pound note and the keys to the car.

"In the car park." she said to Flynn indicating with a movement of her head where he would find the parked vehicle.

Once again O'Neill couldn't resist a jibe at the woman.

"I knew you were sitting on a fortune," he said, "but I thought it was inside your jeans not just in the pocket."

Brendan stood and headed for the toilets leaving Flynn and the woman at the table.

"Keep him out of trouble Paddy, he's beginning to get on my nerves. I want a foot soldier along for this but I'll dump him if he steps an inch out of line when it matters."

Flynn nodded his head at Laura.

"I know he's a prat, but I can handle him. If he screws up, you needn't worry, I'll bury him for good."

For the few minutes they had alone Laura told Flynn that she needed to try to make some contacts with some of the sailors from the base and it was better that she stayed away from the peace camp. She began to tell him the outline of her plan when Brendan appeared.

"We'll talk later," she said, "don't let him get too pissed down at the camp."

The two left the Ardencaple Hotel heading for the car park and then the Somerfield Supermarket just off the main road of the town. Laura headed towards the guesthouse. With the watery afternoon sun high in the cloudless sky the walk back was an ideal time for reflection. In no particular hurry and with the afternoon to kill before she would be able to find sailors in the Helensburgh pubs for the evening she strolled slowly along the waterside path until she found a bench. The rain had stopped, it seemed to have rained since their arrival the day before, and she sat looking out over the water. In the distance, to her left, she could clearly make out the Helensburgh town pier jutting out a short distance into the Gareloch. As she turned her head to the right a few dozen small yachts were bobbing gently at their moorings close to the press centre and the yacht club. A calm and peaceful scene to be enjoyed for a while as she steeled herself against an evening in smoke filled bar rooms, courting the Royal Navy at play.

"Can I join you?" a soft English voice broke the silence and Laura looked up at a woman of about her own age standing to her side by the bench.

"Of course, please excuse me, I was miles away," replied Laura.

The young woman seated herself and seemed intent on continuing the conversation.

"I come down here every afternoon when it is dry," she said. "It helps somehow if I can see the water."

Laura looked at the young woman and her puzzled expression caused her to continue.

"I'm sorry, I should have said, my husband is in the Navy and he is away at sea just now. I know it is silly but looking at the sea somehow seems to bring him closer."

The two women shook hands and introduced themselves.

It seemed that Laura's new friend was Emma Courtney and that she was married to Nigel, the Navigating Officer of HMS Harwich. Emma was clearly delighted to have someone to talk to and before long was recounting secrets about her personal life that she wouldn't have considered telling her friends and neighbours. This was only Nigel's second job as a Royal Navy Lieutenant and they didn't celebrate their first wedding anniversary until August, and then only if the ship returned from a planned mine hunting exercise on time.

Laura was a good listener.

She had that uncanny skill of listening but yet making the speaker feel that both were contributing to the conversation. Emma had given up her job in London and her flat to follow the man she loved. The school system in Scotland, she discovered was different from the one she had trained under in London and as a consequence she wasn't able to get a new job. She had applied for several and seemed, on paper, well qualified for them all. Even worse, at interview one head teacher had told her that she was a great catch if only she had a Scottish teaching qualification.

Emma had investigated what was required to gain the Scottish teaching accreditation; almost a further two years at college going over the same ground that she had already covered. What was the point she thought, Nigel had a two-year appointment to Harwich and then he was all but guaranteed a return to Portsmouth for his next job. She didn't regret coming north to be with Nigel, she loved him far too much for that, she told Laura, but it was all desperately unfair. So Emma kept their small married quarter clean, looked for jobs, and sat on her bench on dry afternoons thinking of her husband away at sea.

An hour passed, and then another.

"Why don't we go and have a coffee," Laura asked, "My treat."

Emma Courtney agreed immediately. It was wonderful to chat to such an attractive and obviously well educated woman and they were just beginning to explore their mutual experiences of life in the big city.

"Better still, why don't you come for supper this evening. It would be a treat to cook for someone other than myself."

Emma blushed and lifted her hand up to cover her mouth too late to stop the words she had just spoken.

"Oh I'm sorry, of course, you must have other plans Laura, I didn't mean to be pushy, please forgive me."

Laura leaned across to Emma Courtney, touched her hand and smiled with a genuine expression of pleasure.

"Emma, I would be absolutely delighted. That is a wonderfully generous offer and if you still mean it I accept. But I do have to get back to my hotel before ten thirty."

Emma gave Laura details of how to reach her married quarter in Smuggler's Way in Rhu and they arranged to meet again at seven. Laura would take a taxi, she said, and she would bring a bottle of wine to make the evening more special. The two women parted company as friends, both looking forward to their next meeting.

Fifteen

"Duty Naval Base Officer, good evening," said Lieutenant Commander Colin Walker into his telephone.

"Sergeant McKinnon here, Sir, just to let you know there is a new car at the peace camp, Sir, a blue Vauxhall Cavalier."

"Have you PNC'd it, George?" asked Walker, inviting the Ministry Of Defence Police Sergeant to comment on whether the registration number of the vehicle had been checked with the Police National Computer of vehicles.

"Aye, Sir, it's registered to a hire car firm in Edinburgh, Leith Auto Rental."

"OK George, can you make sure you tell your Chief and get the details passed in to the Base Security Officer in the morning. Is there any increased activity at the camp?"

"Nothing as yet Sir, if there's anything happening I'll give you a buzz."

"Thanks George."

Colin Walker made an entry in his computer-based diary of events. He knew that down below his office, in the Police Control Room of Base Defence Headquarters, the Ministry of Defence Police would have added the new vehicle to a board detailing the comings and goings of the happy heroes at the Faslane peace camp.

It was Thursday evening and Walker had just started his seventh and final night shift for this week of duty. At seven o'clock the following morning his twelve hour shift would be over and he could set off for home and a two week break. He, like his four working colleagues, had now been in post as the Duty Naval Base Officer for a little over two years and still he declared himself happy with his lot. Walker was a retired Royal Navy Officer who had completed his career six months earlier than the normal retirement age of fifty in order to take on the newly created post.

As a retired Officer, although still in uniform, his salary was considerably lower that when he had been on Active Service but he now collected his pension as a Lieutenant Commander and that pretty well maintained his standard of living. On the plus side, he no longer took work home at the end of the day and once the shift reached a close he was relieved from his post and replaced by another of his group of five retired Officers' who would pick up exactly where he left off. For almost the first time in his working life Colin could plan ahead. He could book a holiday for the following year if he wished, and barring major upsets he could all but guarantee the dates.

No more apologies to his wife and family, no more short notice changes to ship's programmes.

It was wonderful.

Colin had no regrets about leaving the active list. Today's Navy was even more about budget cuts and stretch and strain than when he had left, and then it had been bad enough. He considered himself lucky. Lucky to have had a good career and he had. Not unlike the story of his four contemporaries he had started out as an Artificer Apprentice and had made it up through the ranks until finally he had passed all the examinations to qualify and be selected as a Royal Navy Sub Lieutenant on the Special Duties List of Officers. As an Engineer Officer he had made it to the ultimate job at sea, The Marine Engineer Officer of a sea going warship. In Walker's case he'd made it twice with two appointments as Head of the Engineering Department of two Leander Class Frigates. The Leanders were all gone now, come to think of it so was every other ship Walker had ever served on. All converted to razor blades or whatever fate retiring warships were consigned to.

The new job could be quite satisfying too, he thought. It was mostly reactive and that suited him well. His job description as the Duty Naval Base Officer stated that he was to act as the Incident Commander in the event of any occurrence that affected the Naval Base. That included fire and flood and pestilence and famine and disease, the four horsemen of the apocalypse were never far away. But, most significantly he was to take charge in the event of a nuclear accident or acts of terrorism or breaches of security. The first couple of hours were vital in any emergency and Walker and his team worked in shifts to cover every minute of the day and night throughout the year.

Walker's office was on the second floor of BDHQ, a most unattractive two story concrete structure to the side of Maidstone Road South, the major thoroughfare running through the naval base from South to North. The lower floor housed the nerve centre of the active base security effort and the Control Room, manned by a mixture of Ministry of Defence Police, Ministry of Defence Guard Service staff and a Royal Marine, monitored the base surveillance systems and defences. There were screens showing the images from each of the numerous perimeter fence cameras, all inter-woven to cover every inch of the fence line and still offer some overlap in case of breakdown.

There were alarm panels which reacted to the perimeter intruder detection system, and mimic boards which lit up to indicate the precise location of a problem on the outer defences of the base. Thermal Imaging cameras played constantly over the water space area surrounding the base and locked on to any movement where a temperature difference could be recorded. Radar monitored movements, fire alarms covered every building in the vast base, and everything showed in the control room.

In the adjacent Incident Command Cell, Walker had a space age technology computer system at his call. He could project a map of the base showing every feature, he could pick a single building and activate a video fly through programme that would take the viewer though the interior of any building showing exactly what was to be seen. Vital props in the defence of the home of the nation's nuclear deterrent. Vital aids when briefing security forces on what they may encounter entering an unfamiliar building fallen captive to terrorists. Luckily, in his two years, Walker was yet to encounter a terrorist. Leaving aside the more determined of the anti-nuclear brigade who could be, and had been, successful at gaining entry to the base, albeit for only a matter of minutes, his bread and butter security difficulties came from the happy heroes up at the camp. There was always the summer camp in August. That was going to be a nightmare. Walker had checked his shifts and he would be on duty right in the middle of the Trident Ploughshares period and there was no way one of the others would want to swap.

***

Laura's taxi pulled up outside the Lomond Guest House and she paid the driver and included a small tip. The evening had been a complete success and Laura now had Emma's telephone number and an invitation to visit at any time. She had more than that though because now she knew the dates and details of the programme for all the ships of the Third Mine Countermeasures Squadron.

Emma had talked and talked all evening.

Laura Latimer recognised easily the brittle signs of loneliness in the other woman, she had experienced the feelings herself just after her mother and father had been killed in Beirut. She had sought out company, physical contact. Laura could see that Emma would be reluctant to pour out her inner feelings to her neighbours for fear of appearing weak, of not being able to cope. It would be hard for such a young and newly married woman, miles from her roots, surrounded by experienced wives for whom the separation had become more commonplace. Laura must have appeared like a welcome spirit. Emma Courtney could unburden herself and then feel confident that no real harm had been done, nobody would know.

Safely in her room she took out her diary and marked down what she had learned. Ten thirty; she made a cup of coffee and sat on the bed quite content and more cheerful by half a bottle of rather good Bordeaux that she had managed to get from the quality section of Tesco's wine selection before travelling up to Emma's home.

***

"That's the Cavalier just left the camp at 2230, occupants two males but we didn't manage a good look, Sir."

"Thanks George, hopefully they are all bedded down for the night now,"

"The outside patrol reckoned they saw Sheila Boyd around the camp about 2100 but she didn't seem to be involved with the Cavalier so we'll keep looking in case we can spot her again."

"OK," said Walker and turned back to *Newsnight* on television where the presenter was concluding a programme about the troubles in Indonesia and the departure of the President after thirty years of dictatorship. 'I wonder how our happy heroes would cope with a regime like that,' he pondered, 'they certainly wouldn't have managed to set up camp outside a high security military base for sixteen years and make a fucking nuisance of themselves.'

***

Flynn and O'Neill knocked on her door and were invited to enter.

The evening had gone well and Sheila Boyd was anxious to meet with Laura the next day. It seemed that the August gathering was gaining momentum and Boyd talked confidently about numbers of up to three hundred. In a quieter moment she also suggested that the focus for the gathering would be at a place called Peaton Glen Wood close to the armament depot at Coulport. She told Flynn in confidence that her organisation thought little of the drop outs and drug addicts who gravitated towards the camp.

"They are cannon fodder in the struggle for progress," she said.

Boyd also had some pretty solid ex-Navy contacts from whom she had managed to get some of the technical details which Angela Young had incorporated in the Tri-Denting It Handbook. Laura listened with interest until the men had completed their brief. She recounted her own experience from the evening and declared that she now had all she wanted from this visit and would return to London the following day after meeting with Boyd. Laura wanted Flynn to accompany her the next day and so she made sure Brendan O'Neill had some spending money and told him to make his way back to London first thing in the morning. Filled with the evening's beer and pocketing the money proffered by Laura, O'Neill made no objection. The night was at an end, or would have been had not O'Neill decided on one final comment. He was content enough to take her money when it was offered but he still had difficulties with taking orders from a woman, a good looking one at that.

"I still can't get over you shagging that bloody wimp from Fulham," he started. "I'll bet you've never had a real man have you?"

"What is a real man like then Brendan?" challenged Laura, quite out of character, but mellowed by the evening's wine.

"More like me, that's for sure. Someone who uses his tackle for more than stirring his tea."

"And I suppose you are better endowed than the rest of your sex are you?"

"Certainly better than that wanker from Fulham," said O'Neill, the best he could manage by way of reply.

Laura looked first at Flynn and then directly at O'Neill. Flynn did no more than raise his eyebrows a fraction, O'Neill had challenge written all over his face.

"Why don't you let me be the judge of that Brendan."

The slightest hint of uncertainty crept into O'Neill's voice as he replied.

"What do you mean?"

"Simple, Brendan let's have a look at your magnificent weapon."

"What?"

"Yes, come on, put up or shut up."

O'Neill's bravado began to return with the woman's direct challenge and he reached with his left hand to grasp the waistband of his trousers whilst, at the same time, his right hand moved to the top of his zip. The Irishman paused.

Laura transferred her gaze from O'Neill's waist up to his face and lifted her hands, palms stretched upwards in a gesture of expectation. The standing man started to unzip his jeans to slowly reveal rather ordinary looking boxer shorts. He hesitated. Nothing happened. He pushed his jeans down to his ankles, looked up at the two people sharing the room with him. He expected an instruction to stop; he received none. Flynn shrugged his shoulders and kept his face expressionless. O'Neill focussed his attention on Laura.

"Oh come on Brendan, we haven't got all night," she said in a voice dripping with impatience, "I don't suppose it's that good so don't build up the excitement too much."

"Fuck you," mouthed O'Neill defiantly as he pushed his shorts down to join the jeans around his ankles. Laura eyed the man with apparent interest, looking first from one side and then the other. She leaned forward and stretched out her upturned, cupped, right hand and with the lightest of touch weighed him in her palm.

O'Neill began to react as only a man could and nervously tried to lighten the moment. "See, you don't get many of them to the pound," he said.

Laura kept up the gentle weighing action and reached forward with her left hand. She slowly curled her fingers around the man's erect shaft and maintaining just the lightest of contact moved her fingers first up and then down his firm manhood. O'Neill took a quick gasp of breath as shock was replaced by excitement.

"Told you it was a good 'un didn't I."

Emboldened by what he saw as the superiority of his position the Irishman pushed out his chest and half closed his eyes to savour the intense pleasure he was feeling as the woman continued the same back and forward motion. O'Neill moved his own hand down to cover Laura's and applied more pressure to the stroking action. Laura responded briefly and then almost imperceptibly withdrew her left hand. O'Neill continued on his own, oblivious to the two people watching the scene that was unfolding in the room at the Lomond Guest House. Laura watched for a few seconds more and then closed her cupped right hand quickly and firmly around the man's testicles. O'Neill screamed aloud as the searing pain shot up though his body. She released her vice like grip and O'Neill stepped backwards, tripping over his jeans and underwear, and clattering to the floor.

"I think we have established who the wanker is don't you," Laura said in a calm, half mocking voice as she stood up and moved towards the wash hand basin in the corner of the room. She made washing her hands into a theatrical gesture and looked over at O'Neill who was grasping himself as if his touch would reduce the pain.

The injured O'Neill scrambled to his feet and in a comic stance, trousers and underwear around his ankles, one hand comforting himself and the other pointing an outstretched finger at Laura snarled, "You bastard, I'll get you for that."

Padraig Flynn looked at his countryman with a half smile and said, "You had it coming, Brendan."

"Very witty," replied the injured man, clearly still in some pain but now able to re-adjust his clothing.

"Yes, Brendan, no hard feelings OK," Laura added.

"Right, let's get all the jokes over with now shall we."

"No," said Padraig Flynn abruptly, showing that he too had begun to run out of patience with his fellow countryman, "let's cut out the crap and get down to business."

Laura stood, rested a hand on Brendan's shoulder and gently guided him towards the door of the room. She opened the door and stepped out with him onto the landing of the upper floor of the guesthouse.

"Seriously Brendan, let's forget this and move on. I'll see you back in London soon. I do have a job for the three of us and I do want you with me." Her tone of voice and the hand still on his shoulder did much to disarm O'Neill and he limped off to his room slightly pacified. He wasn't happy but Laura thought he was less likely to strike out and spoil her plans.

Flynn and the woman talked for an hour and Laura laid out her ideas for their ploughshares contribution. They passed ideas back and forth between the two of them and gradually a firm plan began to emerge. Hardware was needed to make it work. Items that Laura, even with her contacts in the world of Middle Eastern terrorism would find difficult to source within Britain.

She knew that from the very beginning.

She also knew whatever she wanted to achieve would only

be possible with a partner and a network closer to home. She had contacted Flynn for that very purpose. Laura and Padraig developed a shopping list and he confirmed that each of the items could be obtained through his own contacts either in London or back in the Province. They parted for the night and agreed to meet for breakfast at eight the following morning.

Brendan was finishing his breakfast coffee as the other two entered the small dining room at the Lomond Guest House. He had already told the taciturn landlady about his early departure and she had made no comment. As his final act of defiance he had told the proprietor that Laura would pay for the untaken night so that the woman would not be disadvantaged. She almost managed a smile. Laura allowed the Irishman his little victory. Events of the previous evening had gone further than her iron discipline would normally permit and she was not keen to alienate O'Neill completely. Breakfast on the Friday morning was a repeat of Thursday's and Laura felt sure it would be so every day that the guesthouse was occupied. She stuck to the cereal and over cooked toast.

Brendan muttered a farewell to Latimer and Flynn and set off to walk to Helensburgh station and the journey back to London.

"Paddy, I've just remembered there are two leather briefcases under my bed, would you mind grabbing them and putting them in the back seat of the car whilst I sort out the bill with the landlady." Flynn took to the stairs and returned a few seconds later with the cases. "I'll explain later," she said and they headed for the car.

Padraig drove. He stopped at the peace camp long enough for Sheila Boyd to get into the rear seat with Laura and sped off in the direction of Garelochhead. Boyd and Laura established an immediate rapport and Laura set out her proposals for action. Boyd listened quietly. The plan was daring and dramatic and although there were massive risks it had the audacity to succeed. Boyd gave an unqualified agreement, was enthusiastic and very willing to participate.

From the front of the car Flynn remained silent.

He listened in admiration as Laura Latimer spun a web of truth and lies to catch the Trident Ploughshares 2000 leader and suck her ever deeper into the deception that was their own plan. In her turn Sheila Boyd told the two of them about her Naval contacts garnered over years of association with the peace movement and the camp and demonstrations of all kinds across the nation. Things were looking good. Flynn pulled up in the lay-by adjacent to the peace camp and Boyd prepared to leave her new friends.

"One more thing, Sheila," said Latimer, "just for a bit of fun and mischief, take these two briefcases with you. They each contain three rectangular biscuit tins and one of them has a house brick in it. I have sealed the flaps with superglue so it is almost impossible to get to the contents without major surgery. When a decent opportunity arises and your team manage to stage an incursion through the Base perimeter fence, get them to take these through and try to hide them as cleverly as possible. When the Defence Police finally find them they will assume they are dealing with a bomb and will have to waste hours and lots of manpower getting the bomb disposal team in to deal with them. In the middle of the night it will be even better because all the sleeping sailors will have to evacuate their accommodation blocks until the action is over with."

Sheila Boyd's face lit up into a beaming smile. "Why on earth haven't we thought of that before now," she said. "It is absolutely brilliant, thank you so much for the idea."

Boyd got out of the car and placed one case on the tarmac of the lay-by so that she could wave her new co-conspirators a smiling farewell. She picked up the case and with one in each hand entered the camp. She returned to the peace camp brimming with ideas and reeling from what she had become a part of.

A greasy cup of tea half finished and suddenly the peace camp lost some of its attraction.

It had become vitally important that she head south to speak with Angela Young her co-founder at Trident Ploughshares 2000 and share all the exciting new plans for the coming days and weeks.

By lunchtime Padraig and Laura were well away from Helensburgh and the naval base and were heading for the M90 motorway. Flynn knew exactly what was expected of him when Laura dropped him at the Granada service station at Kinross and she continued on to her first stop in Edinburgh.

Sixteen

Flynn found the Kirklands Hotel in Kinross without difficulty and booked himself in for one night. The small public bar at the front of the old coaching Inn was warm and welcoming and he relaxed on a bar stool with a pint of the guest ale.

Bobby was a genial host and the two men talked amiably about anything and everything until another lunchtime customer joined them. The landlord made the introductions and explained to the newcomer that Flynn was staying the night at the hotel.

Padraig Flynn bought the beer and was ready to listen.

Bobby visited the kitchen and spoke to Janet, his head cook, and then retreated to his small office to begin the daily business of preparing a lunch and dinner menu on his computer. The two men talked and the landlord came through to replenish their glasses twice more before his resident was once again alone. Flynn felt the need for some fresh air. He walked through the town and down as far as the park at the side of Loch Leven. For a couple of hours he watched the boats and the fisherman who were casting their fly rods in search of the famous brown trout.

The loch was calm.

The ruins of a castle out on a small island in the loch turned the scene into an artist's dream, solid form against the backdrop of water and hills. Flynn walked to the end of the grassy park where a small boat was moored against a short pier. Boat trips to the island. He read the tourist information boards displayed around the pier. Mary Queen of Scots had been imprisoned in the castle he learned. The Scottish midges swarmed around the water's edge and Flynn swiped with his arms to keep them at bay. A couple of bites were enough. His head was now clear of the afternoon's beer and he decided to make his way back to the hotel.

***

Laura paid the balance of the car rental in cash and headed for the station.

It would be four hours back to London.

She was looking forward to a long hot bath at her flat and some decent clothes but knew it would be late into the evening by the time she had cleared up at Collier Street, sent out her electronic mail message to her controller and waited for any response. She was certain that her ideas would be welcomed. The train journey would give her the time she needed to put her plan into words.

There were weaknesses of course; every plan had areas of greater risk. Ship programmes could change. On balance she felt it would achieve its objective and generate the reaction she sought. Things were going well, this would be a major feather in the cap of Leila Latif, and the more so because she would be able to assure control that her identity would remain a secret. Laura toyed with the thought of telephoning Coleman from the station before boarding the train south but decided that the attraction of her bath outweighed the prospect of sex with him. Tomorrow would be soon enough to renew contact; after all she had at least a fortnight before the next phase of the plan would begin.

***

Distribution of the August edition of Envirocare was complete and Daniel felt a considerable satisfaction at the response so far.

He had tried something a bit different and it was working. Perhaps he should target one major issue each month in future. He had to acknowledge that Laura had provided most of the inspiration, but then he had begun to think of them as a couple after she had stayed with him at the flat for those days earlier in the week. His routines were upside down, he had finished writing and editing and production well ahead of his

89

usual schedule, and now, with distribution over with there was a gap to fill.

Daniel had replaced his whisky supply and treated himself to a haircut.

He had hunted around in the spare room and found his old sleeping bag. Laura had talked about going up to Scotland for the demonstration. He hoped that she meant it. It occurred to him that he should have a laptop computer if he was to report from the field like a proper journalist. Daniel checked his building society savings account to see if he could afford the expense. It was easy enough to persuade himself that it was a vital tool of his trade and so he visited the Tottenham Court Road and bought a rather swish Toshiba complete with a carrying case and a battery pack. Coleman was ready to face the world's press.

***

With Annie down in Petersfield Alan South felt less guilty about putting in an eleven hour day at the office and had done so each day this week. He wouldn't be able to get away on leave until after the August demonstrations were over with and that meant his period as a bachelor would be longer than he welcomed.

He'd miss seeing the children too.

It wouldn't be fair for Annie to leave them during their respective summer breaks so she would stay with them and he would have to fend for himself. This afternoon he would sit in on the Commander's fourth Trident Ploughshares committee meeting and update himself on the latest intelligence. Start day, according to the group's own publicity was just two weeks away and there were already signs that this series of demonstrations were likely to be the biggest and best organised for many years.

He knew that Young had requested coverage from the St John's Ambulance organisation for a period of three weeks, almost the whole of August, and that she had been targeting the more sympathetic of the newspapers for some time. He had tried his best to persuade the Fleet planners that having a 'bomber' in the base during August was a risky strategy and that it was providing just what the demonstrators sought to find. Trouble was, he fully accepted the age-old argument about changing plans and giving in to external pressure and so his heart wasn't really in the bid to have his Naval Base empty of submarines.

At least he had managed to fend off the proposal from the US State Department for the visit of an American vessel. With their somewhat inflexible rules of engagement the spectre of someone actually getting shot at whilst attempting to board a US missile carrying sub' was more than he wanted to contemplate. There was certainly enough happening; the month alone would fly by.

***

Carolyn Smart collected her thoughts and set off for the Command Building Conference Room and her committee meeting. She felt a sense of expectation, butterflies in the tummy. It wasn't the thought of chairing this meeting it was more about what the meeting represented. All the plans were in place, she was sure of that. The overtime bill for the month of August to pay for all the extra shifts undertaken by the Ministry of Defence Police and the Guard service would be astronomical. If no one turned up it would be so hard to justify, if the whole thing were a damp squib there would be some hard questions to answer. There were always choices, decisions to be made, let's hope we get some of them right she thought.

***

Sheila Boyd drove her car hard as she headed for East Anglia and the Norwich home of Angela Young.

The two women, the driving force behind the Trident Ploughshares 2000 action group, had met countless times and spent hours preparing their strategy for the August meeting at Faslane. They both recognised that support for the peace camp had waned over the years. If they were to make their, hoped for, impact they needed to spread the appeal of the demonstration beyond just the long haired, slightly seedy, group that occupied the Faslane Peace Camp and include a more intelligent, international, and more presentable gathering.

They needed some 'names', a few television personalities anxious to have their pictures in the papers in support of nuclear disarmament; an MP would be a distinct advantage, a Euro' politician a godsend. It mattered little to Boyd and Young that the various affinity groups had agenda of their own. It was fine by them if the Naval Base was subjected to a host of uncoordinated actions.

What the women wanted were film crews and television outside broadcast units and newsmen from the world's press, they wanted magazine coverage, radio programmes, and questions for the Prime Minister in the House of Commons. Boyd and Young knew without shadow of doubt that publicity was the fuel that their particular cause would thrive on. There were no shortage of people who, when fired up with the excitement of demonstration, could be led into cutting the perimeter fence around the base, or getting into a canoe. Whatever the danger, or the risk, there were willing hands who the two women could manipulate.

They were good at it.

Sheila Boyd had been arrested so many times she had forgotten the number but still she had her freedom.

Young was the same.

As she drove she replayed in her mind the meeting with Laura.

This woman, who would have looked at home on the fashion catwalks of Paris, or could have graced the Summer Garden Party at Buckingham Palace, was as tough as nails. Boyd thought of herself as a warrior but she saw from her brief meeting with Laura qualities she knew to be lacking in her own make-up. Sheila had agreed in an instant to the plan Laura had laid before her. She had agreed to discuss it with her partner, but had left Laura in no doubt that Trident Ploughshares 2000 wanted to be included in the action. If

Angela agreed then she herself would be the spokesperson.

Seventeen

Dusk descended over the Gareloch and the lay-by that was home to the Faslane Peace Camp.

Even the incessant drizzle, so unwelcome in August, could not dampen the spirits of Jenny Graham. She had experienced quite the best week of her long stay in the damp and dingy caravan that was her home of the last six years. For the previous seven days Jenny had played house matron, tour guide and general advisor to a host of people from all over the United Kingdom and Europe.

They were arriving to take part in the month of action at the Royal Navy base just across the A814 road from her chosen home. They came from the Home Counties in hire cars and carried enough professional camping equipment to mount an assault on Everest. They had accents more suited to the wine bars of Tony Blair's Islington.

Others disembarked from the cabs of passing lorries having hitched lifts from Wales and Cornwall and the West Midlands. A steady stream of people arrived by train at Helensburgh station. The ubiquitous Volkswagen Camper Van had arrived in a dozen different colours and an equal number of different style registration plates from Sweden and from the Netherlands and Denmark and Belgium and Germany.

The camp had been vibrant again.

The place buzzed with a polyglot of voices. Mostly Jenny had handed out the information packs produced by Sheila Boyd and her Ploughshares Group telling the new visitors all about the Base and what was planned for the month. She had then offered directions to the much bigger camp site and action centre at Peaton Glen Wood a few miles further round the end of the loch past the village of Garelochhead. Some of the old stagers had stayed for a few nights and the party had been in full swing. Jenny had been re-united with several groups who had visited the camp before so there was an atmosphere of carnival much of the time.

More significant for Jenny was the appearance of Georges from Brussels. He, and his friend Paul, arrived on foot and declared themselves too tired to move on to the other site that day. By evening a party had begun and the twenty or so gathered around the campfire had been in great form fuelled by warm beer and the generous amounts of cannabis passed, hand to hand, between the revellers. Most were in natural pairs; they had arrived as couples and stayed that way at the fireside.

There were two pairs of women together but it was clearly a matter of choice for them and that was fine too.

Of the new visitors only Georges and Paul were without the closer companionship of a sexual partner. By late evening as couples drifted away to sleep in their vans or tents Jenny and June and Georges and Paul were left at the fire, spirits still high but now bathed in a more comfortable glow from an evening of laughter and raised voices and exploring new friendships.

A pairing was inevitable.

Before long June and Paul had moved together at the makeshift table and were deep in their private world of whispers. If Jenny had been made to guess she could imagine June explaining to her new Belgian friend about her young daughter, sound asleep in her caravan. She knew what a damper the young Rosey could put on the ardour of the newly arrived Belgian who by now was probably thinking of taking the friendship further. Jenny's attention was brought sharply back to the present. Georges leaned forward and very gently closed his teeth on her left ear, the warmth of his breath a mixture of the evening's beer and their last shared joint.

It was a closeness, an intimacy she hadn't contemplated.

For all that, she found it pleasant; no, more than pleasant, it added to her glow of happiness. Jenny turned her head towards Georges they were inches apart. Their first kiss was inevitable. It was at first tentative and tender but gradually increasing in intensity and becoming a true embrace, a

95

meeting of desires. He broke away first and for several seconds the two remained close to each other as Georges searched the girl's eyes hoping to find the answer to his unspoken, but nevertheless obvious question.

The answer when it came, owed more to June and Paul.

They rose together and crossed, hand in hand to June's caravan. From their movements, their attempts at silence made all the more difficult by the frisson of the moment Paul knew he would not have June entirely to himself. In their whisperings at the campfire they had discussed what they would do. Georges and Paul had erected their tent before the party got to full swing but June was cautious about letting her little one wake up in the caravan alone. It hadn't happened before. The child knew of nothing other than the Peace Camp. She had been brought there as a toddler when June's relationship with Rosey's father had broken down completely and their lives had been plunged into turmoil. June had grasped the 'peace movement' with both hands, an anchor in her unsettled life. She owed the peace camp a huge debt of gratitude and although in reflective moments she missed her middle class family life and her parent's middle class values, she was happy.

They'd take her back, and Rosey, in an instant. She knew that well enough. There wouldn't even be any recrimination. No mention of the string of minor convictions gained in the pursuit of her life as a Faslane Peace Camper. No, "I told you so," from her father. June dismissed the thoughts from her mind, raised a silencing finger to her lips and opened the door. She and Paul disappeared from view as the caravan door gently closed behind them.

Left alone Jenny and Georges fell into a silence.

Expectant, tense, waiting for what must come.

They followed her friend's example.

It had been a long time for Jenny.

She was not what could be described as conventionally pretty and was not, generally, promiscuous. She kept herself in good shape more by the uncertainty of her diet, her lifestyle, and a lack of money than by some pre-determined health plan. To look at her in her normal garb of sloppy jumpers and

96

jeans it was difficult to decide what lay underneath. In the gloom of the caravan lit only by a camping gas lamp set at a low burn Georges tenderly lifted the sweater over her head and followed it with her tee shirt. It was at least a year since Jenny had stood in front of a man dressed in only jeans and a bra but she felt her instincts flooding back quickly enough as she reached out to Georges and unbuttoned his thick plaid shirt.

The earlier giggles of laughter at the campfire had now deserted both of them, replaced by feelings much more immediate, more serious. Jenny ran her hands over the man's chest; firmly muscled, lean and athletic, hairless, smooth. She shivered as she studied his upper body, his shoulders, his neck and face. Georges was fit and active, that much was abundantly clear to her; she couldn't recall contact with such a body before. Her bra fell to the floor and she felt the pressure of both his hands on her breasts, circling, smoothing, teasing, and finally gently rolling a nipple between his fingers.

Jenny hadn't thought about her breasts for a long time, they were just there. Now she realised that they were really quite good and she gave herself to the experience with more confidence, even some pride. Both reached for the fastenings of jeans but the undoing of belts and buckles was soon left, by mutual decision to themselves. Georges was first. After sliding his hand inside his waistband to free his urgent erection from his underwear, he slid jeans and briefs to the floor of the caravan. Georges stood proud in front of Jenny who, having lagged behind by only a second, now bent forward to remove her own remaining clothes.

Perhaps the dim light accentuated his size or perhaps it was the excitement and anticipation of the moment, whatever, Jenny gasped at what she saw and as she straightened to full height she never took her eyes off Georges' middle. He explored her curves and liked what he felt. Days later when Georges and his friend had moved on they would discuss their respective conquests. He would confide in Paul that he wasn't sure whether the shapeless looking woman at the peace camp was a good choice but that as soon as he saw her naked he lost that uncertainty.

For Georges, stroking soon turned to gentle probing and for Jenny her desire turned to a hunger that could only be satisfied when they were finally joined. The bed that had served her for six years and was well suited to her single existence was now less than adequate as she and Georges sought space to make love. They shuffled their bodies on the narrow bunk, touching and moving apart, until finally they met in a few moments of sheer passion. Even in the briefness of their first encounter Jenny had never known such physical pleasure, such focussed sensation, she tingled from head to foot but she burned in the centre of her being. They lay together in silence, breathless, two people who had met only hours before but were completely at one with each other.

The peace camp was in complete silence as Jenny and Georges, still naked, sat at the dying embers of the camp fire an hour after their lovemaking. The gentle drizzling rain continued. The makeshift awning slung over the centre of the camp kept them dry and the chill of early morning didn't reach them through their warm afterglow.

All was quiet.

Traffic on the main road just beside the camp had reduced to the occasional flash of headlights as cars sped on their way south to Helensburgh or north to the naval base and beyond. Neither could contemplate sleep. Both waited with anticipation for the other to make the move that would take them back to the caravan. Georges spoke first. Their second time was different. The urgency was gone, replaced by the need to make the act more lasting, almost a competition between two healthy young people trying to satisfy both themselves and each other. Jenny reached orgasm and that was another first for her. Finally sleep came and for three or four hours confined in the small bunk they renewed their strength for a new day.

The dawn light speared through the gap in the shabby caravan curtains and hit the couple, lighting up a path across their middle. Jenny woke first. She was cuddled close to his back with her knees drawn up slightly, matching his, and with her arm thrown casually over his chest. She was on the inner side of the bunk and furthest from the window and the source of the light. She withdrew her arm and traced the spear of morning sunlight across his body with her fingertips reaching down until finally she touched his sleeping manhood. Raising herself slowly on her other arm Jenny could see over Georges' body to where her hand had come to rest. Even the lightest of touch seemed to affect the sleeping Georges and Jenny watched enthralled as his body came awake even before his eyes opened.

"My God," she thought, "look at me, boring Jenny Graham. Here I am with a gorgeous Belgian guy about whom I know absolutely nothing except that he has given me the best night of my life and I am trying to wake him up for more."

Georges obliged by opening first one eye then the other. He quickly realised where he was and the source of the pleasant sensation spreading though him and turned towards his partner of the night before. He turned half way to be lying on his back. Jenny stopped him moving further. She slid her left leg over his waist and moved to a position above him. She grasped his firm erection, guided him to her entrance and lowered herself slowly.

It felt right.

Jenny reached for Georges' hands and lifted them, one to each breast. She leaned her body forward and pinioned the man to the bunk with her hands on his shoulders. Georges started to move but she stopped him. "My turn," she told him simply, and with that she began a gentle raising and lowering of her hips. "Tell me when to stop," she demanded and she obeyed his instructions, easing up whenever Georges came to the brink of climax.

It was their best yet.

Even though Jenny was determined to prolong the pleasure forever she found herself unable to do so as her animal lust pushed all thoughts of improved technique out of her mind. Georges cried out in orgasm and Jenny collapsed onto his chest as the two gasped for breath until their pulses stopped racing and returned to nearer normal.

The first good news was that Georges and Paul decided to delay their move to the Peaton Glen camp for a few days. They would stay at the Peace Camp. It seemed that June was as pleased as Jenny and that the presence of young Rosey had not posed the two of them any major problems. Certainly there had been a naked man in her mother's bed when the child had woken in the morning. But neither Paul nor June had paraded their nakedness in front of the child and in the close environment of the Peace Camp the little girl had probably seen a hundred times worse in the last few years. Paul made genuine attempts at conversation with the child and gained some favourable reaction for his efforts.

The next few days passed in continued activity, new arrivals were given the welcome information and shown what could be seen of the Naval Base from the perimeter fence and the two principal entrances, the South and North gates. Jenny Graham led different groups on little sorties along the fence line where they deliberately rattled the fence to activate the alarm systems.

Her friends, old and new studied the reaction of the security forces, developed a feel for the speed of their response. They harassed the police as much as they could without provoking arrest. Jenny knew that the Ministry of Defence police would never arrest them for just rattling the fence wires and setting off the alarms, there wasn't a charge that would stick. The hours of paperwork needed to bring the culprits to court made such a gesture of frustration totally futile.

They had visited the South Gate on several occasions and just hindered the traffic going in to and coming out of the base, nuisance tactics she knew, but it all helped to keep the security forces on their toes. She was happy enough with the way things were building up. The nights, of course, were the real bonus when she and Georges could disappear to the privacy of her caravan. Even June, her best friend of many years made the comment that she would wear the poor guy out soon, not that Georges looked exactly distressed at the turn of events. The two Belgians were moving around the loch to the main site the following day. Jenny was determined to mark their last evening with a victory against the forces of her perceived evil and then celebrate their success with a night of activity of a very different kind.

Jenny remembered well what Sheila Boyd had said about co-ordinated action against their targets.

She managed to persuade the peace camp residents of the day to join together in one glorious assault. Around the campfire in the drizzle of the August evening the group had just finalised their plan of action. They would wait until midnight and then move out in their groups together, each with their own objectives. There had been no partying this evening. Everyone was sober and no one had offered the cannabis at the end of the evening barbecued supper. June had elected to stay behind when the action started, she couldn't leave Rosey in the camp alone, and naturally enough Paul had offered to keep her company. Jenny could see a second agenda for the two of them but she was so buoyant after three nights of glorious sex that she could hardly deny her best friend a taste of the same fruit.

At ten thirty Jenny gathered her troops around the fire for a final briefing. She felt like a General. She was plotting a military operation. Jenny climbed up onto a wooden bench and gently called for quiet. The peace camp residents responded.

"OK everyone," she said, "tonight is in two phases. First of all, when we finish here now, we go out in our groups and do some nuisance stuff. Rattle the fences; go down to the loch side by the slipway and wander around; one group down to the South Gate and the last group to the North Gate. Try to upset the MDP and the MGS, make them deploy their dog teams to the gates, but don't get arrested or detained. Whatever you do, remember to stop short of getting caught."

She paused whilst she surveyed the nods of understanding around her audience and then continued: "After an hour, no more, everyone returns here for the big one. OK."

The groups began to discuss which of the first activities each would undertake and within seconds agreements were made. They all looked to Jenny to give the order to start the action and Jenny was bristling with pride at what she had achieved. In the six years of her residence at the camp she could hardly remember one time when the peace campers had set out with a plan, let alone a plan involving more than one strategy.

She raised her hands again and waited for the murmuring to stop.

"Oh and when we get back here," she said, "remember to change into dark, close fitting clothes and rub some dirt onto your faces to make yourselves more difficult to spot."

Jenny Graham got down from her bench and mingled with her friends offering more encouragement.

More nods of agreement greeted her words and she was so delighted with herself that she punched the air with her fists clenched tightly and called out in a loud voice, "Good luck everyone and let's give 'em hell."

***

"Foxtrot Alpha Two-One to Foxtrot Alpha Control"

"Two-One send," came back the response to the radio message from the Ministry of Defence Police mobile patrol who were attempting to contact their Control Centre within the Base Defence Headquarters of the Naval Base.

"Four 'Papa Charlies' on the south approach road heading for the South Gate; over"

"Roger Two-One they're on camera."

At the console in BDCR Sergeant George McKinnon studied the bank of monitors and picked up the images of the four people walking slowly towards the southern gate. Two cameras had been moved by push button controls to pan on to the approaching group and would follow their progress down the hundred yard straight road until they reached the security gates. The approach road was not Ministry owned and so the 'Papa Charlies,' the peace campers, would be allowed free and unhindered access until they reached the gate. Almost at the gate but to the west side of the road was a small privately owned ship repair yard called Timbacraft who had workshops, some office space and a slipway down to the water's edge of the Gareloch.

The Ministry of Defence should have bought out the owner years ago and demolished the little shipyard but they hadn't. Now it offered an area of private property between the main road and the base that any demonstrators could try to hide in. The group moved beyond Timbacraft and stopped at the gate. Traffic to and from the base was pretty sporadic at just after ten thirty at night so the closure of the outer gate caused little inconvenience. Electric controls were engaged and the twelve-foot high steel wall rolled across the road closing off the southern access. Within minutes a Land Rover Discovery vehicle painted in the livery of the Ministry of Defence Police arrived on the south approach road and edged its way slowly towards the demonstrators.

The group of four found themselves in a sandwich between the vehicle and the closed gate.

The MDP Shift Commander, Chief Inspector Bill Campbell and the Duty Naval Base Officer Lieutenant Commander Colin Walker had both heard the radio exchange in their respective offices and had made their way to the Control Room.

"Better call Strath' Pol' Bill," Colin Walker suggested quietly, and his Police colleague directed one of his constables to contact Strathclyde Constabulary via a direct line telephone sited in the Control Room.

The relationship between the Royal Navy Officer acting as DNBO and the Ministry of Defence Police Officer who was the MDP Shift Commander was an unusual but reasonably healthy one. The policeman had operational control over the security forces comprised of the MDP and MGS, and the small Royal Marines Response Force whose job was the protection of the Trident submarines and berths in the northern area of the base. But the DNBO had Operational Command over all the agencies within the base, including the security forces, in the event of any incident. It took patience and gentle progress to reach the stage where the police accepted that a uniformed Naval Officer held sway over their actions and it was a position reached not without tears. Colin Walker and Bill Campbell had worked together happily for over two years now without a falling out.

"Fence alarm at Camera 36," called the MGS security man watching the large mimic board in the Control Room. The map of the base perimeter now showed a red light burning in the area of one of the fence cameras. The Control Room altered the pan and tilt of a further pair of cameras and peered at the monitor screens looking for some signs of disturbance around the affected area of fence. The operator zoomed in and out as he moved the camera head but saw nothing out of the ordinary.

"Can't see anything at three-six, Sarge," he called out.

Bill Campbell interceded and directed his Sergeant to send another outside patrol vehicle to examine the area of the fence covered by Camera 36.

"Two-One to Control."

"Two-One send."

"Taxi just arrived at South Gate with four sailors returning from shore, do you want the gate opened or shall I send them round to North?"

"No, Two-One, get the pedestrian gate opened and let them through."

George McKinnon knew only too well that the taxi driver wouldn't want to back track along the south approach road with his disgruntled passengers and then charge them an additional three pounds for the extra drive to the North Gate. He knew even better that asking the four sailors to end their 'run ashore' with what amounted to almost a six-mile hike wasn't the way to win over their support. From the South Gate the sailors could all but see their accommodation blocks, if they went to the North Gate for access they would then have to walk the length of the Base inside the fence before they would get to bed.

"Just make sure the 'Papa Charlies' don't make a run at the gate when it opens." said McKinnon

The small group of peace campers knew only too well that the arrival of the four sailors offered the chance for real mischief and they moved up close to the small pedestrian opening at the right side of the large gate. The sailors paid off their cab and made their way towards the gate. They too knew what was going on, there had been so many instructions lately about dealing with demonstrators and keeping cool under provocation that the four young men were sobering up fast from their night out.

104

"Two-One to Control."

"Send"

"Control, these four 'Papa Charlies' are blocking the access."

"George," Bill Campbell attracted his sergeant's attention, "send a dog team down to the South Gate *toot sweet* and ask 'Jack' to hang on a few minutes."

McKinnon did as he was instructed and the minor stand-off at the gate began.

"Foxtrot Alpha Two-Two to Control."

"Send Two-Two."

"Nothing seen at the fence line at Camera 36 Control."

"Roger Two-Two resume patrol."

"That alarm at three-six hasn't reset, Sarge," from the MGS man monitoring the fence alarm panel.

The telephone at the Sergeant's position in the Control Room rang and McKinnon lifted the handset.

"CSO5 Willmot at the North Gate here Sarge, there's two peace campers turned up at the gate on bikes, one male and one female."

"Two-One Control, Strathclyde Police have just arrived at the South Gate any instructions, over?"

"Yes Two-One, ask them to warn the 'Papa Charlies' for obstruction and let's get Jack off to his bed."

The Strathclyde Police Vauxhall Astra had parked just behind the Land Rover Discovery of the Ministry of Defence outside patrol and the officers of both organisations were speaking together out of the hearing of both the patient group of sailors and the equally patient group of peace campers. The moment the civil police moved towards the group of four they moved away from the gate and began a slow walk back along the approach road in the direction of the peace camp.

The pedestrian gate opened and the sailors passed through unhindered, they had added half an hour to their night out and wiped away what good humour they had left the pub in earlier. The Strathclyde team bade their farewells and carried out a neat three-point turn in the road and headed off. In the Land Rover Discovery the MDP constable turned to his colleague and complained bitterly.

"That's what really pisses me off about these wankers, they give us all this stick six inches outside our property and then piss off like little lambs when Strath' Pol' turn up. We ought to be able to nick 'em right off."

The constables sentiments were echoed in the BDHQ Control Room, if a little less graphically, by the frustrated George McKinnon as he ordered the re-opening of the South Gate and the return of outside patrol 'Two-One'.

"Those two cyclists leaving the North Gate Sarge," reported the MGS watchkeeper who had been quietly observing events at the other end of the base on his monitor screen.

"Is that it for now then, Bill?" asked Walker and he took some notes of the timing of the various minor incidents and headed back to his office to complete his computer aided narrative of the events of his shift. As Walker turned to leave the Control Room the message came through on the radio that the dog and handler had arrived at the South Gate having suspended their perimeter patrols some ten minutes earlier when directed by Sergeant McKinnon. Both he and the dog were directed back to their earlier duties.

***

The two pairs of women who had gone down to the foreshore opposite the peace camp arrived back at the camp first. As the first pair disappeared into their camper van to get changed the second pair looked around for signs of life. It wasn't hard to track down June and Paul they just needed to follow the sounds. They could almost have known from the movement of Jenny's caravan what the couple were up to so they started a conversation between themselves to draw the activity to a close. The two women smiled knowingly to each other and clasped hands. Not for them the sweating and grunting of a heterosexual relationship. They were at peace with what they saw as a more gentle and refined approach to the business of sex and they had been together as a couple for several years, not as man and wife because neither saw herself as masculine or feminine, they were simply a couple.

June and Paul emerged from Jenny's caravan as the

106

occupier herself arrived back at the camp with the other three who had made up the South Gate party. June mouthed a silent thank you towards her good friend and Jenny smiled in return.

The fence team came in next and finally puffing with exertion the two cyclists rode in through the camp entrance. It was just before eleven thirty and as far as Jenny could tell everything had gone according to her plan, there had been no arrests and everyone was safely back at camp.

General Jenny wanted to know what had happened at the other locations and was surprised to hear that the four women who had gone down to the foreshore had sat there for almost an hour without being noticed.

"We just sat there talking amongst ourselves and watching the police boats going up and down," said their spokesperson, "nobody came near us and there we no alarms as far as we could judge."

Jenny declared that to be most unusual because in her experience the Clyde Marine Unit of the MDP, the policemen who patrolled up and down the Gareloch in their high speed launches and rigid inflatable boats, didn't miss much of the activity on the water or the shore line. She'd even heard that they had now extended the coverage of the base thermal imaging cameras and closed circuit TV cameras to cover the southernmost area of the base in much more depth.

The experienced peace campers already knew that there was a bit of a blind spot in the fence camera coverage in the area of camera 36, just by Magennis Gate. Magennis Gate, named after a young submariner who was awarded a Victoria Cross for bravery during the Second World War was a small gate which remained closed off and barricaded with razor wire until emergency access to the base was needed. The report from the couple who had attacked this area of the fence came as no surprise to Jenny.

"Did they send out an outside patrol vehicle to look at the fence?" she asked the fence couple and the man answered.

"Yes, we saw the Land Rover coming and lay down in the grass just behind a sort of contour in the bank. They stopped the vehicle, looked out of the window and shone torches at the fence and then drove off."

"Well done," said Jenny.

"And," came back fence man, "we cut a slot in the fence about two feet long after they had gone and we waited another twenty minutes or so and they didn't come back."

"That probably means the fence alarms haven't reset," said June who felt somewhat left out of the successful action even though she was glowing from an hour's action of her own.

"Even better," pronounced the group's leader, "that means all our missions have succeeded and that two of them have beaten the security team completely, it looks good for tonight."

"OK everyone, get changed and muddied up, don't forget the roll of carpet and the cutters and once again, good luck."

***

Jenny Graham mustered her troops between the caravans of the peace camp and away from the central campfire area. Although the campers had erected a large fishing net, knotted with scraps of coloured cloth, between the fire and the road side in an attempt to prevent the MDP patrols witnessing what was going on in the camp she didn't want to risk her plans being foiled from the start.

From the road the camp looked in darkness.

The month of July had been the wettest for sixty years the papers reported, and so far August was not much better. The drizzle had lasted all day and now into the early hours of the next. They were sixteen adults and one child. Once again June ruled herself out of the action because of her daughter Rosey but she would act as lookout in the camp, she would keep the home fire burning and form the welcome party when the night's activity was over. June had a mobile telephone so that she could contact the newspapers with any information that could embarrass the enemy within the naval base fence. They were all set. The lookout took up her station at the road side to signal a quiet time when the traffic, and more important the police patrols, were clear of their area. She called out that the coast was clear.

Fence man from the warm up earlier in the evening, and his

girlfriend; John and Rachel from Pinner, would start off the real action. They set off on the two bicycles heading south towards Helensburgh. Rachel had her long fair hair covered under a balaclava and both had blackened faces. Tied to the cross bar of John's bicycle and wrapped in a black rubbish sack were a pair of heavy duty wire cutters and on his back a small rucksack.

Georges and Paul dashed across the A814 into the wooded area opposite carrying the first of their one-man canoes. Safely deposited within the trees, they returned for the second. The two Belgians were across the road when a local man from Helensburgh joined them. Hamish was a regular visitor to the camp and arrived a few hours earlier carrying his wet suit and fins. He darted cautiously to the end of the tree line and watched the canoeists as they slid their craft to the water's edge, waded out a few yards and skilfully completed the task of boarding unaided.

The four women who had so successfully avoided discovery on the foreshore earlier in the evening set off, bold as brass, towards the south gate of the base, their mission; to cause as much nuisance as possible without getting arrested. The women had a definite spring in their step and were anxious to enter the fray.

Petey, the other long-term resident of the peace camp, took a couple from Denmark out onto the main road and headed north.

Jenny and her two remaining accomplices waited by her caravan until the others were well clear. She wanted the four women to have reached the south approach road and be enjoying the interest of the security forces before she led her team out. As if in confirmation of her timings a Land Rover Discovery turned on to the south approach road as the three left the cover of the peace camp carrying a roll of carpet and a pair of bolt croppers.

The cycle ride to the car park of the Ardencaple Hotel was totally uneventful and the hotel was in darkness as they parked and chained the two bicycles together behind the hotel. John and Rachel kept their cutters in the black bag and sprinted up the road opposite the Clyde Off Site Centre. The building looked as dark as the hotel except for the solitary light shining from the gatehouse just inside the locked gates and behind the twelve foot high fence. Easily past the single patch of light they crossed the road unseen and reached the fence line. The two came to a halt beside a chain link fence, no different than the one around the sports field at school, he thought, and certainly not as robust as the one he had managed to cut earlier in the evening. They waited. They looked up and down the road and saw nothing. John pulled out the cutters and snipped through the first link.

Nothing.

The two of them were so tense they had expected air raid sirens and flashing lights; there were neither. He snipped again, and again, still nothing. With Rachel watching the road for traffic, and the area of the gatehouse for movement, John snipped the strands of fence until he had fashioned an 'L' shaped incision one metre from top to bottom. Pushing forward, a triangular flap opened in the fence and John hunched his shoulders and back and stepped through. His outstretched hand guided Rachel and they had successfully breached the perimeter of the Royal Navy's Press and Media Reception Centre. Rachel dashed for the darkness and cover of the large prefabricated building and John remembered the instruction from Jenny Dawn: 'if you get in, fold the fence back so that it looks normal'. He did so. The two co-conspirators huddled together in the darkened gloom of the building and fought the temptation to giggle.

"We may just as well have rung the doorbell and entered by the gate," whispered Rachel.

"Let's explore," her boyfriend replied and the two deposited their wire cutters, once more wrapped in the bag, and set off gingerly to follow the outer wall of the building towards the depths of the large compound.

***

Petey and his two new Danish friends had already started their action by hitting the perimeter fence with a large stone they had collected on their walk along the road. Petey was now openly pointing out to the couple the positions of the cameras that were being moved in an attempt to search the affected fence panel. When the camera head lined up on the trio they waved.

They moved slowly north and on reaching the position of the next tall camera pylon they repeated their move. It took less than five minutes before the dog handler and his German shepherd dog arrived at the same place on the inside of the fence. Mission accomplished. Petey knew there were four dog teams on each shift and already his group had engaged one of them. Now it was time for a gentle stroll for the two miles or so left until they reached the north gate, rattling the fence as they proceeded along. He gave a running commentary to his Danish team-mates, waved to all the cameras and sauntered along without a care in the world. For the dog handler there was little he could do except walk the fence line or wait for his Control to move him elsewhere. The policeman knew who Petey was and had already passed the details of the three of them to BDHQ on his portable radio. The dog watched and enjoyed the exercise but was less keen on the rain.

***

Georges and Paul had launched their canoes. Both had canoed before and Paul was a keen water sports enthusiast. The usually orange coloured glass fibre kayaks had been given a skim of black paint during the previous few days and with black paddles, dark clothes and muddied faces they left little for the casual watcher to catch sight of. They had discussed a plan, set off together, and were heading away from the base and out into the Gareloch. The aim was to get beyond what they knew to be the protected area, the area deemed to be Ministry of Defence property, before they changed direction and headed north.

***

Hamish sat patiently inside the cover of the woods, back to a

111

tree, and followed the progress of the two boats. The two were paddling well and covering good distance towards the centre of the Gareloch. Hamish had grown up around this stretch of water and had observed it in every condition that Scottish weather could offer. On a 'dreicht' night such as tonight, with a clouded moon and the constant drizzle they would travel less than a hundred yards before they disappeared from view to the naked eye. After fifteen minutes peering out into the gloom even the last traces of silver as the paddles dipped into the black water were lost to him and Hamish, bent from the waist, ran the few yards to the water and slithered in. Once able to sit down with the water swirling around his chest Hamish donned his swimmer's fins and struck out with a leisurely stroke for the southern most end of the Naval Base.

***

Their appearance gave them away to the Ministry of Defence Guard Service woman nearest the South Gate before they were nearer than fifty yards. They looked like peace campers and not service women, WRNS. For a start, living a week at the peace camp wasn't exactly good for ones state of tidiness. The washing facilities were, to say the least, primitive, and at best could only be described as rudimentary. When all around you smelled of wood smoke and perspiration it somehow seemed to matter less.

Margaret had blackened her face with mud from the roadside as had her partner Jan' and the other couple. As soon as she saw the smartly uniformed woman staring out at her from the other side of the fence and saw the disgust written all over her face Margaret had her first doubts. Instinctively she turned to Jan' for reassurance. Jan' was her rock. They had lived together for three years and it had been the happiest of Margaret's adult life.

Her marriage had been a sham, a mistake from the first.

The physical side of the marriage she had been able to bear although it gave her little joy and less pleasure; it was when the beatings began that life turned sour. At first it was just frustration from her husband and she accepted it with

112

stoicism. But soon it turned to something altogether more sinister; he seemed to enjoy administering pain and humiliation. She had little experience of life even then, at twenty-two, she wasn't a virgin going in to her marriage to Brian but she knew little beyond furtive one night stands behind the pub or in someone's car.

Love didn't really enter on to the scene at all. Sex was a response to the pressure from her friends at the shop where she worked as a sales assistant; it was expected, it was what the others talked about all day long. How big was this boy's dick, or how many times they could do it; Margaret was dragged along by the allure of it all and it led her to the altar with the wrong man. It took her three years to reach the refuge for battered wives in Bath and then she met Jan'. Jan' was a regular visitor to the refuge, almost a counsellor, and the two hit it off from the first. Margaret had never even thought about a gay relationship before the refuge but once there, it somehow seemed a natural step. She soaked up the affection, the tenderness, like a sponge; where Brian's approach was rough, even during the good times, Jan' was gentle. She whispered and she caressed. It took months for her mind to erase the searing pain of Brian's thrusting efforts but eventually the memories faded and she began to pick up the pieces of a shattered life.

Jan' immediately saw the look of panic in Margaret's eyes and came to her. The four had reached the South Gate and were milling around a yard or so outside the line of the gate closure. The security team watched, alert, waiting for an attempt to cross the demarcation line between the local authority road and the Ministry property. Jan' slipped her arm around her friend's shoulders and turned her to face away from the stares of the guards.

"I'm so sorry Jan', I suddenly feel so dirty."

"I know love," Jan' replied, "don't cry, do you want to leave?"

"Oh, yes please Jan' can we go home, I'm just not brave like you."

Jan' approached the other two women and briefly reported their departure and within seconds the pair were making their way south and back to the camp one comforting the other. Before any of the other groups returned to the peace camp from their individual missions Margaret and Jan' were driving out of the area and navigating their camper van towards the motorway. The other pair waited at the gate but suddenly their bravado had slipped away too and they turned to leave.

***

John and Rachel heard the sound of a television set and saw the flickers of changing light from the window ahead of them. They stopped and flattened against the huge wall of the rear of the building.

"Stay here Rach', I'll have a look."

John crept forward, almost on tiptoe, a caricature of stealth. As he neared the partially open window he could pick up words from the programme being screened, it sounded like a commercial, and when he was close enough to risk looking in he could see that the television was playing to an empty room. He took up a position on the opposite side of the window and signalled Rachel to join him.

She set off.

Rachel passed by with her back to the lighted window and the couple continued until they reached the end of the building. Ahead was an open, tarmac covered parking area stretching some twenty paces to the opposite perimeter fence looking out onto the Gareloch. There were some small dinghies on trailers and close up to the side of the building a wooden single ladder ten or twelve feet long. A huge smile spread over John's face and he gestured Rachel to come forward and take hold of one end of the ladder. Between them they carried the ladder and retraced their steps back along the rear wall of the building to the roadway.

***

Hamish surfaced on the southern side of the south dolphin, a square concrete structure which once acted as the permanent mooring for the floating dock which had been a feature of the

114

skyline of the Gareloch for many years. Old age had finally overtaken what had been the Royal Navy's longest vessel in commission and the Government had sold it off to an Icelandic shipping company. The dolphin was now home to an installed thermal imaging camera and a closed circuit television camera.

From Hamish's vantage point he could not be seen from the base and he considered the worst to be over even though he had only covered a distance of some sixty yards from the shore line. Hamish sucked in some welcome fresh air and prepared to cover the swim between the south and the north dolphin, a swim of no more than fifty feet but his last across the brightly floodlight approach to the first of the jetties.

Taking a final breath, he submerged and kicked out to the north.

He covered the first twenty feet underwater without difficulty and broke surface in the centre of a huge patch of light. Hamish closed his eyes against the glare, sucked in more air and submerged again. Twice more Hamish broke surface before he reached the safety of the darkened side of the north dolphin.

Although the crossing was not strenuous for a man used to swimming in the water of the Gareloch he was shaking from a mixture of tension and exhaustion when he grasped the ladder leading to the top of the huge concrete block rising thirty feet above him. One look and he could see the coils of razor wire blocking his access upwards. In the gloom of the early morning and out of the pattern of lights Hamish reached the end of the protruding concrete jetty in a few strong strokes.

From the outer edge of the jetty Hamish could see all along the ship berths and as far as the rising shape of the massive ship lift at least one and a half miles to his north. All the jetties were illuminated both above the structure and below it. Hamish had been here before and knew that a network of walkways extended from where he now was right down to number six berth. The steel walkways, slippery from the rising tide allowed the base engineers to service the multitude of pipe systems that criss-crossed under the jetty areas bringing fuel and water and compressed air and a host of other services to the berthed ships and submarines. He also knew that locked gates broke up the walkways randomly, and that he didn't want to attempt climbing out of the relative safety of the water just yet.

His ship count revealed three Sandown Class vessels on the first berth, two other Mine Countermeasures ships occupying the next two, and what was clearly a Swiftsure Class submarine further down at about five or six berth. His trip around to the other side of the Gareloch earlier in the day had prepared him for what he would see but even the small Sandowns' looked awesome from the water line.

***

The remaining group was lying low in the grass beside the outer fence in the area of John and Rachel's activity earlier in the evening. The place marked the end of the chain link fence surrounding some sports pitches and the start of the secure area. From here onwards they could be seen by camera and needed to take extra care.

Jenny and her companions had crawled the last twenty yards on their stomachs, using elbows and knees to drag themselves forward. She knew that John had cut the outer fence but so far she hadn't found the exact spot. Over the years Jenny had made countless assaults on the perimeter, some more successful than others, but never had she gone to so much trouble to disguise her coming. If the years of experience had taught her anything it was that the fence material would always spring back into place.

That was both good and bad for the peace camper's cause.

Bad tonight because she would have to work mainly by feel to find the incision made by John. Good, often, because the security forces had to do pretty much the same and that meant a small cut could go un-noticed for days or even weeks. The guy bringing up the rear of the threesome pulled a ten-foot long strip of carpet with him and the exertion was beginning to show. As the leader, Jenny had parcelled out the tools to the other two and the girl directly behind her had struggled manfully with the bolt croppers.

Jenny risked lifting her head to look through the fence to the inside of the base; she needed to know whether a patrol was monitoring the area. She saw nothing unusual. Another yard and they would be level with Magennis gate and on target. She signalled the team to crawl on. Feeling the wire with her fingers she moved slowly forward. She wanted to reach the cut without pressing on the fence too much because, for once, she hoped that the fence alarm would not activate.

"Got it," she whispered over her shoulder. "Come on up here and let's see if we can open up the gap."

The man crawled up beside her and wriggled his fingers into the small incision left in the fence. He pulled, at first gently and then with more force as the cut edge began to separate. John was right in his estimation, the cut was almost two feet in length and Jenny thought it might just be enough.

"Pull the edge back as far as you can," she whispered, "I'm going through." The man and woman grasped the sharp edge of the weld mesh wire fence and heaved. It was harder than they had expected but the fence separated leaving a triangular opening. Pushing her arms fully forward in front of her head, and using her feet and hands to inch herself forward, Jenny slid into the small gap. Her head and shoulders slithered through. Jenny's companions strained to keep the gap open.

"It's not enough," whispered Jenny from her position stretched out on her stomach, "I'm coming back."

Jenny Graham dug the toes of her boots into the grass, and with the palms of her gloved hands flat on the ground inside the fence she wriggled and pushed until her head and shoulders were once again outside the perimeter fence.

"There's enough room for me to get through," she said addressing her two friends, "but you'll never make it."

The man nodded and accepted her judgement without question.

"What now," he asked, "do we go back?"

"No way," was the response from Jenny Graham, "we've got this far and I want to get into the base. We'll just have to cut a bit more of the fence."

They shuffled the heavy bolt croppers up to the fence line and with the man holding one leg of the large shears and

Jenny the other, they managed to get them into position at the top of the existing incision.

"What about the alarm?" the woman spoke for the first time.

"Look," said Graham, "it hasn't gone off yet has it; we'd be up to our knees in coppers by now. Maybe they haven't been able to reset the fence alarms."

Jenny held her leg of the cutter still and the man operated his as the big shears cut the first horizontal strand. The metal parted with an audible click and the cutters closed on the next strand. The three peace campers took a deep breath and waited, one second, then another.

Nothing.

The cutting began again, spin, snip, each strand of steel less than a pencil's width from its neighbour. Progress was slow but steady and Jenny was satisfied when the vertical gash in the base defences had grown by another foot. She moved forward on her stomach again and began to wriggle though the widened gap. This time she made it through the fence with little difficulty. Staying on her belly she swivelled around to face her friends on the other side.

"Pass me the carpet and the two dummy bombs."

Jenny grasped an end of the roll and pulled it through inch by inch, two leather brief case followed.

"Wrap the cutters up in the bag and hide them in the grass away from the fence," she directed, and the girl left outside did as she was told. Jenny signalled the girl to come through whilst her boyfriend continued to hold back the cut fence and she slithered through in a few seconds.

"Push the flap towards us," she told the man and once the two women were able to get a handhold on the stiff wire fencing they pulled it inwards.

"Now come through." The man obeyed Jenny's order and the three had soon crossed to the inside.

The wire mesh of the fence sprang back to its original setting. The group found themselves at a junction point where the coils of razor wire turned a right angled bend and passed down a steep slope, following the fence, to Magennis Gate. In the other direction the wire disappeared into the distance as it followed the path of the main road to the north. They stayed in the gap between the fence and the razor wire and descended the sloping bank of grass carrying with them the carpet strip. At the bottom of the bank the ground levelled off and the trio reached a metalled road surface.

To their left, looking away from the base to the south they were confronted by a twelve-foot high gate, securely padlocked shut, they were now on the inside of it. When they looked to the right, towards the buildings in the base, the sight of two moveable barriers blocking the road greeted them. Each element of the barrier was constructed out of coils of razor wire attached to a large metal trellis-like frame. The wires were in round coils of about two metres in diameter with two forming the base and a third fixed firmly on top. The security looked daunting. The tightly gathered razor wires offered an impregnable defence and Jenny's less experienced compatriots knelt on the road, open mouthed, as they contemplated the prospect of scaling this lethal barricade.

"You can't cut the strands of wire," she said quietly, "the loose ends just fly at you like a whip. We'd be cut to shreds."

Jenny went on to explain that sometimes, when work was being carried out at the main entrances to the Base they had to open this smaller gate to relieve the traffic congestion and therefore the barriers they now faced had to be removable. With the man's help Jenny unrolled the strip of carpet and together they threw the loose end over the top of the three coils of razor wire. They had a makeshift bridge.

"This is how we get in, OK?"

Both her companions looked decidedly unsure about this proposal but before they could formulate their objections Jenny crawled on hands and knees on to the carpet and inched her way over the high curls of razor sharp wire. The dense coils held their shape and she was soon over. Jenny stood, or rather crouched between the outer and the inner barriers and called for the cases to be slid across the rolled carpet into her waiting hand.

She beckoned the first of her companions to join her.

The man came first and once his partner could see that the method would accept his greater weight she followed suit. All three were now in a dangerous sandwich between coils of lethally sharp wire. Carefully, Jenny started to pull the carpet strip towards her and the two joined in. Some of the threads were left clinging to the sharp blades of the fence but the bulk came over. Relieved to have succeeded thus far the group set about re-laying their magic carpet across the inner barrier and in the same order they crossed the final boundary into the accommodation centre of HMS Neptune. Jenny stopped the other two and indicated the two camera positions way above their heads, both cameras were trained onto Magennis gate and the three had worked in the blind spot immediately ahead of it.

"Do we go back out this way?" asked the woman as her partner dragged the carpet towards himself over the barrier.

"No," replied Jenny smiling, "I'm sure we can do better than that."

***

John opened his rucksack and took out the tin of paint and the four-inch brush he had carried with him from the peace camp. He handed both to Rachel and set about propping the ladder against the outside wall of the Clyde Off Site Centre. His canvas was the blank side of the building facing outward on to the main road from Helensburgh. John worked quickly moving the ladder along after each four-foot high letter had been completed. The main road was quiet at almost one o'clock in the morning. He and Rachel had encountered no signs of life inside the compound beyond the evidence of the switched on television. Rachel watched.

"That's it Rach', let's get out of here."

He dumped the remains of the open tin of paint on the grass, dropped the brush and quietly lowered the ladder to the ground. Leaving at the same point through which they had entered the couple recovered their wire cutters and were soon on the opposite side of the road turning to admire their handiwork.

Rachel was first. She turned and laughed. John followed and let out a cry of, "Bollocks," before he too started to laugh. The sign read,

"SCRAP TRIDNT"

"OK, so I can't spell," said John, "at least it shows we have been here."

With that the couple ran the short distance to the car park of the Ardencaple Hotel and recovered their bicycles for the ride back to the peace camp.

***

The fence walkers had completed a pass of the Naval Base south to north and had spent a few minutes in desultory conversation with the MGS staff at the northern gate. Petey and the two Danes were now retracing their steps along the fence line rattling each panel along their path. Their passage in both directions, so far, had remained under the watchful eye of the fence cameras and the operators far inside the base at the Defence Headquarters Control Room.

The three were soaking wet from the continual drizzling rain but otherwise in good spirits. Petey called his two companions closer and, out of hearing of the dog handler who continued to track them from inside the fence, suggested the other man go on ahead and try to find the bolt cutters left by Jenny if her sortie through the wire had been successful. The man set off purposefully to put some distance between him and the others. Petey correctly predicted that the dog handler would stick with the larger group and he watched as the policeman put his radio up to his mouth and presumably reported the minor change to his control.

***

Paul and Georges had been paddling northward for almost thirty minutes.

They were trying to keep low in their canoes and dip the paddles cleanly to minimise water disturbance. Both men were cold despite the night temperature being in double figures. Georges was wet and had realised earlier that a small leak in the hull was shipping water. The level had reached the single plank seat in the canoe and that meant his jeans were now soaking up the water, his clothing was like blotting paper. Both men had watched the frequent passes up and down the Gareloch from the police launches and could see that the two launches had now taken up a stationary position to the south of the base guarding the front door. They had gone beyond that point and were gaining slightly in confidence.

As the more experienced canoeist Paul had assumed charge of the pair and now judged the time to be right to start moving closer to the ship jetties and away from the western side of the loch. When the two started out from the foreshore it was without any firm plan of action beyond trying to see how far they could get. But Paul considered that the submarine berthed inside the barrier of large inflatable fenders, at the far end, by the big shiplift had to be the most significant option and so that was the direction he turned the bow of his canoe. Georges followed.

***

The two women and one man who had already penetrated the Navy's outer defences were sticking to the shadows. They had sprinted; half crouched away from the lighted area of Magennis gate and the moveable barriers and had reached the edge of the six-floor multi-storey car park which served the permanent residents of the naval base.

"Loads of these cars in the car park are abandoned by the sailors when they go off on patrol in their submarines," said Jenny to her two companions. "Just go and shove one of those cases underneath the tattiest car you can see on the ground floor." The man, who had been carrying both briefcases all the way so far was delighted to lighten his burden and was back with the other two in seconds.

Even in the early hours of the morning the presence of two women and a man walking through the base would not normally cause alarm but, with muddy faces and clothes, the three would be a dead give-away.

The Ministry of Defence police had permanent patrols out and about, both on foot and in vehicles and that was in addition to the normal business of moving the security staff from one location to another. The accommodation blocks and the car park gave way to the huge sports complex and then to Forth Road South from where they were only thirty feet from the officers' cabins and the Wardroom Mess.

No one challenged them. Beyond the old vehicle repair garage and the stores buildings housing heavy and light goods they had reached a junction between Forth Road North and the main route through the naval base. Maidstone Road was named after the Royal Navy depot ship that had formed the first submarine repair facility on the Gareloch several decades before. This was new territory even for Jenny who had never managed to get this far without being spotted.

She wanted to take stock.

Jenny Graham silently waved her team back from the main road and into the shadow of a small prefabricated building. Although some lights showed from within the building she found a dark area against an outside wall where the three slumped down to rest. Her knowledge of the base was good and she had studied plans describing the major buildings and what they were used for. The irony didn't occur to her of finding herself, in the small hours of the early morning, leaning against the base pass office where all security passes were created and issued.

She tried to think of what she should do next.

Jenny knew that only another fifty yards or so to her right lay the Police Post guarding her ultimate target. First was the Red area, guarded and patrolled, with another fence system inside the one she and her fellow intruders had beaten. If they could breach this new fence, then beyond that stood a further and even more tightly controlled area known as the Green area. The security defences were likened to the many layers of an onion where layer after layer had to be peeled away before the centre was reached. The Green area was the ultimate goal. This was the area of the berths used almost exclusively by the Trident submarines, and also provided the entrance to the shiplift.

What to do?

With ample streetlights, through traffic and guards at every entry point Jenny knew she would not get through even the first obstacle into red area north. It was decision time, what did she want to achieve. For the first time that night she thought of Georges and what had happened already that week. He was leaving in the morning bound for Peaton Glen Wood, tonight would be her last chance to hold his firm body and experience the pleasure she had denied herself for far too long.

**

By keeping close to each of the ships and staying at the waterline Hamish had managed to make his way along to the stern of HMS Middleton, the vessel occupying number four berth. So far so good. From here he had a good view of the submarine only eighty feet away from him. He could see the guard stationed in the sentry box at the head of the gangway and the hatch that would take him through the after end of the submarine hull and into the body of the vessel.

The guard appeared to be reading a book.

Shit or bust he thought.

Hamish moved around the stern of the ship and headed slowly towards the inboard side and the jetty. If he could get completely under the long jetty and out of the arc of the floodlights he would be able to make his way right down to the hull of the submarine. Hamish set off to cross the short distance between the stern of HMS Middleton and the jetty. He took two tentative strokes.

"Swimmer in the water, swimmer in the water, Bandit, Bandit, Bandit."

The cry had gone out from the quarterdeck of HMS Middleton where Able Seaman Richard Rogers was enjoying a last smoke before turning in for the night. Hamish froze. Rogers kept up his shout and pointed down at the intruder below. Along the jetty in the sentry box guarding the gangway of HMS Splendid the MGS guard heard the warning and responded with his own shouts.

"Bandit, Bandit, Bandit," he repeated before finally realising that he had a duty to raise the alarm throughout the establishment. He pushed the bandit alarm button sited at his sentry position.

"Dit, Dit, Dit, Dit, Dit, Dit, Dit."

A piercing, staccato siren split the night air. It could be heard throughout the base and in the surrounding area. It could be heard quite clearly by the residents of the few houses on the west side of the Gareloch opposite the base, and on a clear night even up at the married quarter's estate in nearby Rhu, almost two miles away. It meant only one thing; an unwanted attempt to enter the base was underway.

***

"Bollocks, here we go again," said Colin Walker as he grabbed his copy of Emergency Orders and headed for the stairs leading down to the ground floor of Base Defence Headquarters.

"*Bandits, Bandits, Bandits. Bandits in the water at six berth. Royal Marines Response Force muster at Control Point. Duty Watch muster at BDHQ. Close all doors and windows. Entrances to buildings are either to be secured or manned. Movement in outside areas is to cease. All personnel are to remain indoors or go to the nearest building. Vehicles are to stop. Further orders will be piped.*"

The broadcast message was repeated over the public address system and all those people who were not woken up by the rapid fire sound of the bandit alarm siren were roused by the 'pipe' which went out to every building in the establishment. It was fifteen minutes past one on a damp and dismal Tuesday morning in the second week of August. Colin had been on shift since Friday evening and this was the fifth time he had responded to the bandit alarm. Chief Inspector Bill Campbell, the Ministry of Defence Police Shift Commander was in the Incident Control Room when he arrived.

"One swimmer in the water astern of Middleton and heading for Splendid," was the brief from Campbell to Walker. "Looks properly kitted out; spotted by a sailor from Middleton and the alarm raised by the MGS guy on the sub'."

In seconds the Clyde Marine Unit of the MDP were headed towards the incident in two high speed rigid inflatable boats and one of the police launches was closing the scene.

"CMU One to Control, over."

"Go ahead CMU One."

"I have two canoes visible on the loch in search grid area Quebec 24," came the radioed reply from the first of the two CMU launches. "They are just inside the restricted area but pose no immediate threat. Suggest CMU Two take for action, over."

Colin Walker agreed the proposed action by the CMU and the order was passed to the second launch. The presence of the two canoeists was now noted and they would be either arrested or escorted away from the protected area depending upon findings when they were questioned. They were not the first priority for Walker and Campbell.

Walker went into his task of informing his senior management of the two incidents whilst the security forces launched into their well-practised routines. Throughout the Naval Base security teams were isolating the real estate into manageable sections by shutting all gates, internal and external, and setting up control points. The threat of a 'bandit' in the base, even one in the water who had not yet touched dry land required the complete and thorough search of the entire site to ensure no unwelcome packages had been left behind, and no damage caused.

The swimmer was bundled unceremoniously into the police RIB. He was cautioned by the crewman to sit still, and the boat set off at speed for the small craft harbour where a police vehicle was already standing by to escort the man to the prisoner detention centre for cautioning and questioning.

Hamish said nothing.

CMU launch number two had reached the canoes and the Belgians were being invited to comment on what they were doing. Their sortie onto the loch had ended sooner than they had hoped for and their willingness to enter into a phase of belligerence had been gradually whittled away by the time spent getting thoroughly wet and miserable. Both men offered their names when questioned. The CMU Officer in charge of the launch radioed back to his control and the Shift Commander and the Duty Naval Base Officer both agreed that the two should be escorted back to the water's edge nearest the peace camp and left to fight another day. Bill Campbell wisely advised his Naval colleague that the canoes had only just penetrated the restricted area of the base and although the intention to do more was obvious for all to see, proving it in a Sheriff Court was entirely a different matter. Pragmatism won through.

The increase in activity around Maidstone Road and the rest of the base was readily apparent to Jenny and her two compatriots who had also heard the bandit alarm and the broadcast 'pipe'. If getting this far into the base was a new experience for Jenny then she was now in totally uncharted waters. A police Land Rover Discovery braked to a halt within twenty yards of the group and out of the rear tumbled an MDP Officer and an MGS security man. They set to work closing the large gate across Maidstone Road that had once, many years ago, formed the outer perimeter of the base and was known as 'old north gate.'

The MGS man took up station at the closed gate and the vehicle moved on. Jenny and her team had no escape route to the north and would be seen the instant they moved forward from their cover. They looked around for another exit. If they tried to move away from the road it meant negotiating a steep bank and passing between the four large cylindrical sewage settling tanks which served the small town that was the Clyde Naval Base. If Jenny was willing it was obvious her two partners in crime were less so. They could try a run for it down the road and in the opposite direction from the MGS man, but he had a portable radio and it seemed to all three that all they would succeed in doing was delaying the inevitable by a few minutes.

"Right," said Jenny in an attempt to re-establish her somewhat battered authority, "we'll just walk out of here and give ourselves up to the guard. Remember; whatever you do don't tell him or anyone else anything. OK?"

"What about this other case" said the man. Jenny though for a second and finally smiled. "Well," she said, "this building we are hiding behind happens to be the Base pass office so why don't we leave them with a little bit of a surprise for later.

Don't forget, all of you, you mustn't mention anything about bringing stuff into the Base with us tonight. We will be questioned by the MoD plod but they are always very proper and very courteous when they arrest us."

With that the group of three emerged from the shelter of the pass office and approached the MGS guard.

"Foxtrot Sierra One-Six to Alpha Control, come in control," shouted the alarmed MGS guard at the top of his voice, "two females and one male walking towards me at old north gate, over, they're 'papa charlies' over, get me some help."

An ear splitting screech echoed at full volume around the Base Defence Headquarters Control Room.

"Foxtrot Sierra One-Six repeat your message."

"Yeah, I've got two female and one male peace camper walking towards me at old north gate," he answered, "they're here now. Request some back up, over."

Jenny heard the second more disciplined call into the portable radio and almost immediately the sound of a police siren. The three intruders were caught and they knew it. They remained impassive, shoulders slightly hunched, dejected. For them the night was finally over. A small mini-bus slowed to a halt alongside them and two women police officers and one man emerged to complete the formalities of arrest. The three were cautioned, handcuffed and led away.

Colin Walker and Bill Campbell took the news of the three intruders less well. They now had a successful incursion to investigate and that meant a break in the fence somewhere along the three miles or so of wire. In the early hours of the morning finding such a breach could prove a major evolution.

Despite the lateness of the hour the naval base had ground to a complete halt. No traffic flowed except for the emergency services of police and fire department. The procedure activated by BDHQ required a standstill so that any intruders could be more easily tracked and caught. In the accommodation centre of HMS Neptune the Royal Navy personnel slept on relatively undisturbed. For the remainder, night shift engineers and maintenance staff, some clerical workers and cleaners, whoever had business up and about in the early hours of a Tuesday morning; their lives were put on hold until the all clear was given.

"Let's concentrate on getting the base search over with first and getting us safe."

Campbell accepted his colleague's directive and the combined might of the security forces started the business of searching every inch of the base and every building in it. The locked buildings presented little of a problem and provided no evidence of forced entry could be seen they could be checked off on the overall plan of the base in the Control Room. The places where people were living and working were next on the scale of response because if the 'bandit' instructions had been complied with then any human presence out of the ordinary would be obvious. The unmanned buildings and the acres of wooded ground within the perimeter fence where a hideout could easily be made presented by far the greatest challenge and here the team work, expertise and patience, backed up with the skills of the police tracker dogs came into their own. Campbell ordered the dog handlers and their dogs to deploy to various locations within the fence line and the systematic search was under way.

"The furry exocets will soon flush any more out," Campbell offered as an aside to Walker and added that Strathclyde Police had been informed and would be on their way.

The subject of jurisdiction between the Ministry and Home Office Police forces was always an issue that caused grief. MDP had primacy within the base perimeter unless a serious crime was committed. Similarly, if the local boys offered their authority, the Ministry force could act, with full police powers, outside the fence. There was scope for a happy marriage of co-operation. On the ground the marriage was rarely a successful one. Strathclyde was a large region of Scotland and the police force had a huge task. Disturbances at Her Majesty's Naval Base Clyde were common place because the peace camp was but a few yards from the perimeter and as a consequence the local force was called to attend several times during the course of an average week. On each occasion of a disturbance the Ministry force would first ask for authority to act outside the fence line to arrest the demonstrators, that authority was almost invariably refused. Small incidents grew into larger ones.

Where a prompt action by the team on the spot could have prevented serious difficulties, waiting fifteen or twenty minutes for a Strathclyde Police patrol car with two constables to arrive usually guaranteed that the protesters gained the upper hand. A mixture of petty jealousies, professional rivalry and sheer awkwardness resisted all attempts at sensible liaison between the two groups. It caused frustration for all and doubtless had its seat in budgetary control. If Strathclyde acceded to the requests of the Ministry of Defence Police then surely, sometime in the future, some faceless bureaucrat would want to reduce the numbers of policemen on the force. Colin Walker and all his colleagues frequently remarked that they should lock the two Chief Constables in a room together and leave them there until they came out with an agreement. To the copper on the ground it was just more frustration.

Hamish, Jenny Graham and her two co-conspirators were escorted to the prisoner handling centre and shepherded into separate rooms. Two female police officers were on hand to deal with the women and the laborious process of taking statements began. All four had already been cautioned under Section 13 of the Criminal Procedures (Scotland) Act 1995 which required that the detained persons offer their full name and address, Hamish and Jenny had refused.

The officers questioning Jenny and Hamish were well aware of whom they were and in minutes a file was produced which supplied the information they needed. Charges were formulated. For the couple who had accompanied the leader it would be 'aggravated trespass'. For the other two 'perverting the course of justice' would be added because of their refusal to give the information required by the law. If, eventually, a breach were found in the fence then 'malicious mischief' would be added for the three who had entered from land. At almost three o'clock in the morning the statement taking was complete.

At precisely the same moment and by sheer coincidence the searching police team reached the Base pass office and a torch beam picked out what looked like an unattended and therefore unaccounted for object laying behind the building.

"Foxtrot Alpha Control this is Search Four," crackled over the radio network.

"Go ahead Search Four," came the immediate response from Base Defence Headquarters.

"Looks like we've got a suspicious package at my location."

"OK Search Four, message understood. Are you able to give a description from where you are. Over."

This exchange on the radio now had the complete attention of all the team gathered in BDHQ and both Colin Walker and Bill Campbell both let out silent expletives as the bad night seemed to have taken a further turn for the worse.

"Control, Search Four, it looks a bit like a briefcase but I've moved back a couple of yards from it so I'm not exactly sure."

"Roger that Search Four, maintain your present location and make sure no one goes near it."

In BDHQ both Campbell and Walker reached the same conclusion at the same time.

"Haven't we just nicked three papa charlies in that area Bill," asked Walker of his police colleague and the response came back in the affirmative.

"Yes, Colin, I'll brief the arresting team to ask if they know anything about a package but I wouldn't bet on any kind of co-operation from Jenny Graham she's been at this game a hell of a long time and she knows all the rules backwards."

"In the meantime we'd better contact Didcot and get the E.O.D Team cranked up to deal with this one." Walker agreed and the Desk Sergeant in the Control Room began dialling the direct telephone number to the agency that controlled Bomb Disposal assets throughout the United Kingdom. Faslane was uniquely placed in this organisational network by virtue of being home to the Royal Navy Northern Diving Group, and the round the clock team who dealt with unexploded ordnance, mines, washed up shells from the last war and anything else that was suspicious and unexplained. They were kept very busy with a parish that included the whole of Scotland, Northern England and Northern Ireland and all the many Scottish islands near and far from Faslane.

"DNBO, boss," said the Desk Sergeant, "We've got lucky

this time the Faslane team are available and we won't have to go to Edinburgh to get the Army boys over here."

Campbell and Walker breathed a collective sigh of relief at this message from the control position because it meant that an Explosive Ordnance Disposal Team would be available in minutes rather than hours. At this early hour there may still be time available to get the package sorted out and clear all the major routes through the Base and open the main gates before the morning influx of several thousand workers started.

Almost on cue a young Petty Officer Diver rang the bell at the outer door of Base Defence Headquarters seeking admission.

"PO Diver Brown, Sir, what have we got?"

Walker, Campbell and Brown left the Control Room and stepped into the adjacent briefing space. Using a large scale drawn map of the base Campbell was able to accurately pin-point the suspicious package.

"We'll need a 200 metre cordon around the area and a Police Patrol stationed at the entry point." said Brown and Colin Walker reached for a clear perspex template marked with concentric circles each graded, and scaled to the Base map. With the template in place over the centre of the base pass office the three men could readily see the size of the area that would need to remain completely evacuated and guarded until this evolution was completed.

"At least we are clear of all the accommodation blocks and we won't need to get Strathpol to close the main road," said Walker, "and I don't think we need to be too concerned about blast routes do we Petty Officer Brown?"

"Agreed, Sir, let's get the show on the road. I'm going to deploy the remote operated disruptor and just blow it up."

Brown left the Base Defence Headquarters to brief his team of bomb disposal experts and make ready the four wheeled, radio controlled device that would be guided onto the suspicious package from a safe distance. Once lined up Brown would extend the weapon arm of the disruptor to the target and blast a jet of high pressure water to penetrate and disable the package. Many a senior Royal Navy Officer had suffered the embarrassment of having their sandwiches detonated when disembarking from a helicopter and leaving their briefcases standing on the tarmac.

Approaching 3.30 in the morning and with all the remaining base searches reported as completed without further incident Walker and Campbell discussed how best to restore some sort of normality to the small town that was Her Majesty's Naval Base Clyde.

Walker crossed the control room, picked up the microphone for the main broadcast system and prepared to make an announcement to everyone in the base. Conversation from all present ceased and Walker pressed the activation switch on the microphone and started.

"Do you hear there, this is the Duty Naval Base Officer speaking. As you will all be very well aware, we have had a busy night so far and have dealt with several demonstrator related incidents some of which have culminated in arrests. At present we are addressing our last problem in the area of the base pass office and this has required the establishment of a clear zone around that location. I intend to return the south gate to immediate use and allow limited transit around accommodation areas, Messes and places of work at the southern end of the Base. A further broadcast will be made when all restrictions are lifted. In the meantime, stand down from Bandit Stations, stand down from Bandit Stations. That is all."

Walker replaced the microphone in its holder and declared that he would return to his office upstairs and begin the lengthy list of telephone calls required of him to ensure that the management of the naval base were aware of the night's events and in turn detail was available for briefings up the chain of command and even to the Cabinet Office in Westminster. It wouldn't do for a government Minister to be blind-sided by an enquiry from the press or worse, from an opposition spokesman. As the man on 'point duty' this was almost as important to Walker as dealing with the live incidents because the potential for fallout from above was immense.

Next would come the report writing and the briefing to senior officers, and the sweeping up of loose ends. At first

133

light an intensive inch by inch search of the outer fence would begin. As luck would have it the MGS man who had witnessed the earlier raid on the fence by John and Rachel remembered that the fence alarm had not reset.

In the course of the base search the roll of carpet had been found abandoned in long grass near Magennis Gate and so it was an obvious start point for the fence check. Using the same method employed by Jenny hours earlier the cut was found within an hour. Now could be added the task of repairing the damage, getting the engineering department turned out of their homes in the middle of the night and brought on site to commence the work. For the demonstrators, they had experienced their five minutes of fame. If they elected to have their day in court, to plead not guilty, the actions of the courts would drag on for months.

The four from the peace camp would be charged to appear at Dumbarton Sheriff Court within a few days. Hamish and Jenny were taken away by Strathclyde police to spend the remainder of the night in police custody, Jenny in Glasgow and Hamish in Dumbarton. For Jenny there would be no last night of passion with Georges and he would have moved on by the time she returned to the peace camp.

The police on the night shift of Tuesday could only reflect that the night had brought four more cases for the Procurator Fiscal, four more trips to court, and this was only the beginning.

Lieutenant Commander Colin Walker switched on the kettle. A cup of Earl Grey before he started on the "Demonstration and Incursion: signal that would tell the wider world about what had just happened. He was quite polished at producing these signals now; this was his fifth since the previous Friday evening at seven o'clock.

A knock on Walker's office door broke his concentration and he looked up to see Chief Inspector Bill Campbell and Petty Officer Brown framed in the doorway.

"Come in gentlemen, I presume from the fact that you are both here we haven't sent the north end of the base into the stratosphere."

"No boss," said Brown, "job done, I don't think that briefcase will see the light of day again."

"What did you find?" asked Walker.

"Bit odd really, Sir," Brown chipped in, "definitely a briefcase. As to the contents, the best guess I could make would be a couple of tins and a brick."

"Deliberate or accident - what do you both think?" said Walker.

Campbell spoke first.

"It's not exactly illegal to have a tin and a house brick in a briefcase but I'd agree with Buster here that it is decidedly odd."

"Any chance we can definitely connect it to the papa charlies?"

"Honestly," said Campbell, "not a chance in hell and even less chance we could get someone from the base to claim ownership."

"So, what do we do, put it down to experience and let the adults argue over it later today when my day shift relief gives his brief to the Admiral and the Commodore."

"I think that's about the size of it," said Brown and Bill Campbell nodded in agreement.

Walker sat in thought for a few seconds and finally said, "I've got to tell the Commodore that the incident is now over with and we are back to normal so I'll pass on our thoughts about that bit of it as well. If he doesn't like our conclusion he can always let me know."

With that Campbell and Brown turned to leave. "Bill," Walker called out after his colleague, "could you order the stand down from the IED incident and get a broadcast made that all is now well please."

"Aye, Colin, will do." came the reply and Walker went back to his tea and the task of composing a Royal Navy signal message.

Eighteen

Seven people sat at a round table in the back bar of the Argyll Hotel in Oban.

For all the world they looked liked a hiking group in their uniform of loose fitting woollen sweaters, denim jeans and walking boots with a trace of thick socks bridging the gap between footwear and trousers. Exactly the image Laura wanted for her group, precisely what she had briefed them. The seven had not walked a step; they had reached Oban by train, by bus, and by car, but certainly not on foot. For Daniel William Coleman it was just as well. His walking boots were brand new and felt heavy and stiff on feet more accustomed to sandals and London footwear. The group had been together for an hour and the introductions had been made. Conversation had reached a lull and for several minutes each had withdrawn into his or her own thoughts.

Coleman fidgeted.

He was nervous and agitated. Except for Laura, he had only met Flynn and O'Neill before this afternoon and he could sense an almost open hostility from O'Neill already. Coleman was finely tuned to the reaction of others, especially when he felt threatened. Scholarly looking types, like Daniel, soon developed an instinct for spotting danger and all his built in sensors were registering alarm as he tried to stay calm at the table. Bullied at school, and ignored at University his most recent, almost reclusive, years had dulled the feeling of panic that accompanied situations like the one he now imagined himself to be in.

He was drawn constantly to Laura's face, seeking reassurance, feeding on her confidence.

It wasn't that she was distant towards him, that wasn't it; she returned his glances, she just seemed to want to keep their personal relationship separate. There hadn't been much opportunity to speak to her alone since they arrived in Oban; he by train and she by car, and that had made things worse. Daniel desperately wanted her in his bed tonight; he wanted her to give him the courage to deal with these new people and especially the Irishman, O'Neill, who frightened him out of his wits. He reached out to lift his glass from the table and knew his hand was shaking. Coleman fought with himself to keep his eyes away from O'Neill but snared like a rabbit in the headlights of a car he couldn't avoid a fleeting eye contact. The smirk on the Irishman's face said all that was needed and Coleman retreated back into his discomfort, hardly hearing what little was being said around him.

'Fuckin' wimp,' was the thought that ran through Brendan O'Neill's mind as he caught the sideways glance from the red haired, bespectacled man he had first met in Fulham. O'Neill still thought it totally inconceivable that Laura Latimer could have allowed the man into her bed. Short on brainpower but long on machismo Brendan could never grasp that women were capable of sexual cunning.

For him the physical act of lovemaking was something that could only be initiated by the male of the species and it was best accompanied by displays of masculinity. He most definitely subscribed to the 'big muscles - big dick' school and just assumed Coleman would be a lightweight in the sex department in direct proportion to his lack of physique. Whether they were prepared to admit it or not, he had decided, all women really wanted a tough talking, tough acting hunk as a sexual master, not some bookish little jerk who was trying to save the planet.

Just as Daniel Coleman was distracted from his surroundings by his awkwardness, O'Neill could hardly move his thoughts away from the subject of sex. Even as Laura Latimer was speaking Brendan failed to hear what she said. His mind was playing little games of its own with him as the principal player. Unusually for O'Neill he was not getting very far with his fantasies about Laura Latimer. Every time he began the process of stripping her mentally he remembered the searing pain she had inflicted upon him and his mental picture of the beautiful woman faded to nothing. O'Neill remembered Sheila Boyd from their meeting at the Faslane peace camp and had briefly included her in his musings before rejecting her as unsuitable. She must have been about fifty, he decided, and although she didn't look disgusting in her jeans she was relegated to his personal category of woman where desperation and eight pints of Guinness played a part. Deprived of a sex object O'Neill turned his attention back to Coleman.

Boyd was nothing if not a seasoned campaigner. She had spent the better part of her adult life involved actively in some form of protest or another. At forty-nine years of age she could still summon up as much anger at the establishment as she had during the heyday of CND. She could recall vividly the passion shown by Bruce Kent and Michael Foot in the early days when she had just graduated from Cambridge and was marching to ban the bomb.

Then it was Greenham Common and the enormous surge of emotion that came with their attempts at breaching the boundary fences of the air base, bent on causing havoc within. Peaceful demonstration gave way gradually to a more active posture as her efforts failed to move successive governments. Somehow she managed to put her life on hold to get married. She and her husband were childless.

There never seemed to be time.

She tried to justify their condition with fine thoughts about not bringing children into an imperfect world full of manmade danger, but sometimes, if she left herself time to think, she was capable of regret. When Trident Ploughshares started it was like a new lease of life. She was born again. A new cause, or at least a different slant on an old one. She found reserves of energy to begin again. Her husband immersed himself in life as a country parish priest whilst Sheila pursued her agenda of demonstration and mayhem. A gentle and patient man, the Reverend John Boyd was, on the face of things, the complete opposite to his wife. His parish business took up all of his time and he was well regarded by his flock.

What they thought about the excesses of his wife he hardly knew and seemed, strangely, not to worry.

She played her part well enough when she was there and her frequent absences, even for the occasional stay at Her Majesty's pleasure, didn't seem to influence him or his faithful parishioners. His Bishop had never complained and life went on. In many ways life had passed Sheila Boyd by, she had never done a day's paid work since leaving Cambridge and so she would never know whether her degree in Psychology would ever show tangible dividends. Looking around the table she tried to remember the names of those that were new to her.

Daniel was out of his depth that was easy to see. He had the look of a startled animal in his eyes and the antipathy towards O'Neill was obvious. Jim was making an effort. He had introduced himself and seemed willing to talk. If there was one thing that life had taught Sheila it was how to deal with people. She had met some pretty odd sorts over her many years of campaigning so nothing about the human condition surprised her any more. Coupled with her other life as the wife of a parish priest, where she had learned to deal with the sensitivities of her husband's flock, she could be catapulted into any gathering and make do.

The other new man, Dominic was it?

She hadn't formed an opinion about him. Even Laura appeared to be treading carefully with him. Sheila looked upon Laura with something akin to admiration; she had clarity of thought and purpose. She was a woman who would win in any situation. Bright, decisive, confident, she was all those things, but when you added poise and beauty it was easy to see why the others gathered at the table were eating out of her hand. Brendan she remembered from Faslane and dismissed as a thug, nothing more than a hard man who would succeed only by brute strength. Flynn, she thought, was cast from a different mould. He kept his own counsel, balanced his thoughts carefully and spoke sparingly. Of the Irish pair, he was the planner, the leader, and most certainly the one to fear.

Flynn was strangely unsettled sitting at the table, it wasn't exactly failure that was causing him concern because Flynn was a professional and wouldn't permit even the notion that things could go wrong. He had spent his life living on his wits, one step ahead of the authorities all the way and that was how he intended to remain. No, it wasn't failure but the departure from his well-laid plans that made him even more alert.

The Omagh bomb of a week or so earlier had changed the face of the campaign in Northern Ireland and Flynn had been in the area when the deadly destruction and bloodshed had taken place. He was unmoved by the death toll; victims of the struggle as far as he was concerned. More important to him was that the event and its repercussions had all but prevented him from filling his shopping list for this operation. He and Laura had worked out what was needed and he was tasked with bringing it across the water and ultimately up to Oban.

Flynn was the only one of the team fully in her confidence and he had almost jeopardised the mission before it had even started. She and Flynn had spoken together in London the previous day and had agreed to accept the compromise that arose from his shopping trip to his home territory. A voice to his left broke Flynn's thoughts and returned him to the present. McCormack was asking him if he wanted a refill from the bar. Flynn downed the remainder of his beer, nodded towards the man and pushed his glass across the table.

Jim McCormack remembered the drinks order and moved to the small dark wood bar on the opposite side of the room. Accustomed to lunchtime drinking he was ready for a second pint. McCormack's feelings ranged through nervousness to elation, he was doing something even if the whole thing felt alien and strange. There was a feeling of excitement about the secrecy involved.

Of the group gathered around him he only knew Flynn, and he wasn't exactly expansive in his manner today. The younger of the two women was welcoming enough and certainly stunning to look at even dressed as she was, McCormack soon introduced himself to the others. At the bar he removed a twenty-pound note from his wallet. He couldn't resist the temptation to skim his thumb over the remainder of the crisp new twenties. Twenty-four similar notes were left, five hundred pounds for what promised to be less than a week's work. He had given his wife Liz half a story when he left Kinross that morning for Oban.

Flynn had briefed him on what to say and he had stuck to their cover story. He would act as a consultant for a company making a training film for the Navy. They needed an engineer, he told her, someone with the experience gained from running his own ship. Jim looked at the money again. He could have left some of it at home with her.

He should have done of course.

It was funny now he thought about it, Liz didn't even ask about the money. It was most unlike her. If truth were known Liz was relieved to have a break from Jim, even if for only one week. His drinking was beginning to become a problem and the constant drain on their savings worried her almost as much. Things in the house would soon come to a head and Liz had even begun to think the unthinkable, could their marriage be over. McCormack pocketed his change and carried the tray of drinks back to the table. His brief on what was really going to happen had been pretty vague but he had picked up that the older woman, Sheila, was connected with an anti-nuclear group and the rest were there to take part in some sort of peaceful demonstration. The good-looking one was obviously in charge and she had said that they would each be given their tasks later that day.

So far, so good thought Laura as she surveyed the group around her, things were moving along nicely. She had already come to terms with the presence of an addition to her team in the shape of Dominic Cluskey and although she wasn't delighted at what Flynn had thrust upon her she could understand the predicament he must have faced in Northern Ireland. Ever resourceful, Laura was confident she could turn the change of events to her benefit and even now was weighing up the options in her mind.

Laura had complete faith in Flynn, they had worked and trained together in Syria and he was as uncompromising in his idealism as she was. If he said Cluskey had to be brought

141

along as a condition of getting the supplies she wanted then so be it. The immediate aftermath of the Omagh bomb, which took the life of twenty-nine innocent shoppers in the high street of that town, had closed off all Flynn's normal supply routes in an instant. Irish Republican quartermasters simply shut up shop and the flow of weapons and explosives stopped dead. Nothing moved an inch, north or south of the border.

Flynn had the guns by the time of the bomb, but not the C4.

She and Flynn were both experts in the use of the plastic explosive called semtex and known in the trade as C4 and they both agreed that it was an essential for the operation in hand. He had little choice but to approach the group who claimed the incident in Omagh as their own and that group were a small splinter of the IRA known as the 'Real IRA'. Padraig Flynn wasn't sure whether Cluskey played any part in the Omagh bomb and wanted to get out of the island of Ireland until the dust began to settle. But, whatever his motivation it was made abundantly clear to Flynn that if he wanted the C4 then Cluskey had to be involved.

The 'Real IRA' was spawned out of the gathering success of the peace talks in Northern Ireland and included the hard liners who could see nothing less than the unification of the island of Ireland as their goal, regardless of the opinions and desires of others. They were a small group of republicans who had already hit the headlines following some callous and deadly acts of barbarism conducted in the name of freedom.

Cluskey was a natural.

He hadn't known Flynn before their first meeting in the previous week but it was obvious that the hierarchy within his own organisation treated him with the greatest of respect. No fool, Cluskey could imagine that his new colleague was from the very top level in the republican movement and not to be crossed. As for the rest, Cluskey was instinctively opposed to O'Neill. A few words were enough to establish that the two had spent their lives on opposite sides of the religious and political divide in the six counties and although he recognised the man for what he was he was deeply unhappy about working alongside a loyalist. His feelings for McCormack ran less deep but still they reflected a hatred for the establishment that membership of the British armed forces implied. Cluskey was on his guard and knew he needed to stay that way until this little jaunt was over.

"Mac McCormack, is that you?"

The question turned all the heads at the table and the group of seven were drawn towards a clean and smart man in his middle thirties, dressed in jeans and a polo shirt, who had just entered the bar in the company of two other similarly dressed young men. McCormack was unsure what to do and how to respond and was grateful when Laura took charge. She looked straight at McCormack.

"These must be Navy friends of yours Jim, why don't they join us for a drink."

McCormack recognised the approval and encouragement in her voice and with a broad smile rose to greet the man who had spoken. Until less than a year ago he had been a colleague. He was now the Marine Engineer Officer of HMS Harwich, the Sandown Class Minehunter berthed at the town pier in Oban. Chief Petty Officer 'Yorky' York and his two friends shuffled extra seats into place and accepted the pints of beer McCormack had ordered and collected from the bar.

"I never expected to see you here Mac, I thought you lived in Kinross," came the next question from York and this time McCormack fielded it with a growing confidence.

"We're on a walking break for a few days," he replied, and hesitated before attempting to introduce his new companions.

The conversation restarted and it was quickly confirmed that HMS Harwich was due to sail on her return journey to the Naval Base at Faslane early the following morning. The sailors were just having a last beer before returning to the ship and an evening on board.

"Why don't you all come on down to the boat later for a beer," York generously offered the gathered company and the invitation was soon firmed up for after the ship's crew evening meal at six o'clock.

Their pints drunk, York and his two shipmates made their excuses and left the bar. What Laura had been hoping for had happened and a contact had been formed. She'd skip drinks later in the day and persuade Flynn, Cluskey and Boyd to do the same. Laura needed an hour to go over final details of her plan with Flynn and she didn't want Sheila Boyd on the ship that evening just in case she made her feelings about the military known. As for Cluskey, thought Laura, he was too much of an unknown to risk until she was ready. But for the other three, this was the perfect opportunity. It would help to relax Daniel and Jim and perhaps give O'Neill a simple task to prove himself. O'Neill would have to be their eyes and ears on the ship during the evening but she was sure he could cope with what was needed of him.

***

Three extra bodies in the already small Senior Rates Mess of HMS Harwich made for a cosy gathering and with their customary generosity the Chief Petty Officers and Petty Officers made their guests welcome.

Coleman and O'Neill adjusted pretty well to the strange environment of a small warship and both had managed the short journey from the gangway forward to the Mess without banging either, their ankles on the door openings or, their heads on the many obstacles just waiting to catch the unwary.

For McCormack it was an opportunity to revisit the scene of his greatest pleasure in life and he found himself responding, not with the bitterness that had surrounded his redundancy and departure from the Royal Navy, but with a fondness and a willingness to talk. In fact, the lunchtime beer and the pint of Courage Sparkling Bitter, with which he was renewing another old acquaintance had served to unlock his tongue. He had launched into a series of anecdotes about his time as 'Chief of the Boat' in HMS Cromer, a sister ship to Harwich.

The ship's senior ratings were happy to indulge Coleman and the stories flowed freely backwards and forwards between them. Brendan O'Neill thought some of what he was hearing bordered on fantasy and even Daniel Coleman who had absolutely no comprehension of what life in a small cramped warship could be like raised an eyebrow once or twice. The evening was friendly.

"Would it be possible to have a look round the ship?" asked O'Neill.

"Yeah, sure," was the response. A Petty Officer rose from the bench seat in the Mess and O'Neill and Coleman set off to tour HMS Harwich. McCormack settled back in his seat free to accept a second pint.

***

"Emma, how nice to hear your voice, this is Laura Latimer, do you remember our supper together last month?"

"Oh yes Laura, great to hear from you, where are you," replied the young wife of Lieutenant Nigel Courtney the Navigating Officer of HMS Harwich.

"Look, this is a bit of a long shot and I don't suppose it is convenient, but I'm back in Helensburgh on business tomorrow. I will be arriving later this evening and I wondered if you would like to meet up again. Perhaps we could go somewhere for a drink, or I could treat you to supper. If Nigel is at home I quite understand you may not want to."

Laura held her breath for a second and felt her grip tighten on the mobile telephone in her hand. This was the first step in her plan. She needed this to work for her. The reply came back almost in a gush of words.

"I'd love to, when will you be here, why don't you stay the night. Nigel's away until tomorrow evening, they're in Oban tonight."

"Could I, no, that would be too much trouble,"

"Don't be silly, I won't hear of anything else Laura, it would be just wonderful to have a girly evening before Nigel comes home. Let's just stay in, I'll cook. What time shall I expect you?"

Laura agreed that she would make it to the flat in Smugglers Way by nine o'clock that evening and both women completed their conversation with a smile.

Nineteen

The first rays of the morning sun shot lances of light at the funnel of HMS Harwich picking out the sharp lines of the red trident symbol which was the squadron emblem of the Third Mine Counter Measures Squadron.

Finally, the overnight drizzle had stopped and the sun offered the prospect of a better day. Oban town pier was still, peaceful in the dawn light. An early morning delivery van rattled along on its round one or two streets over from the waterfront, tinkling bottles the only man made sound disturbing the Scottish daybreak. Gulls called to each other as they circled and landed all along the pier taking to the air again for no obvious reason. The smell of the sea was clearer, more acute without the hustle and bustle that the new day would bring. In the ship the Boatswain's Mate had finished scrubbing the non-slip, tiled surface that was the deck of the ship's bridge. The bucket of dirty water stood on the deck outside the port bridge wing door, the long handled scrubbing brush leaning between the bucket and the doorframe, a signal that the early morning chores were well in hand. The ship's Quartermaster completed his circuit of the upper deck and rejoined his colleague.

"Ditch the water and then go and do the shakes, OK, I could murder a bacon sarnie."

The Boatswain's Mate acknowledged the order from the senior man and made his way down to the port waist of the ship with his black bucket and its grubby contents. He walked a couple of paces out onto the narrow gangway joining the ship to the pier and tipped the contents into the water below. The bucket safely stowed in a nearby wash-deck locker the young man opened the screen door and entered the red lighted gloom of the main passageway, the thoroughfare from the centre of the ship forward. He flicked the switch to revert to normal white lighting and turned off the red lights, no need to worry about night vision now he thought, time some of the buggers got up.

He was a little over halfway through the morning watch.

At the crew's recreation space, no more than a table with a bench at either side, he started a desultory and whispered conversation with a young man in blue overalls who was the duty stoker, the Marine Engineering Mechanic of the watch to give him his full credit. 'Stokes' was clutching a huge, steaming, china mug full of a dark brown liquid that purported to be tea but looked strong enough to support the spoon unaided.

"Gi's a whet," the Boatswains Mate demanded and the young engineer passed his mug over without hesitation.

"Jesus, you must have washed your fucking socks in this, it's like fucking soup," were all the thanks the tea maker received and he took the mug back and took a long and noisy drink himself.

"Please yourself then, make your own fucking tea."

"What's the weather like, is it still pissing down," asked the engineer and he was reassured to be told that the rain had finally stopped and the day was brightening. "Maybe we'll get a decent passage home then."

A few moments passed in silence and the two shipmates realised they had nothing else to talk about so early in the morning. They rose to go about their business, one heading for the Ship Control Centre, the hub of the engineering world, and the other winding his way quietly down a set of ladders to find the bunk occupied by the sleeping chef. With his torch beam shining directly into the face of the sleeping man the Boatswains Mate rested his free hand on the outer covering of a green sleeping bag and shook.

"Come on 'cooky' time to fuck up some more perfectly good victuals."

The chef raised himself onto an elbow, pulled back the zip of his sleeping bag and swung his legs out and onto the deck of his mess. Naked except for brightly coloured boxer shorts the man scratched openly at his private parts and looked towards the source of the comment.

"What do you recommend for breakfast then chef," the Boatswains Mate inquired.

"In your case, I suggest you fuck off ashore and get some." This the reply from a man well used to banter from the thirty five members of the small crew of his warship for whom he provided three meals a day regardless of the weather and the state of the sea.

Another day was starting in HMS Harwich, much like the last.

***

Laura lay awake feeling somewhat confined in the narrow single bed of the upper maisonette that was home to Emma and Nigel Courtney. She had been awake for an hour already, checking and double-checking in her mind the plans she had laid in place. The point of no return had now been passed and with her in Rhu and the rest of the team still in Oban she was powerless to stop the action. Not that she wanted to; she was high on expectation, on the edge of the unknown, the adrenaline was flowing and she felt even more tension because she could only imagine the way events would unfold now rather than have a direct control over them. The drive to Rhu had been uneventful and she had covered the distance in less than two hours in her hire car.

How Laura managed to pass an evening in social chit-chat with the Naval wife was a complete mystery, her mind was churning backwards and forwards starting every thought with what if this or that were to happen the next day. It was witness to how pleasant she found it being in Emma Courtney's company that she had been able to relax sufficiently to join in. Laura found out that Courtney had phoned home the previous afternoon before she had made her own call to Rhu and therefore the husband was unaware of his wife's house guest. It seemed also that the sailing time from Oban was still set for eight o'clock in the morning so everything was going according to plan. From the window of the small guestroom Laura looked down towards the water of the Gareloch. She realised that from this vantage point she would see every ship or submarine make its transit either up the loch to the base or down it, travelling southwards and into the mighty Clyde. She now had to wait.

***

The Quartermaster recognised Jim McCormack before he made it to within ten yards of the end of the gangway. He didn't know his companions but McCormack and he had served together in some previous ship and he called out a friendly greeting.

"I heard you were onboard last night Jim, how's it going?"

McCormack struggled to put a name to the face of the man who had called out to him from the inboard end of the ship's gangway but he knew that sometime in their past they had spent time in the same ship.

"Oh hi there, good to see you again, long time no see."

Jim McCormack crossed the gangway and shook the outstretched hand of the ship's on-watch Quartermaster whilst the remainder of his group waited ashore.

"Thing is, my mate Dominic here," McCormack swung an arm and pointed to Cluskey who was standing nearest to the gangway, "reckons he lost his wallet in the Senior Rates Mess last night when we came down for a beer, and there's, maybe, a hundred quid in it and some cards and stuff. Could we just slip on board for a sec' and have a look."

The Quartermaster paused in thought.

"I'd have to come with you and the Boatswains Mate hasn't come back from doing the shakes yet, can you hang on a bit."

McCormack plucked the man's name out of the recesses of his memory and was able to respond immediately.

"Come on, Wally, I know where the bloody Mess is," he said with a lightness in his voice that he hardly felt, "I'm not likely to get lost and it's too early for a beer even by my standards."

The Quartermaster ended his personal tussle with the rules and regulations and beckoned McCormack forward.

"Go on then Jim, but be quick for fuck's sake."

Cluskey moved swiftly across the flimsy gangway and before the sailor had a chance to say that he had only meant it was okay for the one man to enter the ship, both had disappeared through the screen door and out of sight.

Brendan O'Neill waited a few seconds to allow the two men to get into the heart of the warship. He knew from the previous evening that it would only take those few seconds to reach the place where he had sampled the Courage Sparkling Bitter. O'Neill reached into his anorak pocket and extracted a packet of cigarettes. He flipped up the top, removed one of the cigarettes and offered the remainder towards the man in uniform. The sailor shook his head. O'Neill patted his jacket pockets looking for matches.

"You haven't got a light have you," he asked, gesturing with the unlit cigarette. The Quartermaster dug into his trouser pocket, took out his zippo lighter bearing the ship's crest of HMS Harwich and walked the few paces across the gangway to reach O'Neill. He flicked open the top and span the wheel with his thumb to generate a flame. Brendan O'Neill put the cigarette between his lips, craned towards the man and cupped his left hand around the end of the cigarette and the flame. In a fluid movement he reached into his jacket and pulled out a Hechler and Koch automatic pistol and jabbed it firmly into the ribs of the startled sailor.

"Now listen carefully. Walk back across the gangplank and don't make any sudden movements or noise, got it," O'Neill said directly into the ear of the Quartermaster from no further than three inches distance. "One mistake and you'll have blood all over the front of that pretty sailor suit."

The two men locked in an almost bizarre parody of a dance step crossed from the pier back to the ship. Sheila Boyd, Daniel Coleman and Padraig Flynn followed quickly behind and Flynn withdrew his own weapon when he set foot on the grey fibreglass of the port deck of the ship.

"Captain's cabin now," O'Neill barked into the Quartermaster's ear and the man set off with his human crocodile closed up at his back.

"Captain, Sir, QM here." said Leading Seaman Walters, the Quartermaster, as he tapped gently on the cabin door of his

Commanding Officer.

"Come in Leader," was the reply that came back from his Captain and Walters turned the door handle and stepped over the threshold into the Captain's small, but well fitted out sleeping quarters, office and home from home. Lieutenant Commander Jonathan Welborne stood at his sink; half his face still covered in shaving foam. Dressed only in the trousers of his paisley patterned pyjamas and with a safety razor in one hand he was less than prepared for the sudden rush made by five people as they quickly jostled for the limited space available. Last in the group, Flynn had to shuffle sideways around the door jamb as he pushed it back into place closing off the scene from the ship's passageway just a few inches away. Welborne stood almost transfixed, frozen in the act of shaving himself; the razor still raised almost to his face. The Officer caught sight of the weapon in the right hand of the nearest stranger and quickly scanned the small room for further signs of danger. Flynn broke the silence.

"Listen carefully Captain," he started. "We are part of a wider group called Trident Ploughshares 2000 and we intend to use your ship as a part of a non violent demonstration against the continued use of nuclear weapons."

Flynn paused briefly, unused to giving speeches of any kind but totally confident in what he had to say, "This is Sheila Boyd, a founder member of the group, and Daniel Coleman representing 'Envirocare' magazine. Our names," Flynn moved his gun arm as best he could in the confined space and indicated O'Neill standing nearest to the Naval Officer, "are not important at the moment. If you do exactly as we say no-one will come to any harm."

A single knock caused Welborne to direct his gaze towards the door of the cabin and as it opened a fraction he caught a first sight of Dominic Cluskey looking in. Flynn spoke again.

"As you see we have more of our people onboard."

Flynn pointed towards the bemused Leading Seaman, who was desperately trying to understand what was happening around him and finding it totally outside the realms of his experience, "you go with him." he indicated, and Walters moved out of the cramped cabin to join Cluskey.

"What do you want me to do," asked Welborne, finally getting to grips with himself and attempting to rationalise the situation he faced.

Sheila Boyd spoke for the first time and Flynn almost managed to shrink into the fabric of the small cabin as he withdrew from centre stage.

"We have our own engineer with us, and the rest of the group will be stationed around the ship to make sure none of your crew does anything stupid."

"But, what do you want," Welborne asked again.

"Simple," said Boyd, "we want you to sail from here as planned and give us passage to Faslane. When we get there we will get off the ship and give ourselves up to the Ministry of Defence Police."

***

In the Senior Rates Mess just along the ship's main passageway from the Captain's accommodation Cluskey and McCormack were looking at the confused faces of the Quartermaster, Leading Seaman Walters, and the ship's Chief of the Boat, Chief Petty Officer York. The mess door was closed and the two crew members had been told in no uncertain terms by Cluskey that they were hostages and that the firearm he held casually in his hand was not just for show.

"You two are gonna stay in here until we get to Faslane. So, just in case any of your mates get any ideas, remember you two will be the first to get it."

Oblivious to the drama unfolding in the Captain's cabin and the Senior Rates Mess the remainder of the ship's crew were setting about the familiar business of starting the day. Not just any day, though, this was a day when they would go home after more than a month away. As the sailors queued for their breakfast the ship buzzed with the double excitement of preparing for sea and of going back to their base port.

"Oh great, 'shit on a raft' my favourite, well done chef," said the ship's Coxswain as he spooned kidneys in a thick, dark gravy on top of the slice of fried bread on his breakfast plate.

The Petty Officer Diver moved off in the direction of his Mess and was surprised to find the door closed. He swung the door open and Chief Petty Officer York barred his entry.

"I'm securing for sea in here," offered York and he went on to advise his colleague to finish his breakfast in his cabin rather than in the Mess. The Cox'n shuffled off towards his sleeping space clutching the plate of food and his knife and fork.

A dull grumble reverberated through the ship as one of the diesel main engines burst into life and, after a few seconds, settled down under the control of its governor. Petty Officer Marine Engineering Mechanic John Churchill swept the engine control panel with a practised eye and made sure that the needles of oil and water pressure gauges aligned themselves in the green arc showing that all was normal. He clicked the exhaust temperature pyrometer switch steadily through the range and satisfied himself that the temperatures from each engine cylinder were increasing uniformly.

Churchill moved a yard across the Ship Control Centre and repeated the procedure for the starboard main engine. Happy that his babies would get him back to Faslane that night and him down to the Imperial in Helensburgh before closing time he turned the two keys to initiate the shut down sequence for both the engines.

The Engine Room Petty Officer carried on with his pre-sailing checks of the steering gear, the fire pumps, the generators, and the rest of the array of machinery needed to get a warship, even a small one, safely out to sea. After two years in HMS Harwich preparations for sea were second nature, a routine for which he no longer needed to refer to the printed list of actions tucked in the desk of the control room. Another fifteen minutes and he would have time for a cup of tea. Fifteen minutes after that he would report his department ready for sea to his Chief of the Boat 'Yorky' York, and in turn York would report to his Captain and the order to start main engines would be passed.

Back on Harwich's bridge the Boatswains Mate had finished his bacon sandwich and made his last entry in the ship's log.

Half an hour to go and he would be off watch. He liked the morning watch from four o'clock until eight. It was a bugger getting up for it but once he had broken through the pain barrier it was quite nice to watch a new day unfold. 'Specials ' would be closing up at their stations soon and he would be relieved of duty just before the ship manoeuvred itself away from the Oban jetty. He looked at his watch, perfectly aware of the time but the action automatic as he wondered where his Quartermaster had got to. His gaze passed the bacon sandwich neatly wrapped in greaseproof paper and waiting for Walters to return.

"Fuck you Wally," he said aloud to himself and reached for the wrapped package, "You've had your chance and it won't be worth fuck all in a minute." A last look around the empty bridge and down the ladder into the main passageway convinced him that Walters had deserted him for good and that he would end up getting a row from the Officer of the Watch for having food up on the chart table. The Boatswains Mate unwrapped the sandwich and for a few more minutes lost himself tucking into his second breakfast of the day.

Welborne picked up his cabin telephone and dialled the number for the ship's Wardroom. Only Flynn remained with him in the small cabin and he had insisted on staying whilst the officer had wiped away the evidence of his partial morning shave and dressed himself for the day. Boyd, Coleman and O'Neill had moved along to the Senior Rates Mess and made it known to the ship's Captain that this was to be their headquarters whilst they remained onboard. The Captain felt some measure of relief that the cabin was nearer normal and felt more in control now that the disadvantage of being half dressed in front of a group of strangers that included a woman had been removed. Flynn, alert to every sound around him, had only to look towards the Captain when the grumbling noise vibrated through the ship to be told that the engines were being tested. He listened as Welborne spoke into the telephone.

"Hello Guns, Captain here, we have six guests with us for the passage back to Faslane and they are going to use the senior's Mess. I want them treated with courtesy by the ship's company. They are making some sort of training documentary about the Navy and someone seems to have forgotten to tell us about it. Ok? Oh, and by the way, one of the group is ex Chief Petty Officer McCormack and he is going to take over as Chief of the Boat for the passage home."

"Aye aye Sir," came the initial reply from Sub Lieutenant Damien Rowlands the ship's Gunnery Officer and the most junior officer on board. "Where do you want them to be for our departure from port Sir, on the bridge?"

"Ms Boyd and one of the gentlemen will be on the bridge, I want the remainder of the group to have free access to go anywhere in the ship without the need for escorts. Pass this on to the First Lieutenant will you."

Rowlands replaced the telephone handset in its cradle and slipped the metal clip that held it in place into position.

"It seems we have five blokes and a woman coming with us for the trip home, father wants them treated like royalty, he's even letting one of them take over as Chief of the Boat."

The ship's second-in-command took in the information in silence and nodded his head as acknowledgement. 'If it is all right by the Captain then it's fine by me', he thought. David Rodgers had immense respect for Jonathan Welborne whom he rated amongst the best CO's he had worked for in his eight year Royal Navy career. As the thought surfaced in his mind he realised that the comparison included some much more senior officers encountered during his two previous sea jobs. Nigel Courtney looked up from his breakfast of natural yoghurt, toast and coffee and addressed Rowlands.

"Gosh, he must like them if he is allowing someone to take over the engine room, I'll bet Yorky York is as sick as a parrot. Who is this new Chief of the Boat then Damien?"

"An ex Chief called McCormack apparently." replied Rowlands.

"I know him," chipped in Rodgers," he was the MEO of Cromer a couple of years ago. I think he got made redundant in the last tranche. I heard he took it pretty badly. I'm glad he is getting it together again, as I recall he was pretty good so we should be in safe enough hands."

155

"Special Sea Dutymen close up, close all screen doors and hatches. Hands out of the rig of the day clear off the upper deck. Assume Damage Control State three condition Yankee."

The familiar call to sea duty echoed around the ship via the main broadcast system and people began to scurry off to their leaving harbour positions. Courtney dashed to the upper deck, flipped open his mobile phone and made a call lasting less than a minute. Despite the detour he still managed to reach the bridge before Rowlands who would now be his officer of the watch as Harwich set to sea.

McCormack donned a pair of borrowed overalls and was waiting beside York when the knock came on the Mess door. York opened the door fully and Churchill was able to see that his boss was not dressed for work but the man with him was.

"We're all ready to go Yorky," came the slightly unsure brief from the Petty Officer, "both *donks* warmed through."

"Cheers John, this is Jim McCormack, used to be MEO of Cromer and he's taking us out, Skipper's orders."

Churchill nodded his assent and started back towards the ship control centre, he had enough to think about without trying to fathom out what the hell the 'old man' wanted. He could send whom he wanted up to the bridge to take the controls, it was his train set. Just as long as this bloke doesn't come down below and start messing with my engines he thought, "those *donks* are mine, I've nursed them for two years and that's the way it stays."

McCormack climbed the ladder to the bridge and identified the younger of the two officers, the Sub Lieutenant, as the officer of the watch. He approached smartly, introduced himself, and reported the engineering department ready for sea. It felt good. The report made, he took up his position at the engine controls and the smile began to spread across his face. Rowlands muttered something to the helmsman about McCormack acting as the engineer officer and the bridge personnel accepted the statement without question, each going through their own list of checks. The helmsman moved the steering joystick to one side and watched as the rudder indicator tracked across to thirty-five degrees of port rudder.

156

He repeated the exercise to starboard, centred the joystick and sat poised waiting for the first order. Rowlands lifted the direct link telephone to the control room and was instantly answered by Churchill.

"Control Room, Sir."

"Start both main engines please PO," he ordered and within seconds the grumbling noise and the puff of white smoke out of the funnel proved that his instruction was being followed. A further throaty roar and a puff of smoke and Harwich was ready to slip its moorings and head out of Oban, bound for Faslane.

The bridge phone rang several times as various members of the crew reported themselves closed up at their Special Sea Duty station and the helmsman ticked them off with a wax pencil on a perspex covered check list.

"Specials closed up Sir," the sailor reported to his officer of the watch when all the columns had been ticked. The small bridge was already becoming crowded when the First Lieutenant appeared. Rodgers, in his turn, took a report from Rowlands that the ship was ready for sea and descended the ladder from the bridge to the main passageway, making his way the short distance to the Captain's cabin. It was his duty as the second in command to make the final report. Rodgers straightened himself up and knocked.

"Number One, good morning," was the greeting from Welborne to his closest colleague, the formality of the relationship something of an anachronism in the modern world of first name contact in the work place. The barriers often came down between the two men but tradition had its place in the way warships were run and this was a moment worthy of some ceremony and they both, instinctively, knew it.

"Ready in all respects for sea Sir, one small problem this morning, we seem to have lost Leading Seaman Walters" pronounced Rodgers from the doorway of the cabin. Welborne explained to his colleague that Walters was assisting with their guests in the Senior Rates Mess and with that introduced Sheila Boyd. Welborne skipped over the introduction of Flynn with a gesture of his hand and the three took a lead from Rodgers as he escorted the small group to the bridge.

157

"Cast off forward, cast off aft," Welborne ordered as soon as he had taken up his station at the centre of the bridge by the binnacle housing the ship's compass.

"Starboard 30," he directed the helmsman who moved the steering joystick to position the rudders.

"Slow astern Starboard, slow ahead Port Chief."

The ship's bow swung gently but steadily away from the pier at Oban and as soon as Welborne had a clear view ahead of him he ordered the starboard engine to slow ahead and centred the rudders. A copy book exit without the need to engage my bow thrust, thought Welborne, who considered himself a good ship handler even though his current charge could turn on a sixpence.

Flynn and Boyd stood together at the rear of the bridge and watched the activity. They were both a little impressed and both a little uneasy. It was clearly a slick operation, thought Flynn, even if the man conducting the orchestra represented just about everything he disliked most in life.

Welborne looked and sounded public school.

In his own environment, where he was the undisputed master, he had confidence and authority; he was far removed from the startled rabbit Flynn had encountered less than an hour ago. Flynn re-assessed the man he now viewed as his adversary; definitely one to be watched carefully. Sheila Boyd felt a similar distaste as she watched the sailors scurry about on the forecastle stowing away the berthing ropes and wires that had secured Harwich to the jetty. Little worker bees, she thought, all responding to the demands of the Queen.

A ringing sound interrupted the ordered discipline of the bridge and for a split second heads turned first one way and then another trying to track down the sound. Flynn was momentarily thrown off balance until he realised the sound was coming from the inside pocket of his windproof jacket. He dragged out the phone and looked around at the smiles on the faces of the bridge crew. Muttering a half-silent apology he moved out to the starboard bridge wing and jabbed at the green button.

"Paddy?"

"Yes."

"Listen. The Navigating Officer, Nigel Courtney, has a mobile phone he called his wife. There may be others, sort them out, Ok. How's it going?"

"Thanks, will do, all according to plan so far."

Flynn pressed the red symbol to terminate the call and slipped the phone back into his pocket. Neither he nor Laura had thought that the sailors would be armed with mobiles but he was certainly pleased she had called to warn him.

"Fall out Special Sea Dutymen, revert to damage control state three, condition X-ray" boomed out over the broadcast and once again sailors began moving freely through the vessel as doors and hatches were opened up to give the normal, peace time, sailing state. Welborne and his First Lieutenant left the bridge together, the former anxious to brief his deputy on the real reason for the presence of strangers on their ship.

In the Senior Rates Mess Daniel Coleman had set up his portable computer and begun to type. He remembered Laura's instructions perfectly, he could write up the events as they unfolded but no mention of her or Flynn. Coleman had started with their arrival in Oban and for the first time in his life he felt the words rushing into his mind without the need to work at it. His fingers moved across the keyboard easily as he described the scene around him and the people he had encountered. It was to be more than a diary, he decided, he wanted to introduce more than just the cold facts in narrative form, he wanted to be *Hemingway*, or at the very least *Jeffrey Archer*.

Walters had slumped at the corner of the mess bench, hardly saying a word. His attention seemed completely taken up by the weapons laid on the table in front of O'Neill and Cluskey and he gazed at them with an expression that left him looking as if he was in a world far away from the present. York was worried. He had heard the pipe reducing the ship from 'Specials' minutes earlier but McCormack had not returned to the Mess. What was he up to, where would he go in York's domain, would he create any extra work or cause damage. He had pretty well dismissed Coleman from his mind and decided that he was on the level, just a journalist, it was the other two that bothered him. Their accents weren't exactly lost on him either, even though both men had kept their conversation to a minimum. York raised his head to greet the opening of the door and was almost pleased to see his former friend, the man who had taken over his job even if only for a day.

"No problems, Jim?" York inquired. Whatever he felt about being confined in his Mess and the manner in which it had happened he still felt a natural curiosity to know if his machinery had performed as well as the other man was accustomed to.

"Yeah, it was a great feeling. The 'old man' isn't a bad driver is he, didn't bother with the bow thrusters, just took us straight out on main engines, my skipper in Cromer wouldn't have done that. Is there any chance of a cup of tea Yorky?"

York looked at the two men he was beginning to think of as his captors and posed the question, "Can Wally whet a pot of tea for us all, he'll need to go to the Jackson in the galley?"

Neither Cluskey nor O'Neill had the first idea what the Jackson was but on instinct and because he wanted a drink himself O'Neill rose and invited Walters to show him the way. Walters awoke from his trance like state and collected a polished steel teapot from the cupboard York indicated and made for the door. Like many places in Harwich the galley was only a few paces away from the Mess and sited off the main passageway. As soon as Walters entered the galley and began the task of filling the pot with boiling hot water O'Neill solved the puzzle of the Jackson. A shiny water boiler was mounted on the bulkhead of the galley close to the door and the maker's name was boldly displayed on its front.

Flynn pushed open the door to Welborne's cabin and entered without either knocking or being invited. The two officers stopped their conversation and looked up startled at an intrusion unthinkable in normal circumstances.

Padraig Flynn spoke first, "Captain, we have a bit of a problem. I have found out that one of your officers has got a mobile phone and I suspect there may be others on the ship. I want them all collected up and handed over to my people without delay. They can be returned as soon as we reach

Faslane but I must make sure no messages about us spoil our little surprise at the other end."

Flynn knew from McCormack that the use of mobiles whilst the ship was on passage was forbidden and also that the crew were expected to register them with the coxswain when they were brought on board.

David Rodgers stood up. Like most men he felt uncomfortable about opening conversation with a standing man.

"If you people want to keep up this sham about making a film it's going to be very difficult to make our team understand why you want their phones confiscated isn't it."

"Look, I don't care a toss how you manage it, just get all the phones collected up OK," was the instant reply from Flynn who held the gaze of Rodgers without the slightest hint of uncertainty. Welborne sensed the immediate friction between the two men and rose to his feet.

"I'm sure we can arrange what you want but I at least want to tell my officers what this is all about and the coxswain too. If I could get them together in the Wardroom for a few minutes it will make things much easier for all of us."

Flynn considered for only a second and replied, "Right, do it now."

Rowlands consulted the admiralty chart spread out flat on the bridge chart table and moved his rolling parallel ruler to line up his triangular fixes marked in pencil. Harwich was on track. The radar showed nothing within five miles of the ship and the visibility was still good. Open water ahead and only seven hours to go to reach the safe haven of a berth alongside the naval jetty at Faslane. The phone rang.

"Officer of the Watch."

"Captain, I want all officers and the coxswain in the wardroom in five minutes, First Lieutenant is with me."

"Aye aye Sir, I'll pipe for the coxswain."

***

The two groups had taken opposite sides at the table without

161

prompting. On one side sat the Navigating Officer, the First Lieutenant and the coxswain. On the other were Bryce, Cluskey and Coleman. The leaders, Welborne and Flynn, stood alongside each other and looked at the slightly upturned faces of the assembled company. The demand was made quickly and clearly by the Captain and with equal efficiency the coxswain briefed that there were six personal portable telephones registered, with the ship's mobile making seven. O'Neill and the Petty Officer set off on a tour of the ship to collect them up and Lieutenant Courtney started by handing over his. In ten minutes Flynn was looking at a pile of seven mobiles of various shapes and sizes and feeling satisfied that the risk had been removed. Now was the time to properly position his troops and he sent Cluskey to the ship's radio room, the communication centre of the warship, Bryce to the bridge, and O'Neill to patrol the ship.

As quickly as the phones had been gathered in the remainder of the ship's crew knew that making films had little to do with the reason why they were sharing their space with civilians and the rumour machine took off. If there had been any women in the crew it would almost certainly have been off to white slavery in some Arab potentate's palace.

All John Churchill knew was that his wife had just given him his new Sony mobile as a gift and he wasn't surrendering it to anyone. He'd only used it half a dozen times, trying to keep the bills down, and sure as hell he wasn't going to pay for someone else to call who knows where at his expense.

Churchill slipped the phone into his overalls pocket and silently thanked his luck that he hadn't told the coxswain about it. He'd meant to. The two of them were run ashore oppo's, they had been out in Oban just the previous evening together. Fresh air was what Churchill needed now that they were safely out to sea. He swung the two metal clips that held the starboard screen door in place round on their hinges and pushed the door outwards onto the upper deck.

The sea looked as flat as a mill pond under the late August sun and the engineer made his way past two inflatables' stowed on the boat deck and descended the ladder to the quarterdeck and the part of the ship furthest aft. Churchill found himself a free space at the guardrail and dipped into his pocket for his packet of Benson and Hedges and lighter. The lighter fired up at his second attempt and he drew the smoke deep into his lungs, the irony of going out into the sea air for a cigarette completely wasted on a man who had followed the same routine, every time the weather conditions allowed it, for many years.

Churchill felt a chill, even with the sun bright in the sky, and pressed together the two Velcro strips that closed up the front of his blue overalls. Running his palm down the join his fingers touched the bulge of his telephone and he pulled it out of his breast pocket. The instrument all but disappeared in the palm of his large hand and the novelty of handling it made him press the on switch with his extended thumb. The screen lit up with a range of symbols and the phone gave off its bleep to signify that it was ready for use. Churchill lifted the instrument to his ear and listened, nothing. Would it work here he thought, reception was notoriously bad on the west coast of Scotland, he turned inwards from the guard rail, held the phone in front of him in his left hand and began to methodically press the buttons for his home number.

Zero, One, Four, One for Glasgow, Six, Nine.......

The bullet hit him in the centre of his chest. The telephone flew out of his hand, climbing into the air, spinning end over end in a perfect arc on its way to the sea. Churchill heard the sound of the shot after he felt the excruciating pain and for a split second imagined that the phone had exploded. In, what seemed to him, slow motion he staggered half a pace and fell backward. His head hit the grey deck but by then he was dead. His overalls had stayed fastened to the neck and a red stain of blood was spreading, spreading in a huge circle across his chest.

Twenty

Walker shuffled his feet and looked across the crowded Maritime Operations Centre at the assembled gathering of mostly senior officers and civilian department directors.

The Deputy Queens Harbourmaster was rattling on about ship movements for the day from his position at the briefing lectern and Walker was to be next. Alan South, the Admiral, was the senior man present and the briefing was directed at him. The weekly Tuesday morning Command brief had developed almost to the point of theatre with 'PowerPoint' computer generated slides and maps and charts and any other embellishments that the Operations Room staff could introduce.

The Duty Naval Base Officer usually briefed well down the pecking order. He came after the Staff Public Relations man and after the Visits Liaison Officer. He was after the base Facilities man who talked endlessly, about which cranes were serviceable and which weren't, and about what power supplies would be isolated that day. He went on and on interminably about what was, for most of the audience, of little importance.

The start of Trident Ploughshares 2000 had changed all of that and now he found himself third man in after operational matters and harbour movements. What was even more satisfying was that Walker could now sense that the entire audience greeted his security brief with an element of expectation. If anything he was bringing in the crowds, not discouraging them. It wasn't really surprising because with all the activity of the last few weeks involving peace campers and demonstrators from the world over, this was the place to get the real low down on what was happening and what had occurred during the previous twenty four hours. All five Captains here this morning Walker noted, as well as the

Admiral and the Commodore. He could only make a guess at the collective incomes of all the people seated in the room but it represented the great and good of Faslane that was for sure.

DQHM completed his brief and moved away. Walker strode forward the few short paces to the lectern and pressed the right mouse control to change the computer slide. The screen lit up to the naval base crest and the title 'Security' with Walker's name and rank below it. Any attempts at humour had been largely stricken from these briefs a long time ago. It was a factual account of events delivered without emotion. Walker told everyone that he had banned all humour, hypothesis and hyperbole from his brief and he knew they were the losers for it. Walker thought of it as a shame. He didn't dislike standing up in front of an audience and had a dry enough sense of humour to add a little flavour to the normal diet of what he described as daily trivia.

Trident Ploughshares 2000 had changed that too, now his brief was frequently greeted with questions about matters of physical security within the base, even names and descriptions of the people who were laying siege to the Naval Base. Everyone had been affected by events of the last weeks. It may only have been the delays in traffic movement whilst the gates were closed. It may have been the need to stay in an office whilst a search of the base was completed. Whatever it was the six thousand base workers all knew who Trident Ploughshares 2000 were and what a pain in the arse they had become.

"Good morning Admiral, gentlemen, Security incidents from the last twenty four hours..."

Walker launched into his brief looking only occasionally at his notes as he described the attempt by three swimmers to enter the base the previous evening. All arrested, but not before they had reached the huge inflatable barrier of rubber fenders that acted as a water borne fence between the Gareloch and the northern berths where an SSBN of the Vanguard Class was berthed.

"Two Dutch women and one Finn Sir, entered the water on the western side of the Gareloch and swam all the way across, quite an achievement weighted down with waist belts containing wire cutters, a hammer, plastic bottles of glue and paint, ropes, a torch and emergency flares."

"Glue and paint" the Admiral interjected, "what the hell is that for Colin?"

Walker explained, "the Trident Ploughshares handbook suggests pouring substances like glue and paint into any openings on the casing of the submarines, with particular emphasis on any area around the missile tubes. If they can gum up anything sensitive they see it as a major coup towards making the missile system inoperative." The Admiral seemed satisfied and nodded to Walker. He continued.

"For one of the Dutch women and the Finn this represents their second arrest this week. They were caught by MDP in the Oil Fuel depot two nights previously."

South interrupted once again, "Have Strathclyde police agreed to a policy of three strikes and they're out this time Colin?"

"Yes Sir, they have but we've already got a couple of people with four arrests in the last two weeks. I think there is some concern about custody space for all these people. We could end up filling every police cell in the district. These three women have been charged with bye-law offences and should appear in court today."

Walker was reaching the end.

"It may be of interest, Sir," he continued, "of these three women, two were vegetarians and the third a vegan."

"Why should I find that even remotely interesting, Colin?" the Admiral retorted, and Walker smiled.

"Well Sir, as you know the MDP have a duty of care for any prisoners held in custody for a long period. These arrests were timed at half past eight last night, and because we had them at the prisoner reception centre for over four hours we had to feed them."

"You're joking surely," replied Alan South voicing the same thought that had occurred to everyone else in the room, "what the hell did we feed them, and who provided it?" South asked, clearly amused at what he had been dragged into by Walker.

"We have had a chef on call throughout this period so far

166

and all three women were given a fresh salad. When I told the chef he had a vegan to cater for he thought we had a character from Star Trek in the base. We settled on the salad."

"So they have got salad in the galley then," chimed in one of the Captains, "haven't seen any in the Mess for weeks. I didn't realise we were just keeping it for guests."

Walker rounded up his brief with a description of the main ploughshares site at Peaton Glen where the drizzle had reduced the entire area to little more than a mud bath and where the gathered demonstrators and activists were having a decidedly unpleasant time for late August. He waited through the remainder of the command brief and ambled back to his office thinking of tea.

***

O'Neill lowered his weapon and looked down at the prone figure on the deck below. The shot, taken two handed with both arms extended, was a classic marksman's effort and he felt professional pride before any other sensation. He could already see, without closing on the body, that he had taken the man in the centre of the chest. Always go for the largest body area, that's what he had been taught, if you get a big enough gun you'll kill the target regardless. Flynn arrived first, closely followed by Welborne, each the others shadow it seemed. He took in the scene in an instant and realised just as quickly that O'Neill had destroyed any chance of reaching Faslane without further confrontation. Film crews didn't shoot sailors, at least not with handguns. What struck him more forcibly was the thought that peaceful demonstrators didn't assassinate servicemen either and he knew that Boyd and McCormack and Coleman might now have to rethink their positions in this little escapade.

Welborne spoke first. "Oh my God, what have you done what could Churchill possibly have done?" He rushed down to the quarterdeck half thinking he may be able to do something for the stricken Petty Officer. The spreading pool of crimson blood oozing away from the blue overalls persuaded him that he was too late. "He's dead," the ship's commanding officer turned back towards O'Neill and shouted, "you murdering bastard, you've killed an unarmed man in cold blood."

"He was on a mobile telephone," said one Irishmen to the other. "He was making a call so I took him out." Simple as that thought O'Neill. The situation had arisen and he had dealt with it. Flynn would have done the same, he was sure of that.

"You'd have done the same, Padraig, you know you would."

Flynn looked back towards the dead man and said, his voice under complete control, "where's the fucking phone then Brendan, I can't see it anywhere." O'Neill told his countryman that it had flown over the side with the shot. Flynn shook his head from side to side more in a gesture of exasperation than one of disbelief. "Push him over the side and hose down the mess, and for Christ's sake don't shoot anyone else unless I tell you to OK."

O'Neill set about his task, comfortable now that he had an order to follow. Padraig Flynn descended the ladder to the quarterdeck and turned to Welborne.

"We can deal with this situation in two ways," he said to the man in uniform. "We can do it the easy way and hopefully avoid any more bloodshed, or," Flynn paused for a second, "we can take the other route and end up with World War Three right here in your ship. What's it to be?"

"This isn't a peaceful demonstration at all is it?" Welborne asked. "What exactly are you going to do with my ship and my people? Are you really going to give yourselves up to the Ministry of Defence police when we get to Faslane? It's going to be a bit difficult with a murder on your hands don't you think."

"Your job is simple Captain, keep your sailors under control until we get to the base and they won't get hurt, OK. I told you people no phones didn't I. That man didn't follow instructions. He paid the price; don't let it happen to anyone else. I hope that is clear."

Flynn walked away from the naval officer and headed back up the ladder and into the artificial light of the ship through the starboard screen door. He followed the passageway forward until he reached the door of the radio room and entered without knocking.

"Dom' outside a minute," he said to Cluskey, and the man followed him into the passageway. "Brendan's just topped one of the sailors, we've moved up a gear OK. Nothing, but nothing is to go out on the radio, all right. Get that sailor out and lock the place up."

Cluskey nodded his understanding and set about the task. Leading Radio Operator Trevor Russell wasn't accustomed to taking orders from civilians but the sight of a pistol levelled at his stomach persuaded him to obey the snarled command to leave his place of work. Cluskey turned the key in the door lock and tried the handle, all secure. It looked like a pretty substantial door.

"Jim, show me round the ship." Flynn commanded and McCormack rose from his position on the upholstered bench seat in the senior rates mess. "Bring my daysack as well." Flynn indicated a small green shoulder bag that had sat next to Coleman, almost forgotten, since they first arrived on board HMS Harwich.

Coleman continued to type, tapping away at the keys of his lap top computer, words still flowing forth. In his narrative he had just reached the ship and was describing the encounter at the gangway between O'Neill and Leading Seaman Walters. The quartermaster of the morning watch had once again withdrawn into his own thoughts, captive within his own home.

On the bridge Boyd was battling with the idea that she had heard a shot a few minutes earlier. The bridge door was clipped shut to maintain the integrity of the air conditioning within the ship but she was certain that the noise had been a gunshot. Rowlands and Courtney continued with the business of navigating the warship along its charted course but they had started to whisper to each other since the noise and she suspected they had reached the same conclusion. Both Officers had seen that the three Irishmen were armed so it wasn't a long distance for the thought to travel.

The arrival of Welborne, looking pale and angry, was all the confirmation Sheila Boyd needed, even before the whispered conversation between the three officers. No way had she bargained for someone being hurt or worse killed. The

169

struggle was worth a few bruises, even a broken bone or two if it made her case more convincing but she wasn't sure about the ultimate sacrifice to the cause. O'Neill followed shortly behind and the small bridge seemed as crowded as it had done for their departure from Oban barely three hours earlier. It was obvious by the expressions on the faces of the three officers that they knew O'Neill was responsible for whatever atrocity had taken place and Boyd shuddered as she looked at the man. No sign of emotion from him, his mouth turned upwards in a sneer as the three men observed him in silence.

"Where are we then," O'Neill inquired of Rowlands, "show me on the map."

"It's called a chart at sea, and we are here," Rowlands picked up a pair of brass dividers and extended the legs to form a pointer, he laid the point on the chart at their current position.

"How long to Faslane then," he asked as he looked at the unfamiliar chart, able to make out the shape of the mainland coastline and the islands dotted alongside it.

Rowlands folded his dividers, concealed his face in the cowl of the radar display and answered. "Four hours to Perch Rock and another half an hour from there to the Base."

O'Neill tired of navigation and turned his attention to the view out of the bridge windows. The sea remained calm and visibility was good. Harwich made its way ahead. It was more a gliding sensation than carving her way through the waves and what little sea motion there was O'Neill found rather pleasant. He stood behind the helmsman. Absorbed with the moving tape of the gyrocompass the helmsman altered the ships head with gentle adjustments of the steering joystick and the ship answered his instructions smoothly and quickly. O'Neill could see the two engine order telegraphs both set at half ahead and as he peered at the controls in front of him he identified two instruments showing what he assumed to be the speed of the shafts and propellers in revolutions per minute.

"How fast we going," he asked the sailor as he tapped him on the shoulder to gain his attention. "Revs for thirteen knots," was the response and O'Neill wanted more.

170

"What'll it do then, how fast, flat out."

"'bout eighteen knots downhill." came the reply and O'Neill once more lost interest.

"God, I'm fucking starving, when do we get fed," he asked next and Welborne answered.

"Lunch will be available from twelve o'clock. I suppose you have worked up an appetite with what you have done this morning, if you go to the galley now I'm sure the chef will feed you early."

O'Neill laughed out loud and headed down the bridge ladder and out of sight.

"Do I sense you are getting in over your head Ms Boyd," Welborne asked of the woman who stood alone in silence on his bridge. "Whatever these three men are here for it certainly isn't what you described to me earlier is it?"

Sheila Boyd looked into the eyes of the ship's Captain and saw warmth and compassion. His eyes were older, somehow, than his face. They at one time registered pain at the death of one of his crew and concern for the rest of his adult family of sailors. Boyd saw in him what she often saw in her husband, the soul of a good man. She swallowed and drew a breath, ready to speak. Flynn appeared at the bottom of the ladder and made his way up to join the group, the green rucksack hanging limply from his left shoulder. The moment was gone, perhaps forever and Boyd turned away to look out of the side window of the bridge. Welborne cursed silently to himself but had learned a little more about the bizarre mess he found himself in. Flynn was cold and efficient.

"Captain, work out the absolute minimum number of people you need to keep us going towards Faslane, include my expert, and get the rest of the crew down to the lower mess deck in five minutes. I want all non essential people together and out of harm's way."

"What about Chief York and Walters," came back the response from Welborne and once again Flynn recognised how quickly his adversary had sized up the situation.

"You can have them back too."

The First Lieutenant, David Rodgers, organised the move of his ship's company to the lower mess deck without fuss and then he joined them. Left on the bridge were Rowlands, Nigel Courtney and the Captain. At the helm sat an Able Seaman, the helmsman of the watch. Jim McCormack would alternate between the bridge and the ship control centre and Cluskey would go with him. O'Neill was the minder for Coleman and Boyd and the young chef still engaged on the preparation of lunch. Flynn would become the baby sitter for the bridge. All neatly arranged, Flynn decided, any further risk of disaster reduced to a minimum.

Welborne tried again.

"Look, I don't know what to call you, what is your name," he asked Flynn.

"Paddy will do," was the Irishman's reply.

"My chef has prepared a meal, can we get everyone fed. It shouldn't present a problem now you have them all together."

Flynn agreed.

***

Thirty men crowded together in the lower mess deck of HMS Harwich. Seated four to a bunk there was little room to stretch. They had filed up and down to the ship's galley and tucked into a hot lunch of stew with potatoes and tinned carrots. Not the most sensational lunch but certainly better than nothing. The usual banter between the diners and the chef had departed and although the sailors were more contented now they had full stomachs their normal humour had all but deserted them.

"So who's left up top then?" asked a sailor of the man next to him.

"Skipper, Navi, Thrombosis and Jonah on the bridge, and the chef in the galley. Fucking chef gets all the good numbers."

"I dunno about that," commented a young engineer. "We've left the chef with all the washing up to do so that'll pay the bastard back for the rubbish scran."

There was a brief pause in the conversation.

"Who's thrombosis," another man asked from the same bunk.

172

"You know, the gunnery officer, Rowlands, Subby Rowlands," answered the man.

"Why's he called that then?"

"Fucking obvious isn't it; thrombosis, what is fucking thrombosis, it's a clot on the move isn't it."

David Rodgers checked that the hatch above him was closed and called for quiet from the sailors crammed into the small sleeping space.

"Right, listen up everyone," he started, "we may be stuck down here away from the action but that doesn't mean we can't contribute. I want a record created of anything and everything we know about these people so that when this is over with they get caught."

Rodgers looked over at Leading Seaman Walters.

"Leader, you're the best cartoonist on board and you have seen them all close up, I want some drawings. Best likenesses you can come up with. Chief York, all the details of what has been seen and heard, names, accents, absolutely anything that comes to mind. Anyone got a couple of notebooks in a locker down here."

Writing paper and pencils were produced and a general swell of conversation began as both men began to sketch or write. Rodgers moved between the two men checking, adding what he had seen and refining the results.

York looked up from his efforts when Rodgers was alongside him.

"Sir, I can't believe Jim McCormack is deep in this business. They must have tricked him somehow; he just isn't the type to sign up with a bunch of Irish terrorists whoever they say they represent. The writer bloke, he's another one I can't figure out. He has done nothing but clack away on his computer so far, I don't even think he knows what is going on around him."

***

"Captain, Sir, Officer of the Watch," said Damien Rowlands into the direct telephone connecting the bridge to the Captain's cabin below.

173

"Captain," came back the immediate reply.

"Perch Rock one mile and visible Sir."

"Roger, Officer of the Watch," replied Welborne.

Jonathan Welborne left his cabin and climbed the ladder to the bridge. Padraig Flynn stood next to the small chart table watching the actions of the bridge crew carefully. Nothing suspicious so far, he thought. Welborne checked the Admiralty chart spread neatly on the table and noted the series of 'fixes' marked in pencil and showing the ship's progress along its planned course towards Faslane. Rowlands had learned his craft well and Welborne considered himself lucky to have such a competent junior officer with him in Harwich. He knew full well what some of the ship's company called young Rowlands but frankly, he thought, they would have called him something or other however good he was; almost a tradition for the youngest member of the Minehunter's management team. The captain looked up from the chart table and made eye contact with Flynn.

"We would normally be talking to the Base at this point in our entry plan to find out which berth they have allocated us," he said. "Unless you want them to start chasing us I suggest we do it now."

Flynn withdrew his handgun from the outer pocket of his jacket, a wordless warning to Welborne that a departure from the normal practice would end badly for him or one of his crew.

"OK," was all the Irishman managed in response.

Welborne instructed his Navigating Officer and Courtney acted.

"QHM, this is warship Harwich at Perch Rock inbound, request alongside berth, over."

The normally quiet and disciplined bridge team from HMS Harwich listened expectantly for some contact from outside their threatened world. Seconds passed and Flynn began to fidget, concerned but unwilling to break the lengthening silence.

"Warship Harwich; QHM; berth two bravo, bows south. Welcome home."

Courtney broke the tension.

"Sir, we need more people above decks for Special Sea Dutymen, we won't cope with ropes and wires as we are, and we'll look a bit odd."

Welborne accepted the comments as good advice and turned to Flynn, the question asked in just the nod upwards of his head.

Flynn agreed to the captain's request and with O'Neill in attendance the upper deck team was allowed to leave the seclusion of the lower Mess deck to take up their positions for entering harbour.

"Special Sea Dutymen close up, close all screen doors and hatches. Assume Damage Control State three, condition Yankee" boomed out across the ship's main broadcast and the few sailors nominated went to their places.

Through the starboard bridge windows the town of Helensburgh was clearly visible and both Flynn and Courtney picked up binoculars and moved to that side of the bridge.

Twenty One

Laura Latimer looked at her wristwatch and noted the time, half past two.

The ship should be close now, she thought. Laura and Emma Courtney had spent a leisurely morning. Emma had tried to immerse herself in housework, vacuuming the carpets and polishing the furniture, anything to fill in the hours until her husband Nigel arrived home. She had a special meal planned for the evening and a nice bottle of white Bordeaux chilling in the refrigerator. The separations were agony and she still couldn't get used to Nigel leaving for weeks, sometimes months at a time whilst he went off to sea. If the separations were agony then the reunions were pure ecstasy, almost a re-affirmation of their love for each other every time they came together again.

Emma had heard all the jokes.

She had heard one wife say that she collected all the green smarties from the children's sweets so that she could scatter them on the lawn for the kids to find as soon as their dad came home, anything to buy some time for the first frenzied moments of passion. She didn't care today. Emma had deliberately left the bedroom curtains closed when she rose this morning and knew that the neighbours would notice; better than shutting them in the early evening she thought. Laura had been great the previous night and this morning, they got on so well together. She had promised to stay right up until Nigel phoned from the ship to say he was ready to be collected and then she would start her journey back to London.

Laura too had busied herself during the morning. There was the legitimate business of running Latimer Imports to contend with; phone calls to make, paperwork to process. Her other persona, the successful businesswoman, was an easy mantle to assume and Laura achieved it effortlessly. She'd made a few short trips away from the apartment whilst the cleaning was going on. The pretence of business in Helensburgh had to be maintained even though Emma seemed so wrapped up in her husband's homecoming that she had failed to notice Laura's close attendance. If Emma was tense with her expectation of things planned for later in the day so was Laura.

"Let's go down to the front and watch for Nigel," chimed Emma, her face filled with an almost childish excitement, "we could sit on the bench where we first met."

Laura thought for only a second and agreed with a warm smile. Certainly there was a slight risk, she knew that, but what harm could it do.

***

The two men on the bridge of HMS Harwich scanned the short distance to the shoreline. The Helensburgh town car park was bustling with afternoon shoppers jostling in and out with their bags of groceries from Tesco and Somerfield. They were just lots of ordinary families innocently going about their daily lives totally unaware of a developing drama so close by out in the river. A few fishermen lined the town pier casting out into the calm waters hoping for a free supper but fully expecting to sample the wares of the fish and chip shop on their way home. Courtney focussed his attention towards the narrowing of the channel at Rhu and was rewarded with the first sight of his wife Emma, seated with another woman, on a bench to the north of the town. Spurred by the pleasure of seeing his young wife the Navigating Officer turned to Flynn, almost at his shoulder, and pointed.

"There's my wife, on that bench, in the red coat."

Flynn followed the direction Courtney was pointing and quickly spotted Laura seated next to a woman in red. The two were clearly following the progress of the ship and although the distance was too great the sensation of eye contact felt strong. Flynn could see that the two were in conversation, that

177

they appeared as friends. Rowlands spoke,

"Good fix, puts the ship on track."

Courtney snapped back to the reality of the moment and with only a hint of reluctance put his binoculars back in their stowage and turned towards the chart. Flynn watched the women for longer, fascinated by the apparent ease with which Laura dealt with the wife of an adversary. At this distance and with the aid of powerful binoculars he could make out their facial expressions, their gestures to each other and even the movement of their lips as they spoke. If only he could lip read, he thought.

"It doesn't seem fair that Nigel isn't allowed to come out onto the bridge wing and wave to us," said Emma. "I know he can see me because he always tells me what I am wearing when he phones up."

"At least he's nearly home," said Laura, and that was enough of a spur for the two to rise from their bench and head towards Laura's hire car.

Flynn watched all of this activity from his place on the bridge and remained silent.

The ship passed the black and white edifice that was the Ardencaple Hotel and shortly afterwards the fenced compound that formed the Clyde Off Site Centre. Both were silent, deserted. If anyone on the ship could have seen to the other side of the barn like structure they would have been able to observe two painters obliterating the words SCRAP TRIDNT from the outer wall of the building.

Even at eight knots the ship seemed to be leaving the local landmarks behind quickly and soon the Yacht Club disappeared in her wake as HMS Harwich continued into the Gareloch.

***

Jim McCormack responded quickly and professionally to the engine orders being passed to him by Lieutenant Courtney. If he had felt in the slightest rusty that morning when he had powered the ship out of Oban then that feeling had disappeared completely. It was as if he had never been away. His attention to what he was doing had dispelled all other thoughts from his mind and even the nagging realisation that he was party to the murder of Petty Officer Churchill subsided within his conscience.

McCormack looked up from the engine controls and out of the forward facing bridge window; the base was in sight. He looked again and noted the change in skyline now that the floating dry dock had finally been removed to other duty elsewhere. He could see other ships at their berths alongside the southern jetty.

A Hunt Class, another couple of members of the Third Squadron.

There would be people he knew. What on earth would they think of him when they knew what he was involved in, did they know already. Would anyone believe that he didn't know what was going to happen, could anyone be that naive, that stupid. The signs were all there for him to see, he should have known better, who was going to give an out of work ex sailor five hundred pounds for a few days work.

What the heck was he going to do to get out of this mess?

What would his wife Liz say?

The thoughts tumbled into his mind one on another and a feeling of sheer panic began to rise up in him. He would go to prison. It could be worse. One man had been shot dead already and these three Irishmen didn't look or sound likely to flinch from killing again. What was the good-looking woman's part in all of this, what did Laura do, she seemed to hold sway even over Flynn and he was the coldest bastard McCormack had ever set eyes upon. Where was she? Was she pulling the strings from afar? McCormack now knew. As he sat at the engine controls of HMS Harwich, half ahead showing on port and starboard shafts, revolutions for eight knots set, and the naval base coming ever closer with each turn of the propellers, he knew. This time he was in deep shit.

A few short yards away from the bridge and in the body of the ship three people sat immersed in their own thoughts. The senior ratings mess, which had been the centre of hospitality the previous evening now felt like a prison to Daniel Coleman.

179

The lid of his computer was closed and he sat, head in his hands and with eyes closed. Not one word had been uttered directly about the shooting but Cluskey, Boyd and he knew that it had happened.

The gunshot was the signal for Coleman to stop writing, his appetite for the adventure he had embarked upon disappeared in that one instant. His thoughts mirrored those of McCormack seated at the engine controls up on the bridge. This had all gone horribly wrong. Coleman opened his eyes and glanced at Sheila Boyd. He recognised the dullness in her expression; almost a vacant stare held her face. Daniel Coleman realised that she too was trying to figure out what had gone wrong.

Cluskey rose from the mess bench and headed for the door. His two lifeless co-conspirators looked up.

"Toilet," he grunted as he exited the Mess and headed out into the main passageway.

"What do we do now?"

Boyd spoke first and Coleman needed no further explanation about what she meant. More than that, her few words convinced him beyond doubt that she recognised the situation had gone far beyond what either of them had bargained for.

"Look," responded Coleman, "I'm no hero, and I certainly don't see myself stopping Cluskey or the other two but when it comes down to the odds there are three of them and a lot more of us. We must convince the Captain that we are on his side."

"Agreed," said Boyd, "Let's try."

With their minder out of the room Coleman and Boyd headed towards the bridge ladder and were in time to see the ship pass beyond the southernmost berths of the Naval Base and into what she had always considered the enemy's lair.

"Half a cable to wheel over to starboard, Sir," Courtney announced from the back of the bridge and Welborne moved to centre stage.

"Both engines set at half ahead, revolutions for eight knots set, I have the ship."

Lieutenant Commander Jonathan Welborne shut all

thoughts of terrorists from his mind and waited for the precise second when he would order the first movement of engines and steering. If he could get his command safely alongside the jetty there remained just a chance that this awful nightmare may be ended without further bloodshed.

"Slow ahead port, slow ahead starboard," he directed McCormack at the engine control panel, "starboard thirty."

McCormack repeated the captain's order. The sailor at the helm replied with a traditional "Aye Aye, Sir."

Flynn moved forward. In a flash he drew his weapon and blocked the helmsman in his attempt to move the joystick controlling the steering pumps and motors.

"No, do not carry out that order," he told both men very clearly and both McCormack and the sailor froze at their different controls.

"Keep the ship moving ahead and take it further along the base until you get to the floating barrier, then anchor it."

Welborne paled and knew his nightmare was destined to continue. He had to decide quickly. There was little choice he knew that. Welborne sensed that he had reached a watershed in the whole sorry incident. This was the defining moment, if he tried to over-rule the Irishman a second man would die, maybe even himself. Welborne had never considered himself lacking in courage and what he felt at that moment was closer to anger than fear. He held the balance. The choice between life and death, could the sacrifice of a life ever be worth such a gamble. He looked at Flynn. His face showed not the slightest sign of emotion, or even self-doubt. Flynn had calculated the odds. He had put himself in the mind of his adversary and decided which decision he would make.

"Midships," he ordered in a resigned voice, "slow ahead both engines." He had to cancel his previous instructions to McCormack and his helmsman. It was the professional thing to do, what he had been taught throughout his career. The bridge crew of HMS Harwich felt time stand still as the duel of minds, the battle of wills played to its conclusion in front of them.

"Navigator, prepare the port anchor for letting go."

A sense of sheer relief covered the three officers on the bridge and their unwanted guests.

Courtney moved out to the port bridge wing of the ship and called down to the sailors making up the foc'sle party. "Prepare the port anchor for letting go," he shouted through his hands cupped to his mouth. He had relayed the instruction. Two sailors looked up at their officer in disbelief but moved to the task anyway. The warship continued to glide gently towards the north end of the naval base and towards the barrier of outsize, floating black sausages joined together to embrace the top security berths

"Warship Harwich this is QHM; your berth is two bravo bows south. You are beyond your turn, over."

The bridge VHF crackled out clearly with the message from ashore. Welborne reached out to pick up the microphone.

"Leave it," said Flynn and punctuated his comment by levelling an automatic pistol directly at the officer's head. Flynn had won the first trial of strength; he needed to hammer home the advantage. If the weapon was to make the difference between the two men then so be it.

Courtney consulted the chart laid out on the chart table. No anchoring position was marked he realised, it had never been the intention. He looked from Flynn to Welborne for an instruction.

"Stop both engines," ordered the captain, and Jim McCormack responded by pulling both engine control levers to their upright position. The captain read his navigating officer's indecision instantly and exactly and with as much dignity as he could muster Jonathan Welborne ordered him to anchor the ship.

Courtney moved purposefully through the port bridge door and onto the open space at the wings. "Let go port anchor." His shouted order echoed down to the foc'sle and the rattle of anchor cable split the silence as the sailors broke the Blake slip retaining the anchor cable and allowed it to fall under gravity towards the bottom of the Gareloch.

"Slow astern starboard."

Welborne skewed the warship backwards slightly to allow the anchor and its heavy cable to pay out along the bed of the

Gareloch to give him a secure anchorage.

"Stop both engines and finished with main engines thank you, Mr McCormack," ordered the captain and his temporary engineer officer brought engines and shafts to a stop and shut down the main machinery of the ship. A silence fell on the bridge and the entire vessel as the dull, never ceasing but hardly noticed, growl of the diesel engines were finally made quiet.

Flynn dipped into the inside pocket of his jacket and withdrew a folded sheet of white paper. He took two paces towards Sheila Boyd and held out the note. Boyd instinctively reached forward and took it.

"I want her to deliver that message to someone in authority in the base now," said Flynn to Welborne, "how does the radio operate."

Welborne picked up the microphone and pressed the switch to speak.

"QHM this is warship Harwich: over."

With that he handed the microphone to the woman. Sheila Boyd scanned the words typed in large print on the page and tried to control her shaking fingers. She looked up at Flynn. No words were necessary; Boyd took a deep breath to steady herself and prepared to obey the unspoken command.

"Warship Harwich; QHM, pass your message."

The woman swallowed noisily and depressed the transmit button on the side of the microphone. Her hands shook. One held the microphone and the other, outstretched before her, the paper.

"My name is Sheila Boyd," she read, "I represent the Trident Ploughshares 2000 group and we have taken over this ship. My team is armed and will use their weapons if threatened. You are not, I repeat, not to approach this ship by boat or by any other means. We are holding the crew as hostages and if you follow my instructions completely no one will be harmed. In exactly one hour I want to speak to the Admiral."

Boyd handed the microphone back to the ship's captain and the sheet of paper to Flynn. She shook almost uncontrollably. Sheila Boyd moved away from the VHF and steadied herself

183

against the wooden rail forming the top of the bridge ladder. She grasped the rail with both hands and with her knuckles white from the strength of her grip she slowly regained control of her jangling nerves. The bridge of HMS Harwich fell into a stunned silence.

Twenty Two

Laura replaced the receiver and ticked an entry in the small notebook open beside her in the telephone box sited on Helensburgh pier.

She had now passed the same message to the Scottish Daily Express, the Mirror and Mail, the Sun and the Daily Telegraph. Next would come the local Helensburgh Advertiser and then, finally, the two major television companies, BBC Scotland and Scottish Television.

That should stir up a hornet's nest she thought.

She looked up and scanned the street. Nobody waiting for the phone and very little movement in her direction, she should be safe to carry on with her calls. On an impulse she flicked over the pages in her book and found the phone number for the peace camp. Laura could hardly contain a smile of utter disbelief as she pondered the fact that the group of demonstrators who had been a thorn in the side of the military for sixteen years actually managed to get a British Telecom' line installed at their makeshift camp. Presumably they must pay the bill regularly or they would be cut off. In her country things would be different. In the first place the camp wouldn't have lasted sixteen minutes, let alone years, the security police would have swooped, arrested all the demonstrators and burned the site to the ground. As for the demonstrators, Laura didn't believe they would ever have seen the light of day again and that probably held true for their families and friends too. She liked London and the life style she had assumed but she recognised weakness when she saw it.

"Is Jenny there?"

Laura received an unintelligible reply and moved the phone away from her ear. She could almost smell the beery breath of the man who had answered. The peace camper called out the woman's name and Jenny Graham responded.

"Who is it?"

"I have a message from Sheila," Laura said into the mouthpiece, "I came to see her the other day and we went off together in my car, remember?"

Jenny had some vague recollection of Sheila Boyd leaving the camp with a woman and a man in a car but it hadn't seemed that significant at the time.

"What does Sheila want?" she asked, almost sure that Boyd would want her to perform some mundane task rather than do it herself. Jenny had great respect for the other woman's achievements as a founder signatory and pledger to the Trident Ploughshares 2000 group, but she also saw her as a bossy figure, too important to do the small jobs.

"She wants you to know that she and a couple of others have high-jacked HMS Harwich from the Navy and have made them anchor the ship near the floating barrier around the submarine berths in the base. She wants you to get all the campers organised. She needs as much activity around the fence and on the water as you can manage. She wants all the security people tied up in knots whilst she waits for the TV and the newspapers to get the story. She wants you to lead everyone from the camp and from Peaton Glen, can you do it?"

Jenny made the woman repeat some of what she had said, more from sheer disbelief than because she had failed to hear the message. After the second telling Laura interrupted her.

"Look," she said, "Sheila really has done it this time, if you want proof go on up the road and see where the ship is berthed. You will see quite clearly that she is at anchor close to the barrier and you know as well as I do that the navy would never let a ship do that."

Jenny Graham was more than half convinced. She'd want the proof that the woman caller had suggested, she would go along the main road until she could see the loch but she had a good feeling already.

Jenny drew herself up and a smile spread across her face for the first time since Georges and his friend had left the peace camp. This wouldn't be as much fun as she had had with her Belgian in their couple of nights of passion but it was a great deal more exciting than sitting around the fire watching everyone get stoned or drunk.

"I can do it," was all she replied.

***

Laura hurried back to the small apartment at Smuggler's Way and Emma opened the door immediately. The naval wife looked distressed.

"He still hasn't called, he's never this late, and there must be something wrong." The words tumbled out and Laura reached out to comfort the woman who was both friend and enemy at the same time. The embrace, so natural between the two women, continued. Laura Latimer made the right sort of comments about extra work on board after a long trip, and about the added responsibility of her husband's position as the Navigating Officer. Gradually she felt the other woman relax. Laura offered soothing words of comfort. She gently stroked Emma's shoulder length fair hair and breathed in the faint aroma of a perfume sparingly applied.

Silence fell between the two as they stood cheek-to-cheek; breast-to-breast, and with arms wrapping each other comfortably together. Very slowly Laura moved her free hand over Emma's shoulders. With a slow circling motion she rubbed the young woman's shoulders and back. Her hand came to rest casually on her waist. Emma turned her head slightly and just the sensation of a wet tear touched Laura Latimer's neck. Laura continued her journey over the woman's youthful body.

She rested her hand on her bottom.

Slowly she traced the curve of her firm flesh through her clothing. She could feel the outline of her underwear through the thin material of the woman's summer skirt. For a second Laura smiled. They were close, very close. With her husband this closeness in an embrace would have been followed inevitably by a kiss. This closeness, today, would for Emma have ended in the bedroom. Laura pondered; should she?

She felt a curious arousal. It might be an interesting distraction.

Would it damage what she had already built with Emma Courtney?

Laura sighed aloud and pulled the woman closer until their pelvic regions ground together, she patted Emma's rump playfully, pushed her tenderly away to arms length, planted a sisterly kiss on her cheek and broke the moment with an offer to make them both a nice cup of tea. Emma gushed out her thanks to her new friend.

She was so understanding and it was so good that she was here.

Laura smiled back as they moved apart. 'Such sweet innocence,' she thought. As she turned towards the small kitchen she couldn't avoid the impish thought that there was plenty of time left yet.

***

Jim McCormack took a long pull at his third pint of Courage Sparkling Bitter and put the glass down rather too heavily on the Mess table. The golden coloured liquid slopped around in the glass and a small spillage slid over the cut facets of the pint mug and puddled on the table in front of him. McCormack dipped his finger in the spilled beer and transferred the wetness to his mouth.

"Waste not, want not," he said in a voice much more cheerful than his mood and reached out again for the glass. Raising it to his mouth a few drops fell from the base of the glass onto the front of his blue overalls and he brushed at them impatiently with his free hand. He took a longer drink this time and the level of beer in the glass dropped to well below the half-pint.

"That's your third isn't it?" said Daniel Coleman from his position opposite McCormack at the senior rates mess table. His words marked the first attempt at conversation since McCormack had returned from the bridge and the completion of his entering harbour duties at the main engine control panel.

"So who's counting," he replied, "I may just as well get drunk, at least I'll forget what a bloody idiot I've been getting sucked into this disaster."

"If you stayed sober you might be able to help us get out of it," came back the reply from Coleman.

Dominic Cluskey gave a small grunt and grinned at the two of them. 'Civilians,' he thought and dismissed them both as beneath the contempt of a hardened fighter for freedom like himself.

The group on board HMS Harwich had split naturally into three after their arrival at the Faslane base. Flynn, O'Neill and Cluskey knew what they were involved in and accepted the situation without question. Sheila Boyd, Coleman and McCormack were useful dupes, no more, and would be used by the three Irishmen for whatever purpose they desired. They all knew it. Even those members of the crew still confined to the bridge of the warship recognised that the woman and the two unarmed men were likely to side with them and suffer the consequences of their own stupidity later on.

McCormack raised his glass yet again and as his lips touched the side of the glass the lights in the small room flickered once and died. McCormack, even through the beer, realised what had happened and sat rooted to the bench as the sounds within the ship began to change. Machinery, starved of power, began to run down in speed and stop. Ventilation fans fell silent, the air conditioning ceased to function, even the small refrigeration compressor in the beer cooler beside them ran down in speed with a clicking sound like a playing card in the spokes of a slowing bicycle wheel. A battery supplied emergency lantern lit up and broke the solid blackness of the room and McCormack moved himself to action.

"The fucking generator has gone off," he said to nobody in particular, "nobody has transferred any fuel to the ready use tanks all day, I'll bet it's sucked the tank dry."

McCormack rose from the bench and headed at speed towards the door. Cluskey got up to follow. Once in the main passageway McCormack turned and started to run towards the after screen door and access to the upper deck. He skipped through an open passageway door instinctively lifting his feet to avoid the raised metal doorframe whilst at the same time ducking his head to miss the top.

Years at sea had taught McCormack how to get around a warship quickly and safely. Cluskey didn't enjoy the same breadth of knowledge and in the battery lit gloom of the passageway he lifted his feet but launched himself straight into the metal frame supporting the hinges of the solid watertight door. The protruding metal rim of the frame, which mated with the rubber of the door seal, was at exactly forehead height as Cluskey made his dash to follow the engineer. He bounced off the metal like a rag doll and fell backward to lie flat on his back in the main passageway.

McCormack heard the impact and the yell of pain that followed. He grasped a passageway handrail and pulled himself to a stop. Cluskey was groaning softly and seemed unable to move. His head poured blood from an open gash across his brow and his eyes had glazed over as he slipped in and out of consciousness. The commotion had brought Coleman to the doorway of the senior rates Mess and McCormack stooped down, gathered up Cluskey's handgun and passed it to the startled man.

"Hide that now," he barked and come with me to the bridge.

Coleman obediently stashed the weapon in the Mess and re-emerged to follow McCormack up the bridge ladder and back into the natural light of the Faslane evening. He made his report to the Captain just as he would have done in years gone by, and despite the drink he summarised events clearly and correctly.

"I need to start the emergency generator and then transfer fuel to one of the ready use tanks for the main generators, start one of them, and then remake the electrical distribution system to restore essential supplies."

"How long, Chief?" Welborne asked, calmly.

This was the stuff of command.

This was what he enjoyed about commanding his own warship. It was often frustrating and even more often embarrassing. These problems always arose at the worst possible moments. Some captains would shout and scream.

Some captains would so unsettle their teams that responses were even slower; mistakes would be made. Not Welborne, he had very quickly learned to trust to the training and discipline of all his ship's company; even McCormack was worthy of that trust. McCormack told him half an hour. Jim sensed the calm from the ship's captain and it steadied his nerves. He knew what to do but even so, he had been away from this rush of adrenaline for a year and that had sapped his confidence.

O'Neill, Flynn and Boyd listened to the exchange between the two men and Flynn spoke first.

"Jim

Welborne cut off any response from McCormack and turned towards the Irishman.

"We do not have any communications whatsoever until the emergency generator is started and I endorse what Mr McCormack has just said completely."

Flynn looked at his watch conscious of the deadline he had offered the base. Forty minutes of the hour had passed already.

Jim McCormack looked from Welborne to Flynn.

"I could do it quicker if Yorky helped," said McCormack directly to Flynn and the man nodded his assent.

McCormack turned to descend the short bridge ladder when he remembered Cluskey lying half-conscious in the passageway below. He called out over his shoulder,

"Dom' has a head injury from banging into a door. Coleman will show you where he is."

191

Twenty Three

Alan South was agitated and it showed.

He had been in the middle of a most important meeting with senior Ministry of Defence civil servants who had just one day in Scotland to discuss far reaching budgetary changes for his command area. If he lost his battle today the consequences would be serious. Negotiations were, as ever, tender; a mutual exploration, teasing to see what could be agreed to cut jobs and save money.

The interruption could not have been more unwelcome. He hoped that his staff would succeed in keeping his visitors sufficiently happy to persuade them to stay on for a while longer. South had only the barest detail of what was going on. He listened to the Queens Harbour Master deliver a short brief on what he knew about the incident so far. A glance out of the windows of the Maritime Operations Centre situated deep within the Naval Base confirmed that a ship of the Sandown Class was anchored towards the northern end of the Gareloch.

The ship was close to the string of inflatable rubber floats making up the waterside barrier around the berths normally occupied by the Vanguard Class SSBNs and certainly not in an approved berth. South looked around at the faces of his hastily gathered team. Carolyn Smart as the Commander responsible for security issues was seated to his left. Colin Walker, the Duty Naval Base Officer stood next to Smart having hardly had time to take over his night shift before being summoned to the Operations Centre. Bill Campbell shuffled uneasily next to Walker trying to weigh up any possible involvement for the Ministry of Defence Police in what looked like a genuine terrorist incident. The final member of the small group was the Base Security Officer. He was a retired Royal Marine Major and he waited patiently for the Admiral to speak.

South addressed the group with a single question: "Is this genuine?" He looked first to Carolyn Smart for comment.

"Commander?"

"So far, we know only two things. First, Harwich is anchored in the wrong place. She asked for an alongside berth and was allocated one. The ship is not berthed alongside where she should be. Second, the voice on VHF claimed to be Sheila Boyd and we know that name. My judgement, this could be for real."

"Colin, anything to add?" asked the Admiral.

"Well Sir," he said, "As the commander has said, Boyd is well known to us. She is a major player in TP2000. She and Angela Young are the driving force behind their whole campaign and are the first two pledged signatories. Sheila is capable of enormous mischief and has been involved in some of the more serious attempts at incursion over the last few years. She is intelligent and articulate and capable of drumming up lots of support. All that said, her group is supposedly pledged to non violent direct action so if she and her mob have taken over a warship then she either has help from elsewhere, or her team have got considerably more radical in a very short time. My guess, Sir, it's genuine and she has backing from outside TP2000."

"Chief Inspector?"

"I'd go along with DNBO Sir, we haven't seen Sheila around here for a day or two so that may lend some credence to the claim that it is her. I can't just remember how many times she has been arrested but it most certainly runs into two figures. There is absolutely no doubt that she is committed to their cause."

South looked finally towards Major David Dawes and nodded.

"David, anything to add?"

"I'd say this marks a massive escalation in action but I agree with what I have just heard, this could be bad. We are all working on the assumption that whoever is behind this action is not getting any support from the ship but I think we should invite squadron staff to comment on whether they have any odd balls in the crew."

"Agreed," said South. The Admiral turned to the Queen's Harbour Master, "talk to MCM 3 George, see what he has to say on that one."

South thought for only a further second before directing his attention back towards his team.

"OK, on balance we believe the radio message to be genuine. We have less than half an hour before they want to speak to me again. We can't continue to control this incident from here, it is too busy and I want this kept close to our chests until we know what we are really facing. The Incident Command is with you, Colin, and I want you to operate as normal from Base Defence Headquarters. Carolyn, you will act as the contact between the ship and us. David, I want a full security profile of Boyd and her associates in BDHQ *a.s.a.p.* OK. Finally, Chief Inspector I want you to keep the rest of the base as tight as a drum whilst we sort this problem out, there are enough demonstrators out there to really stretch our resources as it is without the addition of a major single incident. Any questions, no, good. In that case, let's have another 'O' group in fifteen minutes. I want a brief on all the potential problems and some ideas for a solution when we meet."

Admiral South turned away from the group and strode purposefully towards the door. He covered three or four paces, stopped abruptly and turned back to his command team.

"Last thing for now," he said, "let's fly a little kite and see what happens if we move a CMU launch towards the ship. No closer than fifty metres and make sure the crew are kitted out properly and remain out of direct line of fire."

Bill Campbell nodded that he had understood the directive and he and Colin Walker left the Operations Centre bound for their own place of work across the base main thoroughfare, Maidstone Road.

***

The emergency generator diesel engine turned over under the influence of its starter motor and fired almost immediately the

194

initial roar settling quickly into a regular deep toned growl. Chief Petty Officer York was already making electrical switches and checking systems whilst McCormack had begun the process of refilling the small generator ready use fuel tanks from the ships larger tanks. He was manipulating fuel transfer valves and directing the pumped fuel to where he wanted it. They were making good progress. The two men were working quickly and efficiently together despite York's undisguised look of disapproval when he found the reason for the loss of power and the smell of beer on McCormack's breath. Both men knew that they would have to deal with that issue later but for now they were united. There was an engineering problem to deal with and nothing else mattered.

Flynn stood over the prone body of Dominic Cluskey and noted the seriousness of the open head wound and the flickering of the man's eyes as they rolled around in their sockets. Cluskey made an occasional groaning sound but didn't seem to respond to the voices around him. He certainly didn't look right and that about exhausted Flynn's medical expertise. If he had been looking at a gunshot wound things would be different, he knew only too well how to deal with that circumstance, and this was different.

"Who is your medical expert," said Flynn to Lieutenant Commander Welborne who stood at his side looking down at the face of the injured man.

"The Coxswain is the ship's medic but he is pretty well restricted to first aid. This man needs urgent hospital treatment or at the very least a qualified doctor."

"Get him."

Flynn demanded that the Coxswain be brought to the main passageway to examine the casualty. Once again the hatch leading to the lower Mess was opened up to allow a member of the ship's company to leave the dark and stuffy confinement below.

Pleased to be out of the claustrophobic and now hot and sweaty atmosphere of the lower mess deck the Coxswain was delighted to see that the reason for his summons was an injury to one of the Irishmen.

The Navy Petty Officer knelt by the injured Cluskey and looked him up and down. Something of a showman he recognised that he commanded an audience and that they were relying on him to pass an opinion on a topic where his knowledge may just exceed theirs. Flynn waited with almost an air of expectancy for the man to pronounce.

"Well," said the Coxswain, "in my opinion, he's still alive but he's only just conscious and he's got a hell of a cut on his head."

"I know that," said Flynn full of frustration, "can you sew up the cut and sort him out?"

The Petty Officer looked aghast and directed his reply to the Irishman.

"Look mate," came the reply, "the only thing I've ever sewn up, apart from a few homeward bounders in my socks, was a button on the outside of an orange when I did my first aid course. What a game that was," he continued, milking his audience, "all these hairy assed divers and muppets sticking these bloody great needles into a poor orange. Made a right mess I'll tell you. Juice everywhere. Now if you want a fucking great Burberry button on this bloke's forehead I'm your man. But, if you want him to live through it I suggest you get him ashore *tout* fucking *suite* OK." Despite the seriousness of the situation Welborne could hardly suppress a smile as he watched his Coxswain move back in the direction of the lower Mess deck having quite clearly dismissed the whole situation as having nothing more to do with him. Never one to shirk away from having the final, final word, the Petty Officer threw one last suggestion back at the dangerous man standing in the passageway of his ship.

"And, I'd get him in a Neil Robertson damn quick and up to the upper deck."

Welborne explained that a Neil Robertson stretcher was a contraption fabricated from canvas and strips of wood used to transfer injured sailors up and down hatches and through the tight confines of a warship. As if further explanation might be required the Captain opened a tall red locker in the passageway and showed the man what he was talking about.

"Do you want your man moved ashore?" asked Welborne.

"Put him in that stretcher and get him moved up top."

"I'll need some men."

"OK, bring a couple up from down there," said Flynn pointing back towards the space where the remainder of the crew was confined.

Welborne set about getting his Cox'n back to the scene of the injury and briefed him to get a couple of hands to achieve the task. Once again the lower Mess deck was opened and this time three more sailors tasted the fresher air of first the passageway and then the Faslane evening air.

**

Walker and Campbell stood side by side in the small Clyde Marine Unit Operations cell off the Base Defence Headquarters Control Room. The CMU Station Officer flicked a switch and spoke into a microphone.

"Control to CMU One"

The Cox'n of the police launch responded to the call and took the information from his control. The three members of the launch crew quickly donned their body armour made up of seventeen inter-woven layers of kevlar material and assisted each other to insert the half inch thick ceramic plates that offered additional protection to the chest and back. Weighed down by the heavy protective armour they took position in the bridge of the launch. The Cox'n took the engine controls with his crew manning binoculars and the radio.

"Close the ship at anchor to no more than fifty metres and observe," were the instructions passed to the launch and the boat gathered speed in a direct line towards the stern of HMS Harwich

**

McCormack and York completed their final checks of the port generator and York applied electrical load to the machine. Within seconds the familiar and comforting ship noises began again as ventilation and air conditioning was restarted and lights and other services like pumps to supply the firemain were restored. Harwich was back to a normal harbour condition within twenty minutes and both men were pleased with their efforts. In the privacy of the Ship Control Centre McCormack tried to explain to his old colleague and friend what had caused him to get dragged into the situation he found himself in. He genuinely believed he was needed to make some sort of documentary film and although in repeating the story it hardly became more credible York felt at least sympathy for the other man's plight. Jim McCormack told York about Cluskey's gun and suggested that he recover it from Daniel Coleman and get it down to the Officers in the lower mess deck.

***

"One man on the starboard bridge wing armed with a handgun," reported the CMU officer with the binoculars, "no sign of any other activity on the upper deck. Wait a second," he said, "there's a woman standing just inside the bridge, she's in civilian clothing so she isn't a sailor."

The message was passed back to CMU Control by radio and Colin Walker and Bill Campbell realised that they faced a genuine terrorist incursion to the restricted area of the base.

"Train that camera on the ship," Walker instructed the Guard Service operator seated at a console within the Clyde Marine Unit control room. "Perhaps the CCTV camera will give us some decent images of the people on the bridge."

Walker and Campbell were joined first by Carolyn Smart and next by the Admiral himself as they crowded around the Thermal Imaging system monitor in the small room. The operator adjusted his controls and the bridge of HMS Harwich came into sharp focus. Campbell leaned forward slightly, more for emphasis than because of a need to improve his view of the woman now clearly visible inside the bridge.

"Definitely Sheila Boyd," said the policeman, "we've arrested her so many times I couldn't fail to recognise her."

Walker once again addressed the console operator with instructions, "I'd like the pictures from this camera recorded on video and please set the other camera up to sweep the

Gareloch particularly in the area around the floating barrier and the north end of the base." The operator nodded his understanding and the group filed out of the small control room heading for the briefing room nearby.

"OK lady and gentlemen, we now confirm Boyd and at least one male accomplice, hopefully the TI system will give us some more information soon. What we now need is an immediate action plan to contain the problem and then a solution. Let's start with problems. Carolyn?"

"There are thirty odd sailors in Harwich, many of whom will be expected home tonight. We need to open up the Families Information Centre to handle inquiries, and we need a statement to give to all the families. If they hear about this on the television news the shit will certainly hit the fan. Next, I believe we should open up the Clyde Off Site Centre to handle the media. If we know one thing about Trident Ploughshares it is that they advertise all their capers to the press very quickly. I'm surprised DNBO's phone hasn't started ringing already."

"Agreed. Colin what have you got for us?" asked Alan South.

"We already have a Bandit situation given that the vessel is within the restricted area and intruders are onboard. I'd like to raise the base to Bandit stations and get the Royal Marines response force to their final denial positions along the finger jetty and 12 berth. Should any of these people on the ship intend to mount an incursion into the base we need to be ready for them, especially since they are armed. Problem with that, Sir, we will shut down the entire base and all movement will have to stop. I suggest we shut down fully and then relax all but Red area North and the Green area."

South turned to his Commander as if seeking confirmation and Carolyn Smart nodded.

"OK Colin," said the Admiral, "set it up."

"Chief Inspector Campbell how is the rest of the threat at the moment?"

"There has been a lot of activity at the peace camp in the last hour with vehicles moving up and down the A814 and visiting the other site at Peaton Glen Wood. My guess, they have a good idea of what is happening out there on the water and they are building up to something very shortly. I think we can expect trouble."

Alan South acknowledged a knock on the briefing room door and the Base Defence Control Room Sergeant nudged his way into the brief.

"Four canoes just entered the water on the southern foreshore and we have about ten demonstrators gathering at the North Gate."

David Dawes spoke for the first time, "That seems to confirm what the shift commander has said about them having some intelligence about the ship. They must know what is happening out there, it's been relatively quiet for the last 24 hours and this looks co-ordinated."

"Anything on the Int' front yet David?" South inquired of his Base Security Officer and the Royal Marine explained that he had recalled his staff and they were trawling through security reports and sightings to see if they could make a connection.

"That seems a reasonable flavour for the immediate problems and actions," said the Admiral, "now the exam question, what are we going to do about it."

Dawes answered first. "I think we should let them declare their hand at the radio call in a couple of minutes and then formulate strategy from there. However, I think we should contact DSF in London and see how quickly we can get an SBS company up here."

General agreement greeted the proposal to call Director Special Forces. Admiral South turned to Carolyn Smart and invited her to open the batting with DSF to gain tasking approval to deploy a company of the elite Special Boat Service at Royal Marines Poole on the south coast of England.

"Liaise with the MOC on that one Carolyn," said South, "I want them to take over that bit of the negotiation to leave you free to talk to Boyd."

The group broke up and Walker initiated the call to bandit stations within the Naval Base and once again the staccato *"dit, dit, dit"* of the alarm boomed out over the main broadcast system.

"Sir, you'd better see this," came the call from the Ministry of Defence Guard Service security man operating the controls of the thermal imaging cameras mounted high on the roof of the massive shiplift building at the other end of the base from the centre of security operations.

Walker and his police colleague moved to the operators shoulder and focussed on the small CCTV monitor. Walker spoke first.

"They have a casualty, that is a Neil Robertson stretcher being man-handled onto the upper deck."

The screen showed two men, obviously sailors from their blue working uniform, at either end of the laden stretcher edging gingerly to a space on the upper deck close to the guard-rails.

"CMU One to Control."

"Pass your message CMU One"

"Activity on the upper deck of the ship, looks like they are bringing someone out on a Navy stretcher, over."

"Can you make out any detail of the person, over."

"Hard to say, Control, the stretcher is wrapped around the person pretty tight but from the size I'd say it is a pretty big man."

Walker and Campbell headed away from Base Defence Headquarters and made for the Maritime Operations Centre. Slightly breathless after the sprint up three flights of stairs the two walked into the Op's Room just as the Ship to Shore VHF crackled into life.

"Admiral, this is Sheila Boyd can you hear me."

Sheila Boyd had taken on the look of a very frightened rabbit as Flynn stood at her side ready to stage-manage the proceedings.

She looked around the ship's bridge from face to face searching for comfort or sympathy and found just a flicker of something etched around the eyes of Jonathan Welborne.

Carolyn Smart looked towards the Operations Room's duty officer for confirmation of how to activate the VHF radio and pressed the transmit button.

"This is Commander Carolyn Smart, the Commander of

HMS Neptune, I am authorised to speak to you on behalf of the Admiral."

Twenty Four

The two women had slipped into an uneasy silence during the last hour.

Emma was wringing her hands together and checking her wristwatch every few seconds, her expression when she looked up at Laura Latimer was almost pleading her new friend to make things better for her and bring her husband safely through the front door. Laura was equally on edge but for very different reasons. She too was conscious of the time. What was happening out there, had Flynn managed to keep everything going safely, were Coleman, McCormack and Boyd behaving. It was nearly time for her to phone Flynn but she didn't want to overplay her hand and lose advantage.

"It's half past seven," said Emma, "He's never been this late, there must be a problem. He's got a mobile phone, I'm going to try ringing it."

Emma Courtney lifted her phone and punched in the numbers for her husband's mobile. She had never done this before. She knew how Nigel felt about his job and she recognised his ambition, his dreams of making it to a senior rank in the navy. The last thing she wanted was to become a whinging wife sitting at home agitating every time her man was a few minutes late. But this was different, or at least Emma thought it was. Emma listened.

"It's just that awful message telling you the phone is switched off," she told her companion and hung up the receiver. Emma had hardly replaced the telephone when the ring caught both women by surprise. Emma Courtney was first to respond. She flew out of her seat and snatched the receiver from its cradle almost breathless as she tried to give her number to the caller. Laura listened and watched the other woman's face intently.

"Yes, this is Mrs Courtney. Yes, my husband is an Officer in HMS Harwich."

Emma listened intently to the caller.

"What do you mean an incident? What sort of incident?"

Emma paled visibly and sat down heavily in her armchair. She listened for almost a further minute in complete silence struggling to comprehend the message being delivered to her. Finally her thoughts overtook her feeling of helplessness and she interrupted.

"Is this some sort of joke," she said to the caller, "are you trying to tell me that someone has highjacked my husband's warship? But it's a Royal Navy warship for God's sake, it's bristling with weapons, how can a bunch of peace protesters just capture a warship? Is Nigel all right? What do these people want? Yes, yes, I've got a pen."

Emma reached out for a pen from the coffee table and wrote down a telephone number.

"Yes, I have a list of numbers to call for the link wives organisation on board, yes, I'll call them now, as soon as I can. You will call me again if anything happens won't you?"

She replaced the telephone receiver and turned towards Laura Latimer. Her face a study in anxiety, fear and uncertainty etched in the tiny lines around her eyes.

"Emma, what has happened?"

"Some group of anti nuclear demonstrators called Trident Ploughmen, or something, have managed to get on board and are holding the crew hostage. That was a Chief Petty Officer on the line from HMS Neptune. He says there is nothing to worry about just yet, but would I pass the message on to my group of wives and give them this number so they can get any further news later. Apparently the ship didn't come alongside at Faslane they have anchored instead. I've got some phone numbers somewhere."

Emma busied herself, frantically searching through the drawer in her coffee table as if her life depended on finding her link wives phone numbers. She found the list of names and telephone numbers of the six Navy wives she was supposed to alert in the event of special news coming from the ship. She'd never had to call anyone before but Nigel had impressed upon her how important it was to keep this fast chain of communication available. Each of the Officer's wives had a similar list and she supposed that they would all be telephoning by now. Glad of something positive to do she started straight into her task.

With Emma completely distracted by her new task Laura had a few moments to think. Everything going to plan, she thought. How long will it take for the media to start reporting their coup. She turned on the woman's television set.

"Let's see if there is any news," she commented to Emma who was now gushing out the story of the ship hijack to the wife of one of her husband's colleagues.

Laura rose quietly and headed for the front door. It was the time she had agreed to contact Flynn out in the middle of the Gareloch onboard his ship, she couldn't wait any longer for news of what was happening.

***

"Commander, we have an injured man on the ship. He has a serious head wound and needs a doctor immediately," said Sheila Boyd, "before we discuss any of our demands I want this man taken off the ship by your police launch." Sheila Boyd looked towards Flynn who nodded his head in approval at the way she had handled the first encounter in the battle of words.

South and his team heard Boyd very clearly and were well aware that a casualty lay on the upper deck of HMS Harwich. Colin Walker looked questioningly towards the Admiral and waited for his approval. South nodded. The Duty Naval Base Officer picked up one of the many telephones in the Operations Centre and passed an order to the Clyde Marine Unit of the Ministry of Defence Police. Within seconds the powerful launch holding position just fifty metres away from HMS Harwich nosed its way forward toward the starboard side of the ship.

"Is the casualty a sailor?" asked Carolyn Smart across the radio network and she received the reply that he wasn't.

205

"I'll need his name for the hospital," she returned but it was obvious from the tone of Sheila Boyd's answer that she was following a direction from someone else. So the casualty is one of them and we are not to know his name thought Smart.

"We seem to have reduced the odds against us by one," she said to her Admiral and the remainder of the incident command team.

Flynn and O'Neill both raised their weapons and shepherded the bridge crew of HMS Harwich into the centre of the space, away from the starboard bridge wing door and the windows. Outside two sailors remained on the upper deck with the stretcher.

Padraig Flynn and Brendan O'Neill watched their every move.

The coxswain used the powerful engines of his launch to position himself alongside the warship and the sailors looking down on him from above each caught a rope to secure the vessel alongside the warship. With the launch bobbing up and down alongside HMS Harwich the upper deck party quickly loosened off the top most of the three plastic coated metal wire guard-rails and folded the wire back out of the path of the stretcher.

They lifted the Neil Robertson stretcher with Cluskey firmly secured in the wooden and canvas folds.

Feet first.

A drop of about six feet to the upper deck of the launch had to be negotiated. Two policemen came out onto the deck of the launch from the relative protection of the deck cabin. Weighed down by their protective body armour and uncertain about events unfolding within the warship alongside the Clyde Marine Unit officers tentatively reached up to grab the free end of the heavy stretcher. Cluskey swung clear of the guard wires of HMS Harwich suspended, finally, by a single rope attached to the top of the stretcher and held firm by the two naval men above. He was guided to the waiting hands of the police crew. As he bumped onto the foredeck of the launch the two policemen heard his grunt of pain. Cluskey had his eyes closed and an expression of sheer agony etched into his face. As Cluskey was laid flat on the deck of the launch the two securing ropes were cast off from above and the police coxswain powered up his engines to withdraw from his position at the side of HMS Harwich.

***

Lieutenant David Rodgers was the ship's First Lieutenant, the second in command, and was the obvious choice to be given the handgun collected by the Engineer Officer of HMS Harwich. Rodgers problem was how best to use this newly acquired asset. Sitting with the majority of his shipmates in the lower mess deck he had checked the magazine and found it to be full. He had eight bullets.

Since the comings and goings necessary to deal with Cluskey the hatch to their floating dungeon had been left open. The stretcher party appeared at the hatch and began to descend into the mess, facing away from the ladder in the way experienced sailors tended to manage passage from one deck to another. O'Neill followed them gun in hand. Rodgers gripped the automatic pistol and watched as first the shoes and then the legs of Brendan O'Neill came into view. Less familiar with shipboard life the Irishman held his gun in one hand whilst gripping the ladder handrail with the other. Rodgers felt he had a chance and raised the weapon to the double handed firing position he had been taught throughout his service firearms training.

"Drop the gun," he barked, "I will shoot to kill if I have to."

O'Neill put first one foot and then the other onto the tiled floor of the mess deck and quickly took in the new danger that faced him. Rodgers held a handgun at arms' length, his trigger finger extended across the trigger guard and facing forward. Just the training position the Army encouraged to prevent a negligent discharge of a weapon. In one fluid movement O'Neill swung his own weapon towards Rodgers and fired. The shot echoed in the confined space and was so loud that most of the sailors were stunned into complete stillness. For a second nothing moved until Rodgers, open-mouthed and with his face a mixture of shock and horror dropped first to his knees and then toppled forward onto his face. In the echoing silence that sucked away the sound of the explosion O'Neill walked calmly across the room and collected the handgun from where it lay. He moved towards the ladder.

"Fucking amateur," said the Irishmen, complete contempt in his voice, "lesson one, do it, and don't talk about it."

O'Neill climbed the wide ladder to the main passageway of HMS Harwich, unclipped the hatch to the lower mess deck and let it fall. As the hatch descended towards the closed position the sailors below heard his laughter and his final comment on his second killing that day.

"Fucking hopeless," was what drifted down to the shocked men below.

With equal contempt he kicked the hatch retaining clips back into place leaving the ship's crew confined in their small prison, unable to release themselves and unaware what may be happening in the space above.

***

The small group watched from the Maritime Operations Centre as the police launch withdrew from the ship and headed towards the north basin of the Naval Base. A white Royal Navy ambulance bearing a large red cross on its side waited at the pontoon to receive the casualty. As ever the medical staff would do their best regardless of who the patient might be. This time it would be easy, a Strathclyde police vehicle waited at the south gate to escort them to the Vale of Leven hospital some five or six miles away at Balloch. The civilian ambulance driver had completed the journey countless times but never with a blue light escort and certainly never with a criminal. He could hardly wait to tell his mates down at the pub when he finished his shift the following morning.

***

Boyd spoke into the radio microphone, "Commander, are you listening,"

"Listening," was the immediate reply.

"These are the demands from my group; this is what we want before we will release your ship and your men."

Flynn handed Sheila Boyd a hastily written note and the woman read through the short list before returning to the radio. "First of all," she said, "I want to be part of a press conference to discuss the illegal retention of nuclear weapons by the aggressive British Government. I want the Admiral and a senior government minister, preferably the Secretary of State for Defence to be there with me, and I want to make a statement to the television and the media without interference."

"Next," said Boyd, who had tried to warm to her theme, or at least to the sentiment of what she was demanding. "I want a guarantee, in writing, that no member of my group here will face criminal charges for this action on behalf of peace loving people the world over and in particular the Trident Ploughshares 2000 organisation."

For most of her adult life Sheila Boyd had pledged herself to a moment in time when she would be able to deliver such an ultimatum to the military establishment, to government. Now the moment had arrived. What should have been an overwhelming victory for her ideals felt hollow, almost surreal. It was as if her beliefs had taken a huge knock and now she was mouthing words without feelings.

"Finally, when those two demands are agreed and arranged I want a boat to take my group off the ship and deliver us to a point ashore of our choice."

Sheila released the transmit button on the radio microphone and let out a long breath to release her tension. She replaced the microphone in its bracket and her shoulders visibly slumped, the deed done. Her name was echoing across the airwaves; a conspirator in death. The bridge of HMS Harwich fell silent as those around her tried to take in what she had said.

Welborne was first to speak and he deliberately directed his words towards Boyd, even though Flynn was quite clearly calling the tune. "You do realise, I presume that the cold-blooded murder of two innocent people could never be ignored in the search for any deal for your release. Whatever

209

you may have started out as, you are now a group of terrorists. You gave up your right to be considered as anything else the moment you joined forces with these two men." Welborne turned his hand towards Flynn and O'Neill but kept his eyes fixed on the woman before him.

"Paddy," said O'Neill, "do we need to listen to this toffee nosed bastard any more, do we need any of this lot up here? Why don't we shove them down the hole with the others? We know how to work the radio and if we need anything else we can always bring them up one at a time."

"Yeah, good thinking Bren'," replied Flynn with an uncharacteristic grin, "sort it."

O'Neill smiled broadly and gestured with his weapon for the Royal Navy crew to move towards the bridge ladder and ultimately their incarceration with their colleagues in the cramped sailor's sleeping space one deck below. Welborne had little choice but to conform to the man's order and he led his Navigating Officer and helmsman off the bridge with a resigned shrug of his shoulders.

"Should have kept your mouth shut smart arse. The boot's on the other foot now." O'Neill pushed the ship's captain along the main passageway of the ship with the barrel of his gun and pointed at the ladder leading downwards.

***

Alan South sat at the head of the conference room table on the upper floor of Base Defence Headquarters and surveyed his team. He, Smart, Colin Walker, Bill Campbell and David Dawes had all listened to Sheila Boyd as she had made her demands.

"OK lady and gentlemen what has happened since we last spoke," said Admiral South. Carolyn Smart cleared her throat and replied first.

"SBS at Poole will have a company in the base in six hours," Carolyn said. "'C' company I think it is. They will discuss tactics on arrival but have asked for a Sea King helicopter to be on immediate stand-by on our helicopter pad from the time of their arrival. I presume, although David will be

210

better qualified to comment, they may be considering a *fast rope* descent on to the ship from the air."

Carolyn Smart looked up at David Dawes as if for confirmation and the man nodded in return before adding: "The press cell is all set up at the Off Site Centre and we have received enquiries from several national newspapers and all the major television companies. Someone in contact with the ship has obviously fed the media some advance information. Strathclyde Police Special Branch has been informed and they are sending someone down here to liaise and to attend these meetings from now on. Finally from me Sir, all the families have been informed that the ship has been taken over by anti nuclear demonstrators and they have been given an information telephone number on which to get any updates we are able to give."

South thanked Carolyn Smart and turned his attention to Major David Dawes the Base Security Officer.

"Certainly *fast roping* on to the ship is an option for SB' although I see the request for a helicopter as a fairly standard operating practice in these cases. Special Forces like to keep every option open. I would have thought a sub surface approach might be more likely, the group on board the ship would notice the arrival of a Sea King fairly easily and I think they may retain the advantage. We'd better crank up the Diving Group so that they are available to supply anything needed. If they are able to get here from Poole in less than six hours they won't be bringing too many of their fancy toys with them. I think we need to wait and see how they read the situation when they get here and then try to move heaven and earth to provide anything they may need. Mind you, when they are in place they don't generally give out much information so we may be kept in the dark until they strike. As for intelligence on this group, there isn't much so far. Sheila first. We know all about her of course, but she isn't pulling the strings this time. I think from what we have seen and heard the two men are the key to it all. The man we collected by launch was unconscious when he left for the Vale' so no clues there yet."

Bill Campbell addressed the Admiral. "I've got a wee bit update on the casualty. He is now in the Intensive Care Unit at the hospital and he hasn't come round yet. Strathclyde police have somebody up there to watch what happens. They tell me that the man had no identifying papers on him at all, no wallet, no credit cards, nothing; and that even the labels have been removed from his clothes. Whoever he is he is a professional."

"What about security in the base Chief Inspector, how are we holding up there?"

"Well, Sir, we are pretty stretched. In the last couple of hours we have made sixteen arrests at the north gate, four at south and two more on the water. The Peace Camp and the gathering at Peaton Glen wood seem to be throwing everyone they have got at us. We're coping, just about, but every time we make an arrest it takes two of my officers out of the front line whilst they sort out the formalities. I've called in every off-duty MDP officer I can so your overtime bill is going to be pretty awful this month."

"I think we can stand it provided we don't end up with two major incidents on our hands. What about you Colin, anything to add?"

"Yes Sir, the base is at bandit stations although we have only sealed off the area of the submarine berths and the northern, red area, surrounding it, as we discussed earlier. The Royal Marines are closed up on the submarine berths in their final denial positions, and all the ships and submarines in the base are closed down to their Operation Awkward states. We've got Royal Marines patrolling inside the floating barrier in their rigid raiding craft alongside the CMU team, and I consider the risk area of the base as tightly controlled as we can make it. We continue to record the pictures being offered by the CCTV camera mounted on the top of the shiplift and those images are being examined by the Base Security organisation. The Shift Commander and I have an open telephone link to Strathclyde Police and another to the Off Site centre."

"Thank you all," said Alan South, "I believe that brings us neatly up to date. The final topic for now must therefore be the demands made by Sheila Boyd. Perhaps I'd better start with how I view them."

Twenty Five

Flynn now felt confident.

With all the ship's crew safely contained below his feet in the sailor's mess deck he faced little or no threat. He realised for the first time how much Welborne had unsettled him. The officer came from a different world to Flynn, that much was sure. No doubt he had an upbringing of privilege and prosperity; a good school. He wouldn't have gone hungry, wouldn't have watched his parents destroy each other with poverty and the drink.

Flynn had.

He'd struggled as a child in the south of Ireland. Flynn had witnessed his father drink away every penny he could get and his mother fight a losing battle to put food on the table for him and his siblings. The political struggle was a natural progression for Flynn; it gave expression to his anger. From before his teenage years he was engrossed in the culture of revolution. It permeated every layer of the Ireland he grew up in.

If you were hungry, blame the British.

If there was no work for his father, it had to be the British at fault.

He could choose.

It had to be either the Catholic Church or the IRA. Flynn chose the latter and never looked back. He carried a dark anger to the depths of his soul. He had the intelligence and natural cunning to be of great value to the IRA, and later the offshoot of that organisation which became known as the Irish National Liberation Army. Welborne had caused Flynn to reflect. He had made him draw comparisons between their respective lives. Flynn recognised that his dislike of the man was tinged with an amount of envy. Envy for what might have been. He felt better now that the officer was removed, and was out of sight.

Flynn could now walk about his new territory without looking constantly over his shoulder. O'Neill was stationed on the bridge as a look out and in the fading summer light could still command an easy view of anything that made a move across the water towards them. He couldn't count on the woman, or McCormack or Coleman, but then he didn't really care about them anyway. Coleman and McCormack had moved back to the safety and security of the senior rates mess and when he pushed open the door the two of them were seated in silence, one trying to outdo the other with the hopelessness of their expression.

"Right Dan, see if you can find some food and knock up some sandwiches for the team. I'm starving. Some coffee too, while you're about it." Flynn addressed Coleman with something closer to a smile than either of the two men had seen so far in their brief acquaintance. He addressed McCormack next.

"Jim, I don't want another cock up with the lights. Go and have a real good check round and make sure all the machinery is working properly. I'm relying on you to keep us safe until we leave here. OK?"

The two men rose to their appointed task and Flynn headed for the after end of the ship and the fresh air of the Gareloch on a summer's evening.

"Before I forget, here's another one for you Jim," called Flynn, "I want one of those rubber boats from the upper deck all fuelled up and in the water. We might decide to go for a little spin around the base later on."

Jim McCormack showed Coleman where to find sandwich food in the ship's ready use refrigerator and indicated how to extract hot water from the boiler for coffee. With Daniel Coleman set to work safely McCormack headed for the steering gear compartment and the prospect of a set of Engineer's rounds of the ship, his first since his redundancy from the Royal Navy what seemed like years ago.

Sheila Boyd and Brendan O'Neill were left alone on the bridge looking out at the lights of the naval base. She had dreamed, countless times, of getting this close to the heart of her enemy. She was barely a hundred yards away from the low black silhouette of a Vanguard Class Trident missile submarine and if she could have elected to be transported anywhere in the world at that moment, she could only think of her husband John at home in his parish, their parish. For Sheila this was definitely the crossroads of her life. She knew that if she survived this experience her days as a demonstrator for peace were over.

O'Neill couldn't and didn't attempt to rationalise his thoughts. He was incapable of introspection. His eyes scanned the waterline, backwards and forwards, left to right, looking for signs of danger. If he allowed himself the pleasure of distraction he cursed his luck that the only woman on the ship was old enough to be his mother.

Coleman appeared at the bridge ladder carrying a metal tray laden with sandwiches, all neatly cut across from corner to corner. He deposited his load on the chart table and returned to the galley for the metal pot full of coffee and the sugar, milk and mugs. Flynn entered the bridge from the upper deck and set into the food with relish. The other three followed suit and the pile of sandwiches was quickly whittled away to just a couple remaining.

"Leave them for Jim," Flynn ordered and the three men and one woman turned their attention towards the coffee pot.

"What about food for the sailors?" asked Boyd, immediately recognising that she had just considered the personal welfare of a group of people for whom she had held nothing but distaste for many years.

"Fuck 'em," Flynn replied and the sailors were soon forgotten.

McCormack appeared at the bridge ladder wiping his hands on the sides of his overalls as he moved onto the bridge. It would have been unforgivable to leave oily traces of his presence on the bridge of his own ship HMS Cromer, and he would never consider such carelessness here or anywhere else.

"That should keep us for a few hours," he said to no one in particular. "Good job I had a check round, the oil level in one of the generators was low."

Flynn indicated the remaining food on the tray and Jim McCormack picked up a sandwich between thumb and first finger and took a large bite. Even the old habits come rushing back he thought to himself as he tried to minimise the amount of engine room oil and grease he deposited on his food.

McCormack and Coleman cleared away the makeshift meal and went off together to the galley to get rid of the debris. McCormack checked the ship's main passageway in both directions and was confident that Flynn and O'Neill had remained on the bridge. He pulled the galley door closed and with a finger raised across his lips he signed Coleman to silence.

"I've found something," he whispered. "I think Flynn has placed some explosive devices around the ship." As if by way of proof McCormack extended his right hand upwards to his nose and began to sniff his fingers.

"I think it must be semtex," said McCormack, "whatever it is it's all covered in Vaseline and I think that's what you use to make it pliable."

McCormack whispered out the rest of his fears. "It's only a small piece so I don't think it's meant to blow us sky high. I think it's much more likely to be intended to blow a hole in the ship's side and sink us. There's a kind of fuse or detonator stuck in it and I'm not sure whether it needs to be set off locally or from a distance."

"What have you done with it," asked Coleman.

"Well, nothing," came the reply, "if I disturb it now he is going to know about it and then where will I be, he'll know it was me."

The two men moved apart.

"Come to think of it," said McCormack, "I remember Flynn had a little bag when I showed him around so he must have placed the stuff just after we left Oban this morning."

"How many did you find?" asked Coleman, finally beginning to think about this new danger they were facing.

"One," was the reply.

"There are bound to be others wouldn't you think?"

"I suppose so," said McCormack, "if he only intends to use them to sink the ship then any more are going to be under the waterline or close to it."

"You are going to have to find any others or else these maniacs are going to sink this ship with all the crew stuck down that hole."

McCormack allowed the gravity of Coleman's thoughts to sink in. He agreed that he was surely the only one who would be able to identify any other bombs placed near the hull of the ship.

"He's asked me to get one of the ships boats ready for sea as well," said McCormack, "he was talking about going for a spin around the base. I'm going to need your help with the boat OK?"

"Sure," said Coleman, "I'd be glad of something to do to keep my mind off what may happen next. Let's get back to the bridge before he starts to think about us."

The two conspirators had formed a bond of secrecy between each other and set off to rejoin Flynn, O'Neill and Boyd.

Twenty Six

"Warship Harwich, warship Harwich, do you read me?" The VHF radio spluttered out its message and gained the attention of the four men and one woman holding Her Majesty's Ship Harwich to ransom. Flynn signalled that the woman should respond.

"Yes Commander," said Sheila Boyd into the microphone.

"I have been instructed to tell you that Flag Officer Scotland, Northern England and Northern Ireland has studied your three demands and needs more time to discuss them with the Ministry of Defence."

"How much more time?"

"Well, it is nine o'clock in the evening now and I don't think we will be able to reach the Minister of State until tomorrow morning, so another twelve hours at least."

Sheila Boyd looked across the bridge towards Flynn. The Irishman shook his head from side to side.

"Not acceptable," said Boyd.

"Perhaps you could release some of the ship's company just so that we know they are in good health," responded Carolyn Smart, "a gesture of good faith."

It was important that she continue the dialogue, try to develop some sort of rapport with the woman at the other end of the radio transmission. She tried again.

"Do you have enough food and provisions for everyone on board, I could arrange to send any supplies out to you by boat if you like."

"We have enough of everything thank you," replied Boyd.

"Look Mrs Boyd, you have the ship, why not lessen the risk of an incident and let the crew come ashore. I will guarantee that nothing will be done to endanger your position whilst we get them off the ship."

Sheila turned to Flynn.

"Why don't we let some of them go, what harm can it do now?" she inquired, more from hope that expectation. Flynn could hardly dignify the question with a response but O'Neill, as usual had enough words for the both men.

"Perhaps you'd like to go yourself. Do you want those sailors down there helping to identify all of us, don't be so stupid."

Boyd managed a weak laugh. "They seem to know who I am well enough don't they, it's only you two that are a mystery."

"That's the way it stays," said Flynn and the short exchange, almost the first signs of resistance from Sheila Boyd, was over.

"Tell them I want an answer by midnight at the latest." Flynn said to the woman and she once again pressed the button on the microphone to transmit.

"We would like an answer by midnight."

"I have tried to explain that will not be possible, we simply cannot contact people that quickly. Please Sheila, we need some more leeway here. Above all, we need to know that everyone is safe and well. We've already removed one casualty with serious head wounds and I'm sure you do not wish to see any more. After all, your group are pledged to non violent direct action and we are most anxious to resolve this situation without any accidents on both sides."

Flynn shook his head.

"Just comply with our demands, Commander, and everything will be just fine."

Padraig Flynn reached out and took the microphone gently out of the woman's hand and replaced it in its stowage on the front of the radio transmitter. The discussion was closed. He would make them wait a further hour before speaking again. Sheila knew that things were far from fine; she could hardly imagine how things could get any worse. Two people had died in this ship already and that didn't include Dominic Cluskey who had been taken off by the waterborne police. As the commander had said, he looked close to death. Sheila had only seen him secured in the stretcher but as far as she could judge he was in a bad way; maybe the list had now reached three.

***

A phone rang in the operations room and after a brief conversation was passed to Colin Walker. Walker listened for a few seconds.

"We may have identified one of our terrorists," he said, "may I suggest we go over to BDHQ for a few minutes.

The command team crossed Maidstone Road and headed for the small conference room that was quickly becoming the planning and briefing heart of the incident. David Dawes and a Royal Marine sergeant were already waiting. Dawes waited until the Admiral was seated before pushing the remote controller of a video recorder. Footage obviously taken from the CCTV camera on the shiplift lit up the television screen.

"This video was taken less than half an hour ago," said Dawes, "as you can see there are five people inside the bridge of the ship and they appear to be eating sandwiches. For those of you who may not know him, may I introduce Sgt Crawley of the Landing Craft detachment. S'arnt Crawley."

Crawley took the video controller from the Major and watched the footage roll. He pointed the little black box at the video recorder and pressed the button to freeze the frame currently on view. Although a little fuzzy at the edges the image clearly showed four men and one woman all captured looking towards the distant camera lens.

Crawley spoke. "A couple of weeks ago I was in the Imperial Hotel in Helensburgh having a drink with Corporal Ward and two Marines. Cpl Ward was in Northern Ireland on duty last year at Lough Neagh. He recognised one of the men in the bar."

Crawley picked up a pointer and touched the tip to the television screen under one of the men.

"This man is Brendan O'Neill. He is an LVF enforcer. He is a dangerous thug who wouldn't think twice about knee capping his granny. He has a long record of violent offences and is an active member of his particular para-military group."

Sgt Crawley moved the pointer tip to touch another of the men on screen.

"This man was with him," he said.

"Do you or Cpl Ward know this man?" asked the Admiral.

"No Sir, we don't. But the night we saw them there were three people in the group, the other one was a woman."

"Could it have been this woman here," said Colin Walker indicating the screen once again.

Crawley laughed, "not a hope Sir."

"Why not Sgt?" said Alan South.

"Beg your pardon Sir," said the Royal Marine, "she was a real stunner and this one is a bit of a dog. Also, she is a lot older than the other woman."

"Do you mean the woman you saw in the Imperial was older than this woman on the video," asked the Admiral.

"Good lord no, Sir, the other way around. I'd put the woman in the pub at about thirty-ish, tall too. We gave a full description of her to the security office the next day. No, this one here on the video is an old wrinkly by comparison."

"Thank you Sgt Crawley, that seems like pretty indisputable evidence against Mrs Boyd don't you think Commander?"

Carolyn Smart stood almost as tall as the sturdy Royal Marine and with a wide smile looked him in the eye, "you could certainly dent a girl's self confidence, Sergeant. I'm glad we are on the same side here."

The Admiral thanked his base Security Officer and the Sergeant and demanded that the new information be passed to all agencies that needed to know about their small break through. Dawes assured him that the information process was already underway.

***

The radio pager clipped into the belt of Colin Walker's trousers began to vibrate and then sound its trill warning. Walker pressed the button to mute the tone and read the message on the small display. "Ring COSC," was his electronic instruction as the Duty Naval Base Officer headed upstairs towards his office and the telephone. Walker dialled the number for the

Clyde Off Site Centre, now home to the organisation charged with dealing with the media and announced himself. He listened in silence and acknowledged the information before heading back to try to catch Admiral Alan South.

"Admiral, Sir," Walker called, as he hurried to reach the man before he had crossed the road back to the operations complex. "We now have a television news crew down at COSC and they are demanding an official statement about what is going on. We have managed to avoid featuring on the six o'clock news but I don't think we will be as lucky with the later bulletins."

South moaned loudly and nodded at Walker.

"It was bound to happen sooner or later, Colin. Keep it tight down here and make sure I get any and all updates as soon as you are able. I suspect from now onwards I am going to be stuck down at the COSC."

Admiral Alan South left the building and summoned up his official car for the short trip along the A814 and the waiting glare of the cameras.

***

Sheila Boyd and Padraig Flynn were alone on the bridge of HMS Harwich. McCormack and Coleman had just left through the port bridge door with O'Neill at their heels. They were headed aft, along the upper deck to start the small crane needed to lower one of the ship's two rigid inflatable boats to the waterline. Sheila made an attempt to engage Flynn in conversation.

"Why are you doing this?" she asked. "You are not the slightest interested in nuclear disarmament are you? Is it money you are after, do you expect someone to pay a ransom? I know that you have used me, and Coleman and McCormack, we are just tools in whatever plan you have in mind. Isn't it about time to let us and the crew go before they launch some sort of counter attack against you?"

Flynn said nothing. He could have been deaf for all she knew he didn't even acknowledge that she had spoken. She had never encountered a more taciturn man in her life. In fact she had never encountered a more frightening man either. He was cold to the core. Where O'Neill had shown himself to be hot tempered, this man was so alert and calculating he made her shiver. She felt in the depths of despair. A machine started and Flynn turned to follow the sound. McCormack was directing the lifting of the ship's boat and telling his assistant what he should do. Flynn watched the spectacle and soon the mini crane swung on its hydraulic arc and held the rubber boat high above the upper deck guardrail. A flick of the controls by McCormack and the boat began its descent to the Gareloch. Coleman paid out the head rope carefully just as he had been instructed and edged forward to watch as it approached the water. Flynn moved to the after bridge window and leaned forward, his face pressed against the toughened glass.

"I can see that you are well organised and disciplined," she tried again, "if your mate hadn't been here we wouldn't be in half as much trouble and two people would still be alive. Can't you see that Brendan is a psychopath who is going to kill again? Surely you don't welcome more death?"

This time Flynn was stirred enough to reply, "He's not my mate," he said, "and why should I care about the lives of a few British servicemen, they've been trying to wipe me out for years."

Boyd shook her head in despair and disbelief, the inadequate conversation over with before it had a chance to get started.

She picked up a pair of binoculars from the stowage beside the Captain's chair and idly focussed on the shoreline inside the naval base. She panned along the dockside cranes and buildings and scanned the upper deck of the other ships. This place, this naval base, had played such a prominent part in her life for so many years. It seemed she had been campaigning forever.

She knew, at last, she was tired of it all. Somehow a sense of futility wrapped her completely, tightly, like a thick blanket. She wanted to go home. Her mind was still in turmoil. There had been two deaths already. No she realised, they weren't just deaths, they were murders. Two innocent people had been callously and brutally executed. For what, what was the reason behind it all? These Irishmen hadn't even made any serious demands, they seemed happy just to press her agenda.

What was still to come?

Sheila stared at the back of Flynn's head as he peered out of the window. What is going on in the minds of these two men, these two monsters who hold life to be of such little value. Maybe I could do something, she thought, maybe I could help to bring this sorry disaster to an end. Perhaps even now I could make a small difference. She moved slowly across the bridge towards Flynn and swung the binoculars.

***

Alan South dropped his briefing notes onto the table in front of him and with an inaudible sigh sat down.

He had just delivered his first ever press brief.

It didn't matter that he had done the specialist course teaching him how to deal with the media. All senior Royal Navy officers were required to undertake this type of training, especially if their appointments might bring them into contact with the press and television. It didn't count that he had faced it all in the classroom. The presence of the television camera was most disconcerting. A disembodied eye staring at him, seeing everything he did and catching even the inflection in his voice, not just for the instant but for eternity. Recorded and held in the libraries of two television companies to be trotted out anytime they needed his picture in the future. At least the worst was now over. He had described in outline that a small group of demonstrators had managed to board a naval vessel and were holding the crew.

He had accurately stated their demands.

South knew that the only way to handle the press was to tell them the truth and he intended to do so. He had declared himself willing to answer any questions and had handled that part of the press conference well. There hadn't been many questions from the floor. He had been invited to confirm the name of the ship and had done so. The television reporter wanted to know where the uninvited boarding had taken place and South had agreed it was Oban. There were questions about the group of demonstrators but most of the gathered media representatives seemed well briefed on Trident Ploughshares 2000 and so they were easy to field.

The proceedings were going better than he had hoped. The Admiral had described Sheila Boyd as the spokesperson but had guarded himself against claiming she was the leader. If the press drew that conclusion, so be it. South knew from his daily briefings that the name of Sheila Boyd was well known, certainly to the journalists who regularly reported on events and happenings at his naval base. He had kept the name of Brendan O'Neill to himself, although he had been willing to divulge it if necessary. South looked at his watch and stood up.

"Ladies and Gentlemen, I thank you for your attendance and I hope to be able to give you further news as it occurs. May I assure you that the incident is completely contained and there is absolutely no risk to the submarines or any other vessel within the base. For reasons of security I must insist that press crews do not venture out onto the water and avoid the perimeter fences of the base. As you will be aware we are currently in the middle of a period of considerable activity from the Trident Ploughshares 2000 group both in HMS Harwich and ashore and I would hope not to make things more difficult. Thank you"

South gathered his papers and turned to move away from the table.

"Admiral."

He turned to identify the speaker and made eye contact with the reporter nearest to one of the television cameras. A tiny green light illuminated on the top of the camera and South knew he was being recorded again.

"Would you like to offer any more details concerning the body of a naval petty officer washed ashore just south of Oban this afternoon. We understand that he was dressed in blue overalls, complete with badges of rank and that he had a fatal gunshot wound to the chest. Would you like to confirm that the man was from HMS Harwich and that his death is in some way connected to this incident?"

South paled visibly and turned back towards the gathered press.

***

"Emma, I don't know how to tell you this but I really do have to leave soon."

Laura Latimer held Emma Courtney's hand loosely in her own and prepared herself for an emotional scene. Emma was surprisingly calm. She had now spoken to the six wives on her list and that action seemed to stiffen her resolve, to give her more courage. She had encountered a variety of responses from the other women that ranged from near hysteria to complete calm. Emma was better for the experience. It was as if these other wives in some way looked towards Emma to give them strength. She hadn't disappointed them. Strangely, it seemed to her afterward, she had played the part of the officer's wife. Two of the women had already phoned back and on both occasions it was Emma who was telling them not to worry, that it would all work out in the end. Just as she had tried to suck strength from Laura she had now been called upon to offer it to someone else.

She understood that her new friend had changed all her own plans to be with her and she knew that sooner or later she would have to go. Perhaps it was for the best. Yes, she could persuade herself that it was better to wait for her husband alone. She would busy herself getting the flat ready for his return. Cleaning and tidying. It would be all right after all. He would be home any minute. Emma nodded her understanding and Laura gave the woman a hug.

***

Flynn caught the reflection of Sheila's approach in the glass of the window and spun around. The heavy binoculars glanced his shoulder as his clenched fist struck out at the woman's head. A crunching blow hit her full in the face and blood spurted in all directions from a nose that would forever afterwards be out of shape.

227

She fell to the deck, pole axed.

He grasped the sobbing woman by the collar of her jacket and hauled her roughly to her feet. Blood poured between her fingers and soaked her clothing. She had never seen so much. Her eyes were filled with tears and her head throbbed with pain. She could hardly see clearly and had no strength to resist as Flynn dragged her across the bridge and down the ladder to the passageway below. Boyd fell the few steps to the tiled and polished deck and watched as she left a red trail in her wake. She grasped her nose to staunch the flow.

The pain was unbearable.

Flynn kicked the clips away from the hatch and swung it back into its retaining bracket. He uttered just one word and she descended into the mess deck with the ship's crew. Sheila Boyd looked through misted eyes at the assembled group. She had been frightened before but now as thirty pairs of eyes stared at her she knew they wanted to laugh at her misfortune, to hurt her for her part in what was happening to all of them.

She took in the sight of what could only be the body of the officer shot by O'Neill, the body filling one of the green vinyl covers the sailors used to stow away their bedding each day. Now a makeshift body bag it lay ominously in the small space. Daniel in the lion's den, she thought, each of the sailors waiting to pull her limb from limb in their uncontrolled frenzy of revenge.

Welborne crossed the floor and put an arm around her shoulders. A young sailor pulled a white towel from the inside door of a metal clothes locker and handed it to her. Another man shuffled along on his bunk to make room. Welborne escorted her to the space on a bunk and sat her down. Sheila could hardly believe the kindness she was experiencing and burst loudly into tears for the first time in her adult life

***

"So who's going to speak for us now she is down the hole?" O'Neill demanded in a strident tone.

Flynn looked at his countryman.

The two of them had been thrown together. They were an accident of the lull in Northern Ireland. If it were not for that little blip in history the two would be hunting each other down, one from the nationalist community and the other from the loyalist's. If they had any common ground at all it was their hatred of the British establishment and that loose idealism had kept them together so far. Flynn held his compatriot in as little esteem as he did the remainder of the group; he was just a tool to be used for his purpose. The bridge radio interrupted Flynn's response.

"Warship Harwich, come in please Mrs Boyd."

The rich round tones of the voice of Commander Carolyn Smart filled the bridge of the warship. O'Neill, McCormack and Coleman looked at Flynn the question formed on the lips of each of them. The radio crackled into life and once again the female voice intruded into their space.

"Perhaps, if Sheila Boyd is not available at the moment I could speak to Brendan O'Neill instead?"

Flynn could hardly contain his smile as he grasped the microphone from its stowage and extended the flexible cable towards O'Neill.

Brendan O'Neill looked at once puzzled and intrigued, how had they got to him. He wasn't really known outside Belfast and even then only by the RUC and the army. O'Neill didn't think he'd ever met anyone serving in the navy until that day.

"Looks like it might as well be you, Bren," said Flynn. "See what she wants."

O'Neill barked into the microphone and the rasping tone produced instant discord in the Maritime Operations Centre.

"Have you got an answer for us yet? He said, "Midnight, or we start shooting people." O'Neill replaced the microphone and grinned from ear to ear. This was more like it he thought. Now he could extend his brand of terror to a wider audience. Now he had some measure of control. He would be the spokesman from now on; he would make them dance to a different tune.

A soft ringing sounded on the bridge, growing louder as Flynn pulled his mobile phone from the inside pocket of his jacket. He went outside into the summer evening air and pressed the button to talk. The other three watched. Flynn made the occasional sound and finished his call with an "OK." and switched off.

"Right Bren'," Flynn announced, "Jim and I are going ashore in the boat to collect the woman. If anyone tries to interfere with our boat, deal with it. Line one of the sailors up if necessary, just make sure we can get in and back to the other side of the water."

O'Neill puffed himself up to his full height and stood aside as Flynn and McCormack left the bridge bound for the rigid inflatable boat. The rubber boat was swinging gently by the side of the ship tied by a rope to a cleat on the deck. McCormack pushed a jumping ladder over the side and towards the open boat. Secured at the deck edge the rope ladder with its wooden treads lay flat against the side of the ship, its end reaching down into the boat. The two men climbed down easily.

Jim boarded first and steadied the boat for Flynn as he got in. McCormack pressed the start button and the sixty horse power outboard engine burst into instant life. Flynn loosened the rope from the cleat in the bows and allowed it to fall back against the ship. They were free. With just an arm raised by Flynn to indicate direction McCormack turned the boat and opened the throttle to full ahead.

The boat gathered speed and planed across the smooth surface of the Gareloch towards the western side. Speed and surprise were imperative to Flynn and he saw with satisfaction that they were soon well clear of the warship and that the Clyde Marine Unit launch was still unsighted on the other side of HMS Harwich.

***

"Look, I don't know what is going on out there on the ship," said Colin Walker, "but one thing I do know is that we can't just sit here until the SBS turn up tomorrow like the US cavalry. We need to take some positive action."

"Trouble is," responded the Commander, "we are a defence organisation. We have orders up the *ying yang* for dealing with

230

any situation where the opposition brings the problem to us, but this is the complete reverse. I'm open to suggestions."

The naval base command team discussed the apparent impotency of their position and bemoaned their lack of viable options.

"How about a marksman," offered Walker, "do we have any weaponry in the base to allow an accurate shot at them when they are out in the open on the upper deck?"

Walker looked towards David Dawes for an answer. The retired Royal Marines Major shook his head. "I wouldn't want to undertake a shot like that with an SA80 rifle at even this range; if you miss it could launch a bloodbath on the ship."

"Well how about using the Landing Craft Marines for an assault from one of their boats. That's how we conduct boarding operations off Ireland after all. I know the situation is a bit different but the principle must be the same."

Dawes answered Walker's suggestion again: "There is one marked difference here, Colin. When we board a vessel at sea we have the back-up of a fully armed warship sailing alongside. Even the most determined of people will see their position differently with a heavy calibre naval gun pointing at them."

"What if we try a covert approach then? Boarding by stealth. It's pretty well dark now, could we get a couple of boats out there and alongside. Set up a diversion using the police, anything must be better that waiting for them to give themselves up. Or worse still, start dumping dead bodies over the side. You heard what O'Neill said on the radio, he sounds like a real head case to me and that is what the intelligence reports seem to point to."

Walker's phone rang and broke up the general discussion about tactics.

"Duty Naval Base Officer," he responded. Walker listened attentively and then turned to his colleagues. "We have more video footage to look at, down in the control room."

Carolyn Smart, Walker and Dawes moved to the lower floor of Base Defence Headquarters and collected Bill Campbell, the police shift commander from his office.

"Better have a look at this, Bill, some sort of development on the ship."

The three men and one woman joined the MGS security man in the briefing room. He was standing nervously holding a videocassette not sure of whether his intrusion would be welcome.

The civilian security officer addressed himself to Walker.

"Now it's got dark, Sir, I thought I'd see whether we would get any decent results recording the thermal imaging camera pictures. I'm not all that sure what I have here," he said, waving the cassette in front of himself, "but it looks like one of these guys on the bridge of the ship hitting one of the others."

"Let's have a look shall we," said Walker rescuing the tape and sliding it into the video player in the briefing room. Images in shades of black and white lit up the television screen.

The brightest elements of the picture represented the areas where the thermal signature was at its strongest, where the object in the field of vision was warmest. The structure of the ship was a uniform grey in colour, the water of the Gareloch almost black. Pinpointed in the centre of the screen were the outline shapes of two people.

Precise location was difficult from the image but it was clearly the bridge of the ship and the people were inside the structure. Movements were jerky to watch, as if the trail of body heat moved more slowly than the body itself. The white shapes of the two people appeared to be spreading sideways as they moved around inside the bridge.

"Here's the bit, coming now, Sir," said the guard.

All eyes in the group concentrated on the two white shapes. One shape appeared to move rapidly, a flash of white light, from one area of the bridge and towards the other white shape. The two merged briefly and then the moving shape fell back.

"You're right," said Walker to the guard, "that body is now lying down, he has been hit, or maybe shot."

The others agreed.

Carolyn Smart was the next to speak, "I wonder if this has anything to do with O'Neill coming on the radio. I thought it might just have been a reaction to my using his name, but maybe, just maybe Sheila is the one to have fallen."

***

"Wait here, keep the engine idling," Flynn whispered to McCormack as he slid himself onto the rickety wooden jetty protruding from the western shore of the Gareloch. McCormack threw up the bow rope and Flynn looped it securely over an old bollard. Flynn sprinted silently to the nearby road and confirmed the presence of a car. She had made it. They exchanged a few words before Flynn retraced his steps to the boat.

"Where is she?" McCormack asked as the dark shape appeared beside him.

"She'll be two minutes," came the reply, "come on up and stretch your legs."

Jim McCormack did as he was instructed and was pleased to step back onto dry land even if it was represented by a pretty dubious wooded structure sticking out over the water. Flynn helped the man up. They stood for a second in silence looking back towards the lights of HMS Harwich swinging gently at anchor. In the far distance on the other side of the Gareloch the lights of a small town, which were the naval base. McCormack moved to the edge of the jetty to check the boat and Flynn followed behind. Flynn was an expert in single-handed combat. When he and Leila Latif had first met in Syria, years ago, he was the star pupil in the classes they both undertook. She was waiting on the roadway in a car. She was now Laura Latimer. Flynn reached forward with both hands and grabbed the man's neck. One hand and arm held his head rigid for a split second until the other applied the vicious, powerful twist that snapped his neck like a twig. McCormack sagged silently to the jetty as Flynn slackened his grip. He was dead, a lifeless rag.

Laura Latimer ran silently down the short jetty to join Flynn. Between the two of them they bundled the limp body of Jim McCormack back to the edge of the wooden structure just close to the boat.

"Help me lift him back in," said Laura, indicating that she wanted Flynn to take McCormack's arms and throw the limp body into the boat. In the gathering darkness of the summer evening they allowed the body to slump into the bottom of the boat.

"See if you can tidy him up Paddy," she said, "see if you can prop him up to make it seem like he is alive."

Flynn dropped soundlessly into the small rubber boat and hauled the lifeless shape into a sitting position. McCormack's head lolled forward, almost to his chest. He grabbed the small paddle from the boat and slid it roughly down the man's back inside the neck of the blue cotton overalls McCormack had been wearing since they left Oban that morning. A short length of twine tied the head to the wooden paddle and the boat driver once again took on a lifelike posture.

"See if you can get his hand on the engine throttle," Laura whispered, "it would be good to send him back towards the ship."

Flynn once again set about the task. He manipulated the dead limbs of the man he had so brutally murdered as if he were a puppet or a mannequin in a shop display.

Padraig Flynn looked up at his accomplice standing just above him on the jetty.

"Have you got the controller," asked Flynn, and the woman nodded her head in confirmation. She ran back into the darkness towards the road and within a minute had collected a remote control device from the car. Laura passed it down to her associate still in the boat. Padraig Flynn looked at the black box he held in his hands. This was the reason for his trip back to Ireland some weeks earlier. This is what had made Cluskey's presence in the group necessary. He held a rectangular black box about the size of a large box of chocolates. The top of the box was fitted with a single switch next to a small light. Below the isolating switch were two levers. Flynn flicked the switch to the ON position and the light burned red. He looked up at Laura.

"Can I have the first one?"

Laura Latimer laughed quietly. "Go ahead Paddy," she said. "You've certainly earned it."

234

Flynn moved the first of the two levers to the left. The two looked out across the Gareloch towards HMS Harwich and were rewarded with a small muffled explosion close to the water line on the side of the ship facing them.

"Well done Paddy, did you manage to get all four?" she enquired.

"Yes," came back the reply and Laura stretched out her hand to reclaim the small but very powerful radio control transmitter from Flynn.

"Shall we hit the others now?" he asked.

Laura Latimer smiled back and replied, "No, let them panic for a while."

His work in the boat completed, Padraig Flynn grabbed the wooden jetty and prepared to haul himself up to join the woman. A strong and fit man he pulled up with both arms and was fully head and shoulders above the deck level when she spoke.

"Sorry Paddy, it has to be."

Laura took a careful aim and fired a silenced round. Phut, the weapon kicked in her hand. The shot penetrated the Irishman's skull through his left eye socket and exited at the back of his neck. As Flynn fell backward towards the rubber boat Laura fired again. She was an excellent marksman and at short range she wouldn't need to check the accuracy of her second shot. Phut. Clear into the heart.

She untied the bow rope, guided the bow of the boat towards open water as best she could and let it drift away. The local police would spot the boat soon enough but by then she would be miles away.

Twenty Seven

The muffled bang on the western shore of the loch was an ear splitting roar on the bridge of HMS Harwich and O'Neill darted around the bridge looking for answers. Coleman knew exactly what had happened.

"He has double crossed you," said Coleman, "Jim found a bomb on the ship when he was looking around at his machinery. He's trying to kill us all."

O'Neill struggled to take in what he was being told. Could it be true he thought; could Paddy have just dumped him. He was coming back to the ship with the woman, with Laura, he had said so quite clearly. Brendan O'Neill felt the first stirrings of panic. He hadn't really liked Dom' Cluskey. He was a Republican for a start. He was from a new group, the Real IRA, he didn't trust him and hadn't felt any sense of loss when he had banged his head. Silly prat! Come to think of it Flynn was a Republican too. So that's what it's down to in the end, the Fenian bastards had left him to carry the can. He was the only one now. Stripped of Flynn's leadership he was just a bully out of his depth. He was still dangerous, like a caged animal, but out of his depth nevertheless. Coleman tried again.

"Jim and I reckoned there had to be more than one bomb; we must find them and disarm them before we all end up on the bottom of the sea."

"I need to stay here to watch out for them," said O'Neill waving his gun in the general direction of the naval base. "You go and have a look round, see what you can find. Go and see where that explosion came from, see if the ship is damaged."

Coleman left the bridge and headed aft.

The noise of the explosion had been deafening but he felt sure the sound had been behind him towards the stern of the ship. He peered down into the engine room and saw the smoke. Treading warily he descended into the machinery space, into an alien world of pipes and gauges and machines of every shape and size. The lights had stayed on, he felt slightly less afraid.

Daniel Coleman edged along the metal deck plates of the engine room and crossed towards the quickly clearing cloud of smoke. He could soon see why the smoke level was reducing. It was pouring out of a hole in the ship's side just above the water line. Coleman could see the glinting of moonlight on the still water of the Gareloch.

He could see straight through the side of the warship.

The hole was at least a foot in diameter, maybe two. It was almost perfectly round and there didn't seem to be any other damage in the same area. It was as if a neat hole had been cut with a tin opener. Coleman pulled himself back to reality and began to think again. What could he do? His priority would have to lie with finding any more bombs; this one had done its job and couldn't hurt him anymore.

Daniel remembered what he and McCormack had discussed and headed back to the main passageway of the ship. He had to make a systematic search of the lower deck levels. He had to visit every compartment near the water line, anywhere that Flynn may have visited and left his latest deadly calling card. He decided to start at the forward end of the ship and made his way past the captain's cabin beyond anywhere he had visited before, even during his short tour of the ship the previous evening.

Coleman unfastened the butterfly clips securing a square hatch and lifted it vertically on its hinges. The hatch clipped into a retaining mechanism and Coleman peered down into a darkened space. There was a vertical ladder. He swung his leg over the raised hatch combing and settled his foot on the top rung of the metal ladder.

There was only him.

O'Neill was on the bridge and the crew was all locked up. There was only him, he had to do this. Both feet on the ladder, he lowered himself, first one rung and then the next. How was he going to see anything when he got to the bottom he thought, how do the sailors manage, surely they don't carry torches with them. There had to be a light somewhere. Coleman reached around in the dark with one hand, gripping grimly to the ladder with the other. He found it. The space below flooded with light and Coleman descended to the deck plates below. He was in a compartment full of machinery all of it silent. What should he look for? Beyond a few spy movies he hadn't a clue what a bomb would look like, leaving aside one made of plastic explosive.

On the side of the ship he remembered, concentrate on the sloping sides of the ship. Coleman lay down on the deck plates of the bow thrust compartment and peered into the bilge. He saw a discarded rag and picked it out. He shuffled along on his knees for a further few feet and lay down again. Oily water slopped about at the very bottom and gave off an unpleasant smell that made him gag a little. He saw nothing unusual. He moved again. He saw something, could it be a bomb. It was a small blob of something like putty, no more than the size of an egg. He touched the blob it was soft and greasy. That was it, McCormack had said it was covered in Vaseline; he had found a bomb. Coleman climbed the ladder as fast as he could and ran the short distance back to the bridge.

"I've found one, I've found one," he shouted at O'Neill, "what do I do to disarm it?"

O'Neill was not familiar with plastic explosive; he preferred the gun or knife, or better still a baseball bat to inflict his damage. But it was impossible to move in the circles he had inhabited without some knowledge of the bomb and the bomber.

"Has it got a detonator stuck in it?" he asked

Coleman hadn't a clue and said so.

"Go back and look then."

"Brendan, I really think we should let some of the sailors out to help us. They may know what to do. We are going to get caught anyway so we may as well give up before we end up on the bottom of this loch." Coleman pleaded with the Irishman who did little more that waggle the barrel of his gun to dismiss the proposal.

"Just pull the stuff off the ship and pick out the detonator and then it'll be as safe as kid's plasticine."

Coleman shuffled himself back into position on the deck plates of the bow thrust compartment and leaned his upper body and outstretched arm towards the blob of explosive stuck to the ship's side. He was sweating profusely. Not a hero, and certainly no leader this was the most unnatural thing he had ever encountered in his life.

The entire experience of the last twenty-four hours, the last month even, was bizarre beyond his comprehension. He knew that Laura had snared him with her looks and her body and he had fallen for her hook, line and sinker. This was a long, long way from his flat in Fulham and his pathetic little pamphlet. This was life or death and he had already been witness to murder. If he had been more knowledgeable he would have noticed that the plastic explosive had been shaped into an inverted cone, the pointed end facing inwards from the ships structure.

Flynn had known his trade.

his device would blow another neat round hole in the side of HMS Harwich. He grasped the putty with his fingertips and eased it away from the glass re-enforced plastic of the ship's hull. There was a detonator. He could feel a hard metallic tube pressed into the soft pliable substance of the explosive. He had it all in his hand. Coleman wriggled himself into a sitting position and looked at what he held. He raised the small blob to his nose and sniffed the mixture.

***

"Time for another bang," thought Laura as she moved the lever of the remote controller to the right. Laura had driven away from the little boat jetty at the west side of the Gareloch and was now on higher ground overlooking the naval base and the stricken ship. Her getaway so far was a complete success.

***

The force of the explosion hit him full in the face and he died instantly. Parts of his shattered skull flew in all directions and blood and gore decorated the deck, the machinery and even the deckhead above the body. Coleman lived for his many good causes but died pursuing a bad one.

On the bridge O'Neill heard the bang.

He looked around him and saw that the ship remained safe from threat and left the bridge. A haze of smoke poured out of a hatch towards the bow and O'Neill headed towards it. He peered downwards through the square shape of the bow thrust compartment hatch. Coleman was visible, through the smoke, on the deck below. At least, it looked like Coleman, thought O'Neill.

There was little left to recognise.

O'Neill leaned over the hatch and felt something warm and slippery. He took his hands away from the hatch combing and peered at both outstretched palms. They were wet with blood. There were patches of ginger hair mixed in with the gore. O'Neill retched; his stomach churning and his throat dry, rasping with his attempt to vomit. He wiped his hands on his trousers quickly and in utter disgust.

The sound of a third explosion burst along the main passageway of the ship and a further cloud of smoke rose into the confined space below decks. This was it thought O'Neill; I am going to the bottom. He cursed Flynn at the top of his voice and ran the few paces along the passage until he reached the hatch covering the crew's living quarters. He threw the securing butterfly clips off the hatch and lifted it open.

"Get up here and help me," he yelled to no-one in particular, "the bastard has booby trapped the ship, we're going to sink."

Welborne acted first and was on the ladder in a flash. Before he had reached the main passageway he was issuing orders to his crew and men poured out of their prison as quickly as they could. The captain could regain his command. Jonathan Welborne put his hand out to O'Neill and said one word.

"Gun."

240

O'Neill handed his weapon to the naval officer without argument. He was a beaten man. As the Coxswain emerged from the Mess deck he was handed the weapon and directed to guard the prisoner. The Cox'n wore a smile that spoke for every member of the ship's company of HMS Harwich and O'Neill knew he had no escape.

The ship's main broadcast rang out with orders.

"Damage Control teams close up, damage reports to the bridge immediately."

Sailors scurried all over the ship checking for damage and flooding from the three explosions they had all heard and felt recently. Damage control lockers were thrown open and repair equipment distributed. Reports came through to the bridge thick and fast and the pictorial state board of the ship showing every compartment soon bore the tell tale wax pencil signs of where damage had been found and marked.

Welborne continued to issue orders to his crew.

"Navigator, get the f'csle party closed up I want to raise the port anchor in two minutes."

Courtney responded to his captain's order but looked at his leader with a furrowed brow, a slightly questioning look.

In the midst of the mayhem Welborne found the time to explain himself.

"Nigel, if we let this ship sink right here we will block the exit from the submarine berths for months, I'll bet you don't want that on your record any more than I do."

Courtney dashed off pleased to have shared the small intimacy with his boss.

"Chief of the Boat, bridge," boomed out over the main broadcast and within seconds Chief Petty Officer York swung up the bridge ladder and reported in.

"Let the rest of the department take care of the damage effort, Chief, I want this ship ready to move under her own power in no more than five minutes, can you do it?"

"Yes Sir," York replied and he left the bridge at pace.

Welborne reached for the VHF radio microphone; he was now ready to talk to the agencies ashore. He was ready to give an account of himself. The first explosion had hit him like a sledgehammer and he had realised immediately what Flynn was planning to do. Harwich was a mere one hundred metres from the black hull of a Vanguard class submarine, one quarter of the nation's national deterrent. If his ship had gone to the bottom the submarine programme would have suffered a near mortal blow. The access to the special berths would have been blocked until a complete salvage operation could have been mounted. Jonathan Welborne took a deep breath to calm his nervous excitement and squeezed the transmit button on the VHF microphone.

"QHM this is Warship Harwich at unauthorised anchorage, over."

***

The woman trained her night vision binoculars on the distant ship and saw the increase in activity very clearly. There were sailors running around the upper deck and she could make out the uniform badges, the gold shoulder stripes, of a Lieutenant Commander occupying centre stage on the ship's bridge.

She restarted the car engine.

A puff of smoke billowed out of the ship's funnel. They've started the engines again she noted.

She could afford to smile. It was a job well done.

What will the media make of the British submarine threat bottled up in port by a bunch of ban the bombers?

Leila Latif thought about a warm bath back in London. She could smell the scented oils as she gave herself to thoughts of luxury on her skin once again. She couldn't wait to get out of the cotton underwear and back into silk; no more denim for her. Perhaps she would sip some Champagne as she washed away thoughts of O'Neill and the others. They were all victims to her plans, all expendable to the cause.

Laura started the car and rejoined the A814 along the perimeter of the Naval Base. The ringing of a mobile phone caused her to pull over into a lay-by and a rapid conversation in Arabic followed. News was clearly breaking around the world and her masters were delighted with her efforts. She concluded the call and removed a small plastic box from her handbag.

242

She raised the radio control remote transmitter to the open car window and slid a small switch to the "on" position. A red light turned quickly to green and she pressed the button in the centre of the device. "One for the road," she thought.

One hundred metres away on the ground floor deck of a multi-storey car park, hidden inside a biscuit tin contained within a battered leather briefcase an inaudible click set a red digital display in action.

Thirty, twenty nine.

The numbers began their inevitable decent to zero.

Laura flipped the back off the mobile phone she has taken her call from Beirut with and removed the SIM card and battery. The dismembered phone curved in an arc towards the woods adjacent to the lay-by and its heart went into her bag for disposal later.

Seventeen, sixteen, fifteen.

She engaged gear in the car and slowly pulled out onto the road heading for the Peace Camp and Helensburgh and Glasgow Airport.

Her new instructions were crystal clear; go straight to the airport, abandon the vehicle, collect an airline ticket and go to your new destination; take nothing with you.

Ten, nine, eight.

Laura smiled broadly, she would miss London, she would miss England. This had been a great adventure, a sting to the body of the enemy, a direct hit that would send a shock wave to the heart of the cursed infidels in the West.

Four, three, two.

But New York, what an opportunity.

Epilogue

Lieutenant Commander Jonathan Welborne stood firmly to attention next to his Quartermaster. Both men were dressed in their finest uniforms and standing alongside the gangway on the upper deck of HMS Harwich. Leading Seaman Walters was holding a bosun's call in his right hand. He had spent much of the last week practising to make sure that when ordered he would be able to execute the 'still' perfectly. Use of the bosun's call had all but disappeared from the modern Royal Navy but today was an important day and Welborne wanted it to run as smoothly as clockwork. The 'skipper' hadn't ordered Walters to prepare the bosun's call, he had asked.

Walters had jumped at the chance to show his Captain that he could do it.

From the port bridge wing the Gunnery Officer was keeping watch on the southern jetties of the naval base at Faslane and waiting for the first sight of the Admiral's official car. Harwich had returned to its home port on a sunny day in early November.

The clarity of light on this autumn morning was an artist's dream with the calm water of the Gareloch glistening with bars of silver.

The ship had spent what was left of the summer in dry dock at Rosyth on the Scottish east coast getting her hull repairs professionally fixed and the machinery spaces examined and set to work. She was looking as good, inside and out as the morning's weather.

It had been a turgid summer for the ship's company of HMS Harwich. Not only were they recovering from the trauma of events in the Naval Base but they had all attended the funerals of two of their own.

Petty Officer Churchill and Lieutenant Rodgers had been laid to rest with full military honours and their respective replacements were trying their best to fill vacant shoes.

The Police, Special Branch and finally Royal Navy Boards of Enquiry had been almost interminable throughout the late summer and stories, recollections, evidence had been offered and recorded in countless meetings before the incident was laid to rest.

Findings from all the enquiries completely exonerated the ship and its crew and no collusion of any sort could be linked to the terrorist team who had caused all their troubles.

The crew still mentioned Flynn and O'Neill and just occasionally Cluskey.

They still drew a response filled with loathing and the anger had only abated slightly. For Boyd and Coleman and even McCormack there was less venom as the entire crew realised that they were little more than hopeless dupes. After all, Flynn and McCormack had lost their lives too, eventually picked up in the drifting boat.

The mystery of the two bodies in the rigid inflatable had exercised the investigative services, and still did, but there were few if any leads left to chase up and the incident had been shuffled to a holding file.

Coleman's fate was so much more graphic and it was some time before the forensic teams would allow any sort of access to the bow thrust compartment to begin the job of cleaning up.

O'Neill was, as far as they understood, languishing in prison on remand waiting for his day in court. His utter contempt for the British authorities formed a guarantee that no useful information regarding the incident would be forthcoming from him. Rumour on the Ministry of Defence Police grapevine had it that O'Neill had settled easily and well to prison life and was seen by his fellow inmates as something of a celebrity. That would suit him well they all thought.

Cluskey too had eventually found himself detained at Her Majesty's pleasure.

Sheila Boyd had been interviewed extensively by the Police and Special Branch but the totally traumatised Sheila had little to add to proceedings.

Once the authorities were convinced that she too was a hapless pawn in a more dangerous game she was dismissed and allowed to travel home. The exclusion warning of immediate arrest should she be spotted in the vicinity of any military establishment within one year was as toothless as it was unnecessary.

The world of Sheila Boyd had changed forever and she wanted no more than to make up for all the lost time of the last decade or so.

Jonathan Welborne allowed himself a moment to think back over the last few months.

He had immediately been granted permission by naval authorities to offer every officer and man under his command the chance to move off the ship to another appointment or draft.

To a man they had refused.

The shared ambition to see their ship back on operational duties was a huge credit to each and every one of his crew, and in large part to Welborne's own leadership skill.

***

Today was the culmination of all the hard work.

In a few moments Admiral Alan South would be formally welcomed on board the ship and he would address the ship's company. Welborne had briefed his Flag Officer well, he knew small but important personal details about most of his men and once the official arrival was completed he would take tea with the crew in their recreation space before moving on to the small Wardroom Mess to talk to the officers.

Alan South knew, for instance that Emma Courtney, the wife of the Navigating Officer, Lieutenant Nigel Courtney had a small, closely guarded secret of her own. The Courtney family reunion had been as sweet as it was passionate and the aftermath of such danger and uncertainty had persuaded the two of them that some things they had talked of leaving for their return to Portsmouth mattered so much more now they were together again.

South didn't know, of course that Emma still thought of the woman who had so briefly entered her life and disappeared back in August. Emma had heard Nigel talk about this mysterious woman that was supposed to feature somewhere in the high jacking story but a link just never established itself.

***

"Admiral's car, Sir," called the Gunnery Officer from the bridge wing.

"Attention on the upper deck, Admiral South, Flag Officer Scotland, Northern England and Northern Ireland," rang out of the main broadcast speakers in the ship as the car pulled to a halt at the bottom of the gangway.

"Right, Wally, here's your chance to make Squadron history," said Welborne out of the side of his mouth and Leading Seaman Walters raised his bosun's call to his lips.

Walters had difficulty suppressing a smile as he realised that his Captain had just addressed him by his nickname.

Walters took a deep breath and played a perfect 'still'.

The End

Printed in Great Britain
by Amazon.co.uk, Ltd.,
Marston Gate.